# ONCE UPON A
# SPRING

Various Authors
Foreword by H. L. Macfarlane
Edited by H. L. Macfarlane and Adie
Hart

# TABLE OF CONTENTS

For all the flowers that bloom to signal the end of winter

*O were my love yon Lilac fair,*
*Wi"purple blossoms to the Spring,*
*And I, a bird to shelter there,*
*When wearied on my little wing!*
*How I wad mourn when it was torn*
*By Autumn wild, and Winter rude!*
*But I wad sing on wanton wing,*
*When youthfu' May its bloom renew'd.*

**O were my love yon Lilac fair  (Robert Burns; 1793)**

# FOREWORD

H. L. Macfarlane

Spring is the time for birth, and rebirth, and the beginnings of things that will eventually come to an end. But we do not think of those ends in the throes of spring; we only think of the here and now.

Promises of abundant life. The return of light where before there had been darkness.

Hope, and all that comes with it.

But beneath that hope lurks creatures and ideas that frighten us. Deadly frosts whose fingers creep out to grasp us when we think we've safely left the cold behind. Shadowy figures born from the same energy which brings to us new lambs and the first of the bluebells.

Spring is therefore, dear reader, a time of contrasts and opposites and uncertainty. Of romance and revulsion; of giddiness and fear. It is with such a spirit in mind that this anthology includes just a little bit of everything. Lost souls seeking guidance and purpose from the spirit of the moon. Goddesses dreading their role of heralding in the season. Princesses and witches gardening. Yes, gardening. Nothing could invoke spring more.

I hope you enjoy the stories found within *Once Upon a Spring* as much as everyone involved enjoyed bringing it to life.

# ᛒUT FOR A ᗞREᴧM

Ella T. Holmes

*Do not whistle when you enter the Springwood. Do not whisper when you hear a scuttling, scampering, scurrying in the undergrowth. And do not forget to carry a sprig of wattle where it can easily be seen.*

*The Springwood has fingers, and his chest is empty.*

Once, where the wattle trees painted the dense forest a sunlit-amber yellow, a young man slept with his hat slung low over his freckled face. He was easily overlooked; his hair was the same brilliant yellow as the wattle flowers, and his body was long and thin, hardly much to him at all. Wolves passed him by with dismissive sniffs; ants passed over his boots in distracted trails; crows flew over him with disregard – he had no silvers or shinies to draw their eye.

But the Springwood saw this man. It was a strange enough thing to see a human in these parts, but it was stranger still to see one so uncaring. Usually, when they travelled to the wood from their villages, it was with wicker baskets on hips and in hand, swords and bows and bags in the other, always on the desperate hunt for food.

Unable to tame the hackles of curiosity rising in him, the Springwood rustled his trees and moved the roots beneath the soil. It made the air smell damp and sweet with overturned dirt.

The golden-haired man lifted his hat between pinched fingers and squinted at the blue sky, then brought it lower over his face.

How odd, thought the wood, and pinched the roots of the tree closest to the man, shaking it so wattle balls fell and fleeced his human body, tickling him to a fit of sneezing.

The man brushed himself off and looked around, sticking his head between the trees to peer into the blue-green shadows. "I apologise for taking respite in your shade without asking," he said, no louder than he would if he were talking to himself. "It is so quiet here. I find it is the only place I can sleep."

The Springwood smiled – though the man could not see it. "It is rare that people talk to me."

The man staggered back, though he seemed more surprised than frightened. "It is rare that the wood replies. I had thought you a story." He brushed himself off once more, taking care to look at his brown tunic as he did so, as though he might find what words to say next between stray thread and wattle ball. "I am Cole," he settled on. "Cole from Tain."

The Springwood took shape, emerging from the yellow-thistled trees as a man not unlike Cole, but not like him either. He was the wood made manifest, a body of flesh that shimmered in the sun, of sap pushed by a heart of dandelions, of five fingers on each hand. He too thought hard about how he should be known. "You may call me Brinley," he said, and patted the new tunic he wore. It was soft and seamless, but, of course, strange.

"Are you a prince of the wood?" Cole asked, not daring to step forward. "Or a king? Or perhaps another of the beautiful magic folk?"

Brinley smiled; the human's flushed cheeks were endearing.

"I am the wood, and the wood is me. A better title might be 'friend'."

Cole relaxed a little. "Then you do not mind that I have taken to sleeping beneath you?" He blushed harder. "Beneath your trees, I mean."

Brinley shook his head. "Sleep again, if you like."

"And you would ask nothing in return?"

It was a strange question to Brinley, but nonetheless made way for his curiosity to slink out of the shadows of the underbrush and into the palm of his hand. He held it out. "Only that you would allow me to sit with you, and tell me what you dream of."

Cole ran a hand through his hair, and the short curls stood up like barley, flopping when he nodded. He took Brinley's hand and led him back to his favourite tree – marked so by the flattened grass around the base of the brown trunk. There they lay side by side, Cole giving voice to what thoughts entered his mind the instant they did so. And when he slept and woke, he spoke of all the peculiar human magic of glimpsing wonders behind his eyes. Brinley wished he too could dream, and so asked if Cole would return the next day to teach him how.

Cole pursed his lips. "I do not think such a thing is possible to teach," he said. "But I would like to return anyway, if you would allow it."

"So you might sleep again?" Brinley asked. "I would allow that."

"And if I wish to remain awake when I am with you?"

Brinley's heart lifted with the wind. "I would allow that, too."

\* \* \*

Cole returned throughout the summer, bringing stories from his home. He spoke of his first father baking oatcakes in the clay oven his second father sculpted, and his sister's attempt at carving owls from softwood that had fallen to the forest floor.

Brinley could not leave the wood, and so relished these details – took them in like he did the rains that fell through the year. When he told Cole this, Cole frowned.

"That is a shame," he said. "I wished to ask you if, in three days, you would come to the autumn festival with me." Perhaps he was prone to blushing, or perhaps the sun's warmth favoured his pale, freckled cheeks. "We wear crowns of twigs and berries, and dance until dawn. I started making one for you."

At this, Brinley's neck and face warmed, and he busied his hands by reaching out to a bunch of white tufted weeds beside him. Under the brush of his delicate fingers, they quickly wove themselves into a circlet. When it sat on Cole's head, he found his words again. "I would have said yes."

Cole's chest rose and fell a little faster. "And if I asked to kiss you?"

Brinley grinned. So it was, all the way through autumn, that they whispered and lost themselves in each other.

Winter saw hands meeting hands, fingers trailing, delving, undoing. Exploring dips and valleys. The sun averted its gaze and left them by silver moonlight, still tangling together like the roots of oaks. They lay in the crooks of each other, and Cole smiled at the touch of Brinley's fingers against his bare chest.

Cole procured a little wooden whistle from the pocket of his trousers and played a slow song to the forest and his creatures, for, he said, one's care for another can always be captured in a tune.

* * *

It was the middle of winter when Brinley's dandelion heart took flight, sprouting bright white and fluffy in the palm of Cole's hand. It was so small and delicate that Cole, upon learning what it was, took to shielding it with his whole body.

"It is not so frail," Brinley said with a laugh. "But it is yours, and I would that you keep it safe."

"Brinley," Cole said, and paused. He cupped the little white weed in his hands and shook his head, but he was smiling so brilliantly that the entire forest knew it was not Brinley's heart that he was saying no to. "My heart is rather firmly stuck inside me."

Brinley only laughed louder. "Of course. I know."

Cole frowned, then looked at Brinley. "Close your eyes."

Brinley copied his frown. "And do what?"

"Wait."

"And do what while I wait?"

Cole tucked Brinley's dandelion heart right above his own in the little pocket of his coat. "Imagine the future, Brinley." He smiled sheepishly. "Dream."

Brinley closed his eyes and saw nothing but blackness. No – he saw the entire Springwood, for he was the Springwood and the Springwood was him. He could see the blackthorn bushes and the squirrels scampering past them. He could see flashes of tails as something scuttled up a trunk, and another blurred shape as something scurried into the shadows of the undergrowth, startling Cole. Cole.

Cole with the golden hair. The curious man who slept beneath wattle trees and spoke so readily of dreams. The night-whistler, bread maker, brother, and friend. Brinley imagined what it might be like for them in the future. What of the coming spring? Next summer, autumn, or snowy season? He could see a house made of tightly woven roots, and a carpet of hearty green moss over the roof. He could see Cole's sister and two fathers coming to visit, perhaps to build a clay oven so they might all share oatcakes and tales around a warm hearth – for Cole grew colder than Brinley, and they would need such things. His sister could carve owls for the mantle, and Brinley could make sparrows and nightingales to join them.

So that was what it was like to dream.

"Open your eyes," said Cole. He held out a perfect wattle ball – so big and brilliantly yellow that it was almost a match for Brinley's dandelion. "I cannot give you my real heart," he said and smiled. "But I would that you keep it safe, as I will yours."

\* \* \*

Do you remember how the humans desperately hunted for food in other parts of the wood? Well, not all who come to the shelter of the wood are there to hunt; some hide and lay in wait. It was in the sting of a winter dawn that others came to the Springwood wattle trees – three men, with more weapons than want for meat.

Brinley might have stopped it.

He might have seen the men crouch in the shadows of the tall trees somewhere close to where Cole emerged from the traveller's road into Tain. He might have heard the odd scurrying and scampering of animals running from them, and the whispered plans the men had made for whichever unfortunate soul happened to choose this path out of town. He might have warned Cole not to come this way – might have grown his roots into a wall, a shield, a trap.

But Brinley had learned to dream.

When the men made their move, he was dreaming that Cole was merely asleep beneath the wattle tree with his hat still over his eyes, his whistle and Brinley's heart still tucked in his jacket pocket, his fingers splayed over his chest as it still rose and fell. Had Brinley been awake, he might have saved him.

But, but, but.

\* \* \*

If you whistle when you enter the Springwood, or whisper when you hear a scuttling, scampering, scurrying in the undergrowth, or forget to carry a sprig of wattle where it can easily be seen, best keep hold of your heart.

The Springwood has lost his own.

<u>Ella T. Holmes</u> always dreamed of being a Mad Hatter, Trojan horse, or a cunning princess who is definitely not a witch but reality intervened. Fortunately, she's got a knack for escaping it.

Born and raised around Australia, Ella spends her time avoiding bush turkeys, and drinking enough coffee to bring down the moon. Her work has been published in or is forthcoming in Coffin Bell Journal, Antithesis, and Macfarlane Lantern Publishing Seasonal Anthologies, among others.

You can find her non-fiction work and newsletter over on Substack as '<u>ella has thoughts</u>.'

# FAR FAR AWAKE

**Adie Hart**

I was shelving at the moment my childhood dreams came true. To be precise, I was wrestling an extremely large leather-bound copy of *Oleander's Condensed Traveller's Guide to the Twelve Duchies* onto the second shelf from the ceiling, silently cursing whomever Oleander had been and that he couldn't seem to write a sentence without multiple digressions and sub-clauses, and trying not to fall off the ladder.

I almost *did* fall off the ladder when Fiona came barrelling into the room, shouting my name.

"Cora? Cooooora!" she bellowed, peering round the stacks. "Are you in here? I need you!"

"I'm up here." I gave Oleander one last nudge into place and more or less leapt down the ladder two steps at a time. "Look, I know we don't call for absolute silence in the Library, but you could at least not yell. What's the matter?"

A few of the more scholarly desk witches were already flashing us disapproving glares over their tomes. Before Fiona could answer me, I dragged her gently behind the desk and into the little room which the District liked to call the Librarians' Office, and which we librarians liked to call the Cupboard.

As soon as the door closed behind us, Fiona squeaked, "I have the best news!"

"Did Arven tell you he loved you?" I asked. Fiona was my best friend, and I was fairly used to her bursting in on me breathlessly for advice in the middle of the day; she was a talented archivist, but something of a catastrophiser when it came to her emotions. A couple of months ago she'd *finally* managed to confess her feelings for her fellow archivist, Arven, with a little push from yours truly, and luckily, he was just as head over heels for her as she was for him.

Astonishingly, Fi was looking even more flustered than she'd been that day. She grabbed my hand, practically bouncing on the spot. "No, even better!" She paused her bouncing, registering what I'd said. "Wait, did he tell you he was going to? No, never mind," she cut herself off, "that can wait. Guess what, guess what?"

"I don't know, Fi... The District's declared a two-week holiday? Edwin Holly finally submitted a legible report? A rabid wyvern has eaten Professor Carter?" She laughed at that – strict old Carter was the bane of all of us desk witches – but shook her head. "Oh, just tell me," I groaned.

She grabbed my hand and beamed. "Your castle's awake!"

I snorted. "And I'm the Empress of Benir."

Borealis Castle had been asleep in its ring of thorns for six hundred years, slumbering in the forest to the north longer than the Academy had even been here. They said it had been cursed, long ago, but no one was quite sure why, and over the centuries it had become more an interesting puzzle to theorise about than an actual magical problem. It was a part of the furniture, practically; it had lurked there this long, resisting all attempts to enter, and as far as the District Witches were concerned, it was probably always just going to be there.

And it wasn't *my* castle, anyway. Sure, I'd been in love with the stories as a child. And yes, maybe I'd dreamed of cracking the curse and rescuing the princess that was said to lie enchanted within, and yes, maybe I'd spent years learning Old Linerian and researching the known history of the Borealis court, and yes, maybe that was why I'd ended up here at the Northern Academy, just a stone's throw from the castle. despite my mother finding me a posting in her library in the south. But that was all childhood fancy. I wasn't foolish enough to actually *believe* in the legend.

"No, really. Look!" She brandished a paper at me, waving it far too fast for me to read. "Arven got this report just now. The thorns just disappeared overnight."

I grabbed the paper from her hand and skimmed through it. A merchant had been travelling through the forest on his usual route, looking out for the wall of thorns that marked his turn-off towards Bourton and the Academy, only to end up smacking into a different kind of wall altogether: the outer wall of the castle itself. He'd immediately legged it, spooked, and headed straight for the Academy to "have a witch do something".

Stunned, I looked back and forth from the paper to Fiona, who was still grinning at me. I wasn't sure quite what "something" the merchant wanted a witch to do, but this was big. Someone definitely needed to check it out. To see if there was anyone left in the castle, for a start.

"Wow. That's... that's really... wow," I said. "So who's going to investigate?"

"You."

Ha, I could just imagine that. "No, really, Fi, who's got the case?"

She took my hands in hers, pretty much vibrating with excitement. "You have, if you want it."

"But..."

"Elva can't do it, because she's dealing with those dragons over in Miston, and Marnie's still on holiday, and Kennin says he has an allergy to pine pollen so he'd rather not hang out in a forest in springtime, and what I'm saying is, I recommended you. You speak that weird old language, and you know all about the history and all that, so you're the perfect person to go. Dispatch already said yes."

"But I'm not even a field witch! I'm a librarian! I can't take a case!"

"But it's your *castle*, Cora," Fiona beamed. "You can finally rescue your princess."

"That's just... it's just a story, Fi. It's just a daydream, something I thought about when I was a kid who hadn't yet realised I was way too much of an inside witch to be on active duty. There's probably not even a princess in there." Although, according to my research, the family was known for passing the throne from mother to daughter, so...

Fiona tugged on my arm. "Well, you'll just have to go and find out. Come on," she said, pulling me out of the Cupboard and pushing me towards the door of the library. "I've grabbed a kit from Stores for you. Go and get your cloak on – there's a carriage waiting. And your destiny!" she added, giving me a last shove down the corridor.

Destiny was probably pushing it. A princess was *definitely* pushing it. But I couldn't help the grin that finally slipped over my face at the thought of getting to look inside the very castle I'd been dreaming about for years.

*** 

Seeing the castle – as in, actually *seeing* the castle rather than catching glimpses of it through its wall of thorns – was a deeply strange feeling. It did, and didn't, look like the illustrations in the history books: the four stone towers were there, and the general shape of it looked castle-y enough, but there was lichen and moss where I'd expected shining stone, and the broad wooden door was rotted through, offering hints of a tattered, leaf-heaped hallway beyond. Clearly the enchantment that had kept the castle slumbering all these years hadn't stretched to keeping it in good shape.

That was worrying, if there had been any inhabitants inside. I swallowed hard as the carriage moved off. I wasn't exactly prepared to walk into a castle full of skeletons. That seemed like something you'd want an actual field witch for – although honestly, I wasn't sure if their training covered this kind of thing either. Still, I could head back to the Academy and ask for back up, or a replacement. I could spare myself the horror of whatever I might find inside this decrepit old ruin... but I'd also be denying myself the chance of a lifetime.

What was a couple of centuries-old skeletons if I might be able to find first-hand evidence of the way the Borealis court had lived? Everything would be exactly as it had been: food on the tables, hangings on the walls. And oh goodness, the books. There would be ledgers, letters, *diaries.* The scholar in me couldn't resist the opportunity. This was research heaven. I just needed not to look too closely at the bones. Or think about them.

Focusing hard on the treasures of history I'd find inside, I ducked through the largest rot-hole of the door and into the castle. Leaves crunched underfoot, the record of six hundred autumns. I looked up and down the hallway, conjuring a small ball of light to hover above me, and headed left on a whim. The further I got from the door, the lighter the leaf carpet became, until my crunches became clicks on faded floorboards. Already, I could see that the doors on each side of me were less and less worn as I walked. I poked my head into one at random, and found a parlour that looked only mildly decrepit.

No skeletons, thank goodness. Nor behind the next door I opened, though that appeared to be a linen cupboard, and I was rather glad some poor servant hadn't met their doom among piles of tablecloths. I ran my hands over a stack of embroidered napkins, recognising the Borealis crest immediately.

Any one of these rooms could have occupied me for days;

this castle was exactly the treasure trove I'd hoped for. I was already writing articles in my head, the kind that would catapult me to the attention of scholars across the world. But there was time for that later. I'd imagined exploring this castle a thousand times, and while I might not have been attired in gleaming armour, magic sword in hand, I knew what I needed to do next.

I needed to check for the princess.

In my daydreams, I marched to the tallest tower. I climbed the stairs with a sense of delicious anticipation; I strode into the princess's chamber and saw her enormous bed waiting for me in the middle of the room. I pulled back her bed-hangings with a powerful sweep. I saw the face of my beloved - sometimes blonde, sometimes brunette, sometimes with hair as red as my own, but always stunningly beautiful - lying ethereally in her magic sleep, and I bent slowly, reverently to brush my lips across hers. She woke up, fell into my arms, and... Well, look, I don't need to explain exactly how she thanked her valiant rescuer, do I? I was a teenager. Use your imagination.

Of course, judging by the general decay in the rest of the castle, my princess - if she'd ever existed - was probably not in any state to be rewarding anyone. I was a perfectly good kisser, if you believed my exes, but I was pretty sure not even I could bring someone back from the dead. So it was with a sense of dread bordering on terror that I climbed the stairs to the tallest tower. When I got to the top, there was no striding involved; instead, I pushed the door open slowly, barely daring to look inside.

The princess's bedroom, though, was much as I'd dreamed it. The decay hadn't reached this far inside the castle; this room had bright tapestries and rugs all over the floor, and rich brown logs still sat in the hearth, just waiting for someone to light them. The bed waited in the middle of the room, the soft peach hangings cascading down and obscuring any occupants, skeletal or otherwise.

I couldn't take my eyes off it. I was a woman mesmerised, a

girl half-trapped in a dream I'd lived so many times I didn't know what was real. I had to know, I told myself. I had to know if she was there. If she was waiting for me.

I moved towards the bed involuntarily, arm stretched out to sweep away the silk, ready – terrified – no, *ready* to reveal the princess.

And then I fell over something.

It took me a couple of moments to realise what was happening, thanks to my immediate panic that I'd collided with a skeleton. Turns out my main fear response is to shut my eyes tight and hope everything will go away. I stretched out a nervous hand to feel the lump I'd fallen over, praying not to find cold bone under my touch. Luckily, it was soft.

Warm.

Silky.

Cursing in Old Linerian.

"... in the bloody hell do you think you're doing?" was all I caught, between my panic and my rusty listening skills – look, it's hard to practice a dead language aloud – but there was no doubt from the tone that every word was impeccably rude. The lump shoved my hand away and said imperiously, "Well?"

I cracked an eyelid open. Okay, that was very much *not* a skeleton. Lying on the floor with her legs tangled around mine and her face a mere breath away, cosy as if we'd just shared a delightful night's sleep, was someone who could only be the woman I'd spent my life dreaming of. The Borealis princess.

"Hello," I whispered, raising a hand to hover over, but not quite touch, her face. Was this really happening, or had I fallen too hard and cracked my head?

"You will address me as Your Serene Highness, or at the very least Princess, foul intruder," she said, slapping my hand away again. "Get off me and get up this instant or I'll scream. You will *not* touch the royal personage."

That woke me up from my reverie like a bucket of cold water. "Sorry, sorry," I said, scrambling back from her with my hands held up, but my moment of contrition didn't last long in the face of her petulant frown. "You know, if you don't want people to fall over you, perhaps you shouldn't lie on the floor, Your Serene Highness?"

She huffed angrily. "Yes, thank you for the advice, treasure hunter. I can't get up."

"What do you mean, you can't?"

"I mean, I've tried, you wretched thief or whatever you are. It's like my legs are still asleep – when I tried to leave the room, I ended up here. You don't think I lie around on the floor for fun, do you?"

"I'm beginning to think I don't know anything about you," I muttered. "Er, do you want a hand up? I'm not a thief. I'm a librarian."

"A librarian?" She quirked a perfectly shaped eyebrow at me. "So what are you doing in my bedroom? Where are my maids? Why did no one come when I, um, called for help?" She paused. "Why didn't anyone hear me fall?"

I sighed. "It's quite a long story, Princess. Perhaps I could help you back into bed first? So you're comfortable?" Chalk up another deviation from the daydream; my fantasy princess was only too happy to embrace me and more, but this one eyed me suspiciously before accepting my outstretched hands.

I tugged her up and braced her against my side, careful to keep my hands demurely at her waist lest she call me some dreadful name again. She took a step and stumbled, so I swept her up into my arms, thankful for my years of hefting tomes around the Academy. She didn't weigh much more than a stack of books, actually. Goodness, there was nothing of her. I supposed that was what six hundred years of skipping meals did for you. Perhaps a little longer and she would have been the skeleton I'd feared. I pushed the thought away.

The coverlet was flung back all higgledy-piggledy, but I couldn't smooth it out with my arms full of princess, so I simply set her down on top of it.

"Thank you," she murmured, leaning back against the pillows.

That was more like it. She looked like someone you might call "serene", now. Her blonde hair belled out against the peach silk, and her cheeks had pinkened slightly from the exertion of trying to stand. She had a slightly crooked nose, I noted absently, and two moles above her left eyebrow. Not the kind of detail you'd think to imagine, but her face was charming, beautiful, even, just for being that touch more real.

I swallowed, realising I was gazing at her like a lovesick idiot. "It was my pleasure, Princess."

"Why do you talk like that?" she asked.

"Like what?"

"Like a history book. Like you're speaking to my mother. You're so formal, like you learned out of some ancient language book for foreign diplomats."

"Probably because I learned out of some ancient language book for foreign diplomats," I said.

She blew out half a laugh. "No, really."

"Really." I tried to give her a smile, but it felt awkward on my lips. How did you tell someone even their very language was a thing of the past? "I'm not Linerian. No one is, anymore, really." At her puzzled look, I sighed. "Look, can I sit down? I have to fill you in on some things."

\*\*\*

She took the news surprisingly well, actually. I'm not sure I could have digested the fact that everyone I'd ever known had been dead and buried for five hundred plus years – that my country was just a footnote in the history books – with such equanimity.

It turned out that Princess Camellia had been half-expecting her long sleep her whole life.

"It was one of those stupid curses," she said. "I was supposed to turn sixteen and fall into a deep sleep and waste away to my bones on the whim of some horrible fae woman who didn't get invited to my christening. My godmother added a counterspell so that I'd be fine and could be woken up after a year if my true love kissed me, but how was I supposed to have a true love all set to go? I was just a kid. I didn't have a true love, and I sure as hell wasn't going to find her while I was asleep, so I just thought I'd sleep forever. I went to bed on the eve of my sixteenth birthday completely terrified."

"And now you're here?" I gave her a quizzical look. She was young, but definitely not a child. "I don't mean to be rude, but..."

She laughed. "But I don't look sixteen? No. I woke up the next morning completely fine. And the next, and the next."

"Huh. So the curse didn't go off?"

"Your guess is as good as mine. I panicked for a while, refused to sleep, that sort of thing. Partied all night and nodded off upright in lessons. I don't think I got back in my bed for about a month. But eventually, I went to sleep and woke up fine again, and that kept happening, and after eight years I suppose we all stopped worrying about it. I'm twenty-four." She frowned. "Or six hundred and twenty-four, if you're telling the truth."

"I am, but I don't think the six hundred counts." I patted her hand. "The castle seems to have held you in stasis just as you were. The, uh, the rest of the castle's not been quite so lucky." Now the pattern of decay I'd seen was making sense; her godmother's magic must have put its effort into preserving the princess, but become weaker the further away it got from her. Perfect tower, rotting front door. It was pretty efficient, actually.

"My poor castle. I can't imagine how lonely it's been. And my family – at least we had eight more years, but..." She trailed off, tears in her eyes.

I didn't know what I could say that could possibly be a comfort, so I pressed on. "What did happen, after all that time?"

She closed her eyes for a second, obviously forcing herself not to cry, then gave me a rueful smile. "I don't know. The curse went off after all, I suppose. Goodnight Camellia, goodnight history." She flopped dramatically back onto the pillows, eyes squeezed shut and tongue out.

I couldn't help but giggle. "You're not really how I'd imagined."

"Imagine me often, did you?"

*You have no idea.* I fiddled with my satchel strap, hoping I wasn't blushing. "I didn't expect you to call me a filthy thief, or whatever it was. And I didn't think you'd be on the floor. The legend always has you lying all statue-like in bed, waiting for your kiss."

She reared forward off the pillows, eyes full of excitement. "There's a *legend*? They wrote a legend about me?"

"Oh, yes," I grinned. "Why do you think I was imagining you? Every kid in the area plays at rescuing you at one point or another. My brother has a dreadful scar from climbing through the bramble bush at the back of the garden that we always pretended was your thorn wall. I just... never grew out of it."

"I'm glad," she said, grabbing my hand and squeezing it. "Imagine some awful swaggering prince up here thinking he had the right to kiss me because of some story. No, I'm glad it was you, Cora."

I was lost in her eyes, in her hair, in her perfect mouth. "Princess..."

That perfect mouth quirked up. "Even if you did kick me while I was down." She swung her legs off the side of the bed and winced, then tugged the hand she was still holding. "Come on, rescuer. Give me a hand to try walking again."

\*\*\*

It had still been morning when I entered the castle, but the sun was high over the forest by the time the princess could make it around the room without my support. She'd started slow, tripping and hobbling, with more of her weight on my outstretched arm than on her own feet, but she'd refused to give in, even when I saw tears spring to her eyes after yet another stumble. I hovered beside her like an anxious mother hen as she clung to the wainscoting, seemingly forcing her stiff legs forward by sheer power of will.

I was impressed, actually. She had a determination that could rival Fiona when she had particularly difficult handwriting to decipher, like a dragon intent on something shiny. Again, that dogged refusal to give in wasn't exactly what I'd expected of a princess. In one afternoon, Princess Camellia had done a lot to shatter my preconceptions, I realised.

For one thing, she knew a lot more swear words than I'd even thought there *were* in Old Linerian.

"*Ascolsa betanda,*" she muttered as she completed another circuit of the room and sank to the floor in a heap. She looked pale, drawn, exhausted. Like someone who'd run for miles rather than tottered around a bedchamber.

I sat down beside her. "What does that one mean?"

That won me a laugh, though there wasn't much force in it. "It's hard to explain. Sort of... what's that little guy that eats plants, with a little round shell?"

"I know the one," I said. Somehow the word for snail had never come up in my historical research. "We call it a 'snail'."

"Well, it's like an old word for its blood. So... blood of a snail?"

"Those trade documents are missing some great phrases," I said seriously, hoping to make her laugh.

"What it means," she said, "is that I'm extremely *fed up.*"

She punctuated this with several slaps of her poor wobbling legs.

"Hey." I caught her hand before she could swipe again. "Six hundred years of muscle wastage aren't going to be defeated in a day, you know."

She made a frustrated noise low in her throat. "Why couldn't that stupid spell keep me healthy?"

"It did," I said. "You're just... weak from lying down so long, but you're alive, which really, is more than I can say for most people your age." She gave me a small smile, so I pressed on. "And it's more than I can say for a lot of the castle – you should see the state of the front door."

All of a sudden, the princess's face crumpled. "I'm *trying* to."

"Hey, hey, I know, I know." What were you supposed to do when a princess started crying? If it had been one of my friends crying, my arms would already have been around them, but somehow, despite the fact we'd been touching all afternoon while we walked, that felt too familiar. I was still holding the princess's hand, though, so I gave it an awkward stroke with my thumb. "You're trying so hard, and you're doing so well."

"What would a thief know about it?" she said grumpily. But she didn't snatch her hand away.

"Librarian," I said. "And honestly, I've never heard of anyone under a curse like this before, so it's not like anyone was expecting you to pop right up out of bed. Some adjustment is reasonable, I think."

She looked up at me through tear-drenched lashes, and made a visible, if shaky, effort to stop sobbing. "But my godmother" – sniff – "said" – sniff – "I'd be perfectly" – sniff – "fine."

"You said she tweaked it so you'd sleep for a year? So that spell lasted a lot longer than anyone thought," I said. "Maybe it was wearing out for a while before it finally broke."

She hummed again, and then sat up straighter, and her hand

twisted in mine so that suddenly *she* was clasping me. "Can you tell?" she said eagerly. "You know, do some magic on it, work out what happened? Why I woke up now, and not then?"

"That's... not really my specialty." I grimaced. "If you have any books you need alphabetising, I know a spell to do that for you in a tick."

"Oh, damn, what must the library look like?" she muttered, and I flinched, worried I'd set her off again thinking about the rest of the castle. But she continued, "Never mind. You said there were other witches, that you're part of some sort of organisation? Could one of them do it?"

I slapped my forehead with my free hand. "Of course. I can't believe I didn't think to update them. But I'm not going to go back without you, so— Wait."

I lunged for the bag Fiona had packed for me – yes, there was a sheaf of blank report papers and a quill. I scribbled a note, hoping she wasn't too annoyed at me for not knowing the proper format – and if she was, she could remember that she was the one who'd sent me out here unprepared. Luckily everyone in the office was taught the spell for sending letters to the post room, no matter their department (which came in handy whenever an apprentice got lost in the stacks), so I addressed it, scrawled *URGENT* on the front, and sent it off.

Princess Camellia grinned as the envelope disappeared. "Okay, so you *are* a witch."

"Not a pestilent thief, or whatever you called me?" I raised an eyebrow at her. "I could be both."

"Nah," she said. "I think you're too nice for that." Her gaze was magnetic. I couldn't help but lean towards her, caught in those sparkling eyes. She put her hand on my shoulder, and my breath hitched, but she only used the contact to push herself back up to her feet. "Come on, Witch. Let's go again."

"Fine, but don't call me "Witch"."

"Well then, *Cora*," she grinned. "Don't call me "Princess"."

\*\*\*

Fiona's reply arrived twenty minutes later, appearing in my hand as I guided a shaky Camellia down the hallway outside her room.

*The research department is working on the magic tracing side,* she wrote, in fine formal cadence. *They can do that remotely, though someone might need to visit the castle in a few days. In the meantime, Dispatch requests that you remain at the castle and help the princess acclimatise to her wakefulness. Bring her up to speed on history, politics, and anything else you feel she needs to know. Get her speaking modern Common. Since you aren't used to the Dispatch system, I'll be your contact for the duration. You can requisition materials from the library, and anything else you need, through me, and I'll have them delivered. I'll arrange food and living supplies too.*

She carried on for a few more paragraphs with instructions that sounded as if they'd been polished by years of cases, finishing with a request to check in by note at least once a day. At the bottom, in a postscript that sounded much more like my best friend, she'd added:

*Is she everything you dreamed of??*

I smiled at that and tucked the letter into my pocket. "Well," I said to Camellia, "looks like you're stuck with me for the foreseeable future. I'm to stay here and help you "acclimatise", whatever that means, while they work out what happened to your curse."

"Oh," she said. I couldn't read her face. Was the thought of spending time with me that bad? Or had she just hoped for an answer already?

"Sorry," I shrugged, aiming for nonchalance. "Looks like you'll have to put up with me a bit longer."

Her face reddened. "No, actually, that's... that's really good. I want to get out of here, of course, but the thought of meeting all those people, answering all their questions... I've been quiet for so long. I'm not sure I'm ready to talk to anyone but you yet."

"That makes sense." And took a little bit of the bruise off my ego, I had to admit. "You feeling ready for those stairs?"

Camellia paused. "No, but let's try anyway."

***

Our exploration of the castle was slow, but surprisingly enjoyable. Camellia led the way – or rather, directed me, as she still clung to my arm – through parlours and bedrooms and long corridors. Her steps grew more confident as she grew more desperate to see the home she recognised, and how well the spell had preserved it all. She pointed out her mother's chambers, and her father's library (which I told myself sternly I could come back to investigate later, once her curiosity had been sated) and the study where she had attended to her duties in the mornings.

The study seemed like the perfect place for us to take a break; Camellia's legs were beginning to wobble, and apart from her desk, with its tall, imposing chair behind and two spindly-looking affairs in front, there were two enormous armchairs by the hearth. She sank into one with a sigh, coughing slightly at the dust that puffed up from its stuffing.

"I begged Mother for these," she said with a smile. "She'd always make people perch awkwardly in front of her desk when they came for meetings, but I thought it was... I don't know, friendlier to sit *with* them. More like a chat."

"That was nice," I said.

"Oh no," she chuckled. "It wasn't about being nice. People are much more likely to say things they don't mean if they feel like they're talking with a friend."

I feigned indignance. "Oh, so you're trying to... princessenate me into something, are you?"

"I don't think that's a word," she said.

"Hey, go easy on me, I'm speaking a language I've only seen written down. I don't know if half the words I'm saying make any sense to you."

"Mm," she said, eyes glittering with mischief. "About three-quarters. The rest sounds like you're speaking something from about a hundred years before I was born."

"I suppose that's what we have, mostly. A lot of the contemporary documents from your time were, well, in here with you, and no one could get through the magic thorns. I used to daydream about getting my hands on the sources in here." *And a lot more,* I thought, but didn't dare say.

"You should take a look around, then," she said, waving magnanimously. "Nothing but documents for your studious little heart to enjoy. I'll just... sit here and hate my muscles for a bit."

She leaned over to massage her calf, slipping her hands under the hem of her skirt, and I quickly turned my attention to the desk. There were papers and books scattered all across it.

"You weren't the tidiest princess, then?" I called, running my fingers down the side of a pile of scrolls.

"I know where everything is," she scoffed. "Political requests on the left, trade documents on the right. Personal correspondence got sent to my room for me to read at my leisure."

"What about this, then?" I said, holding up a creamy envelope with her name on the front in elegant blue ink. "This looks personal, and it's right in the middle of everything."

She froze. "That's Mother's handwriting."

"You didn't know it was there?"

"No," she whispered, and then commanded, full princess in her voice, "Bring it to me."

I handed her the letter and tried, unsuccessfully, not to

scrutinise her expressions as she read. By the time she finally put the letter down, there were silent tears running down her face, and I couldn't stop myself putting a hand over hers.

"Are you all right?"

"Yes— Not really. Sort of. She says..." She groaned and thrust the letter at me. "Oh, you read it."

"You're sure?" At her nod, I unfolded the paper tentatively, politely ignoring Camellia wiping her cheeks on her sleeve.

*My darling Camellia,* the letter began. *I'm writing this down in the hope that you are woken soon and will read my words in time to find us.*

*We had long hoped that the curse was inactive, that Coccinelle had forgotten about us, but it is clear she was only biding her time until she grew strong enough to tackle your godmother's counterspell. She has ringed the castle with a wall of magical thorns, and she has put you to sleep after all these years.*

*We have waited six months, my darling, hoping every day to see you wake, but it has become impossible for us to continue on in this place. Thanks to the counterspell, the curse will allow those it considers a candidate for your true love to enter through the thorns, but we are running out of supplies. There are not so many delivery girls in the world, it seems, and fewer diplomats and envoys of the right disposition.*

*We cannot look after our people when they cannot get to us, nor us to them, and so your father and I have made the decision* – here, the paper was blotched with tear-marks, but whether Camellia's or her mother's, I couldn't tell – *to allow our queendom to be added to the lands of the Carusine court. Silvie will be a good queen for our people, and as we had once hoped to unite the lands with a betrothal between our daughters one day (though I will note that the curse did not even allow Davinie to take one step into the thorns, so perhaps that was not a good plan) this does not seem an ill course of action.*

*I cannot imagine ruling further without you to take my place,* was crossed out so vehemently I had to bring the letter close to see it.

Under that, it continued, in a forcedly brighter tone, *Your father and I have decided to retire to his sister's court in Alvary, so if you wake soon, you will find us there. It should be fun to relax. Our people have been given the choice to come with us or to take up service with Silvie; most of them have already left. Without access to the carriages, we cannot take much with us, only what we can carry through the thorns, so I apologise for the state of the castle if it is much decayed.*

*Marina has promised us her counterspell will hold you safe until you wake. I can only hope that you will join us in Alvary soon, and all of this will be forgotten. But if it –* several more scratchings-out here, scribbled through so blackly I could not read them at all – *takes longer, then know that we love you always, and we will be as happy as we can. I hope you will do the same.*

*Sleep well, darling.*

I could not read the signature for the weight of tears in my eyes. "Oh, Camellia," I said inadequately.

"It's good," she sniffed. "It's a good thing. They... they got to live."

I didn't trust myself to do anything but nod. The letter was fascinating from a historical perspective – it explained so much that was missing from our records – but I couldn't bring myself to care, not when Camellia was looking... like that. I reached my hand out to her, and she took it.

"Now I know," she said shakily. "Now I know." We sat like that, my fingers gently stroking her hand, for I don't know how long before she shook her head violently and said, "We can't sit here all day."

"We can if you want," I said. "It's a lot to process."

She shook her head again and pushed herself out of her chair. "No, come on. Let's keep going. The sooner I'm back to full strength, the sooner I can go to Alvary to find out... what happened next."

"Okay," I said. "Where do you want to go?" Everyone dealt with things in different ways, I told myself. I didn't have the counselling training of a full field witch, but I could do worse than simply being there for Camellia if and when she wanted to talk.

"We could see the garden?" she asked.

"Sure," I said, offering her my arm. "Lead the way."

She was creaky to start with, but soon she dragged me along in what would certainly have been classed as a rush, even if it didn't quite qualify as a run. I followed her to a door that looked only mildly rotted – we were still within the limits of the spell, but its influence was clearly not at full strength here. I used my shoulder to shove the door open, and Camellia stepped through into...

A tangled green disaster zone.

It looked like a section of the forest had forced its way into the castle courtyard. Vines hung from every lump and bump in the walls, and weeds as tall as the upper windows waves menacingly in the breeze. From what I knew of contemporary castle design, this should have been a beautifully manicured garden, with meandering walkways between beds filled with tastefully exuberant flowers and ferns. And since the Borealis court had been *the* tastemakers of the time, I expected that this had once been the most beautiful garden I could imagine.

Now, I'd have been hard pressed to tell it was meant to be a garden at all.

Camellia stopped abruptly, and I caught up to her, slipping a hand under her elbow. "Are you all right? Did you trip?"

"No, I just... My garden." She laughed, but there wasn't much humour in it. "I thought the spell might have kept it alive."

"It certainly looks alive," I said, disentangling my sleeve from a bramble that had strayed too close. "But I know what you mean. I think it focused on keeping you safe, rather than keeping things pristine out here."

"Such a shame." She shook her head sadly at a wizened old tree trunk that bent awkwardly under a cloak of moss. "That was the most magnificent magnolia. And there..."

Suddenly, she was gone, tearing free of my support, hoicking her dress up to her knees as she stepped through the sea of weeds to the far corner of the garden.

Of course I followed her. "Camellia," I called, "be careful!"

"I have to know," she said, scrabbling at a mound of leaves and thorny vines. "I have to."

"All right, but let me help, at least." I fished in my satchel for the pair of leather gloves I knew was part of a field witch's kit. "Are you left or right-handed?"

"Right."

"Take this, then." I handed her a glove, which she pulled on eagerly. I was right-handed too, but I'd make do with the left – for starters, I wasn't in such a frenzy to jam my hands into a pile of unknown thorns and stingers. "And tell me what we're looking for."

"It's got to be under here. I can't— I don't know what I'll do if it's not."

"If what's not what?" I said, but she didn't reply, just kept tearing at the plants.

A branch emerged from the mess, then another, then more. They were knobbly-stemmed, with wide, glossy green leaves.

Camellia stopped ripping when she saw them, running her hand gently along the thin bark. "I knew it," she said triumphantly. "Can you get rid of everything that's not this?

Without hurting it?"

I racked my brains for an appropriate spell. Maybe one for removing pages from a failing binding could work? I grabbed a weed more or less at random and recited the words; it, and many of its comrades, dropped to the ground, severed cleanly from the branch they'd been crushing. I did it again, on a different weed, and another, until the twiggy bush stood out proudly from the tangle. There was an abundance of those glossy leaves, and glinting on one side of the bush was a single deep pink flower.

Camellia gasped.

This time, my arms were around her before I realised it. It was just that hitch in her breath, all sadness and memory and relief at once. She sounded... she sounded like someone who needed a hug.

"My Camellia," someone whispered, and I worried for a second it was me until she said it again. "My camellia. It survived." She stretched a hand towards the flower, and I let my arms fall so she could reach to stroke its silky petals.

"Yours? More than all the other plants?"

Camellia smiled. "My father planted this on the day he found out my mother was carrying me. It was her favourite flower, and he knew the moment he heard the news that that's what my name would be. It's the first thing to bloom every spring, and I was the first child to bloom for the two of them."

I couldn't help but ask, "What if you'd been a boy?"

"Borealis queens usually have daughters, even if they don't think so at first," she said seriously, then shot me a small smile. "But I don't think Father would have insisted on Prince Camel."

"Not so pretty, no," I chuckled. "But I like the name on you. It suits you."

"Thank you," she said, but her attention was already back on the plant. "It's so good to see it again. Like a piece of before, still standing. Just. Standing in the wreckage of our homes, I suppose."

"Both of you survived the curse, is what's important," I said. "We can deal with your homes at our leisure."

That caught her attention. "We?"

"You didn't think I was going to disappear on you, did you? Besides, I have to teach you to speak Common, and all of that. We might as well tidy up the garden while we do it, and you're not telling me you couldn't use a little sunshine after six hundred years in bed."

"Oh, I can speak Common," she said, in Common. "How else did you think I managed trade negotiations with our neighbours?"

I'm not ashamed to say I gaped at her. "What? Then why have you been letting me pick my way through the dregs of my Old Linerian?"

She shrugged. "I liked hearing my language again, even if you do speak it really strangely. And it was cute to watch you hunt for phrases. You looked like you were having a good time."

"Yeah, well..." I sputtered. I *had* been having a good time, finally getting to use the knowledge I'd hoarded for so long. "Even Common has changed a bit in six hundred years."

"Fine," she said, eyes dancing with humour. "You can teach me some *modern* words while we set the garden straight."

We both looked out over the mess of vines and brambles.

"Any idea where to start?" I asked.

She looked deeply cross as she muttered, "We had gardeners."

"Ah. And I never had much aptitude for garden magic, unfortunately. But I know some basic pest-removal spells and I can do the snipping spell as much as you like?"

"It's a start," she said, and there was a flash of that

determination in her face again at last. "I know where the gardeners kept the tools, at least."

"I'll get Fiona to send some boots for you," I said, pulling out another blank report from my satchel. "More gloves. Some... seeds?"

"Bulbs. Daffodils. And irises," Camellia added. "Actually, pass me the quill. I'll make the list."

\*\*\*

We were so engrossed in the work, snipping and hacking and clearing and pulling, we barely noticed the first stars had begun to blink into the purpling sky until we heard a loud thumping coming from the castle.

"The door," said Camellia, and wiped a green smudge across her forehead with the back of her glove. "Who could it be?"

I leapt up. "Our supplies! I'll get them. You stay here." Suddenly, it seemed incredibly important to me that I kept whoever was doing the delivery outside the castle proper. Partly because I thought that if the state of the place got back to Fiona, she'd probably make us come back to the Academy, and partly because I hated the idea of anyone else, however nice, penetrating our little bubble. This castle, this garden, this princess, still felt like a dream to me. I wanted to keep it all to myself a little longer.

Luckily, the young journeywizard they'd sent was only too happy to drop off the goods and run. "Rather you than me in this creepy old place," was the only thing he said to me beyond greetings. I checked through the pile he heaved down: there was a letter from Fiona, which I pocketed for later, a basket overflowing with food (with a note in the Head Cook's handwriting saying "IN CASE SHE NEEDS FEEDING UP" pinned to the handle), and a bag containing the garden tools we'd requested (also with a note, again from Fiona, bearing a promise to track down some seedlings tomorrow, and were we sure we didn't want Dispatch to send a witch with an aptitude for plants?).

I sent the wizard back with a reply to that one, saying *no, absolutely do not send a witch with an aptitude for plants*, and then, underneath that, some waffle about how the garden was the perfect project to get Camellia back to full strength. I hoped, probably in vain, that Fiona wouldn't see right through that.

I waited in the rotting doorway until the journeywizard's carriage disappeared into the forest before I felt safe enough to return to Camellia. We wolfed down our picnic in the study, which was one of the less dust-covered rooms.

"What did you call this fruit?" asked Camellia through a mouthful of bread and jam.

I laughed. "Apricots. We must have learned how to grow them here after you fell asleep."

"It's nice to know some good things have happened since then," she said contentedly, licking her fingers. I looked away, for fear of blushing.

"We've done quite a lot, really. There are new kingdoms and queendoms all over. Oh, we have miniature dragons now! Even the whole existence of the District Witches is new, from your perspective."

"Maybe if we'd had some at the time, I'd have stood more of a chance of escaping the curse," she said pensively. "Tell me more about what it is you do."

"Me personally, or the District in general?"

"Both," she said. "I want to know about all the adventures *and* about how you spend your days. Tell me everything."

So I did, while we polished off the rest of the jam. Luckily, I knew plenty of funny field stories from the reports Arven and Fiona shared with me, and I loved any excuse to talk about my beloved Library. Camellia was the perfect listener, laughing and asking questions in all the right places. It was probably her princess training, but she made me feel so comfortable, so *wanted.*

When I ran out of anecdotes, I scanned Fiona's letter while Camellia cut into the enormous fruitcake.

"She says they haven't found anything yet about why the curse broke, but they've ruled out a couple of things. It definitely wasn't an active casting – that means, no one took it *off*, it just stopped. The two things that seem likely are that the spell ran out of power, or that it somehow got triggered by something. Your mother said the curseworker was called Coccinelle? They can look her up in the records, see if she died recently – if so, her curses might have taken a power hit. The one we have to worry about is if it somehow got triggered by someone on purpose. That might leave you in an awkward position, politically."

"In what way?" she asked.

"Well, Fiona says that if some prince or princess has managed to get around the curse, it might leave you betrothed to them. Since the curse assumes true love, and all that."

Camellia bit her lip. I didn't like the sound of the theory, either. She'd spent so long tied up by this curse, I couldn't bear the thought of her losing her freedom again so soon.

"Can we... do something about that?"

"Yes," I said fiercely. "I won't let anyone claim you unless you want to be claimed." Then, worried about the intensity of that statement, I added in a lighter voice, "You never know, it could be a really good-looking prince."

She wrinkled her nose at me. "I'm not sure there's a prince good-looking enough in the world."

"Anyway, don't worry," I said, though I resolved to do plenty of worrying myself. "The research team is really good. They'll have it all solved by tomorrow, probably." A yawn overtook me at the thought of *tomorrow,* when there'd been so much *today.* "I don't know about you, but I could do with a rest."

When Camellia agreed, I pulled her to her feet and we made our way back towards her tower.

She grimaced at the stairs, winding up out of sight. "I could murder whoever built this castle," she groaned.

"Ernesto Valtizan," I said absent-mindedly. "In the rein of Queen Kathryn III." And then, at her quizzical gaze, "What?"

"You really do know a lot about history," she chuckled.

*Just yours,* I thought, but out loud, I only said, "Well, I am a librarian. It's kind of my job to know things."

"All right then, Lady Know-Things, tell me this. How in the nine hells do you get an exhausted princess whose legs won't behave themselves up six flights of spiral stairs?"

I grinned at her. "Like this."

She whooped as I hoisted her up – in a practical over-the-shoulder carry this time, not a romantic side-lift – and set off up the stairs.

We only had a couple of bumping-into-the-wall issues, and once again I thanked my library training for my strength. It was cutting it fine by the time we made it to the top, though. Camellia did weigh more than a stack of encyclopaedias, at least when you were climbing too.

At her door, she poked me in the back. "I can manage from here," she said, wiggling; I tried to ignore the wiggling and everything it made me feel. "You don't need to haul me into bed like a barbarian with his wench."

"Oh, at least let me do it properly," I laughed, putting her down and then, as she smoothed her skirts, sweeping her up into the bridal carry I'd used before. "How about placing you gently into bed like a... respectful rescuer?"

She squeaked as her feet left the floor, but didn't resist, just tucked her face into my shoulder.

I crossed the room quickly, slipped her into her peach-soft

sheets and, almost unconsciously, brushed a coil of hair from her forehead where my shoulder had pulled it loose. She smiled up at me fondly. "My sweet, respectful rescuer."

"Don't get used to it," I whispered.

Why was I whispering? Maybe because her beautiful eyes were fixed on mine and for the second time that day, her beautiful lips were so very close. It felt like a whispering kind of moment.

"I should, um, go and find a bedchamber." I pulled away, rubbing my hand on my skirt to kill the tingles. There had to be some rooms with enough undecayed furnishings to curl up in somewhere. Or I could always head back to that linen closet.

"Yes," she said, and then as my hand hit the doorknob, "No."

"No?"

Camellia grimaced. "Would you mind... staying?"

I tried to ignore the old daydream that set beating wings against my chest with her words. "Staying *here*?"

"Yes. Oh!" she exclaimed, misinterpreting the wobble in my voice. "No, I'm not asking you to do anything... like that. I just..." Her voice was very small. "I'm scared, Cora."

"Scared of going back to sleep?" My stomach dropped. Of *course.*

She swallowed, nodded, swallowed again. "What if... what if I...?"

I was back at her bedside in a breath, daring to sit down next to her, grabbing her hand. "Camellia, you will wake up. You *will.* The magic is gone. The research team said so."

"I know, but—" Tears welled in her eyes again. "What if I don't?"

"I'll keep watch," I said. "The moment you look like you're doing anything other than regular sleeping, I'll wake you up."

She squeezed my hand, sending that flurry of tingles back through my veins. "You promise?"

"I promise, Camellia. I'll stay right here with you." *As long as you need me.* "Now rest, you stubborn creature. You've had a long, weird day."

"Okay," she sniffled, snuggling down into her pillow. "But Cora?"

"Yes?"

Her voice was barely a whisper; she was already drifting off. "Will you keep holding my hand so I know you're there?"

"Couldn't let go if I wanted to, Princess."

I settled back against the headboard and watched as her breathing slowed into sleep. Her hand was so delicate in mine, as soft as her silken sheets, and her face looked so peaceful, with all of the worry and frustration smoothed away by dreams. I closed my own eyes and thought to myself, *oh.*

Maybe rescuing the princess wasn't about striding in here and waking her up. Maybe it was about staying with her so she wasn't afraid to go back to sleep.

\*\*\*

As it turned out, I didn't manage to keep my eyes open all night. The next thing I was aware of was Camellia shaking me awake as sun streamed in through the tower window.

"Come on," she said, full of more energy than anyone ought to have right after waking up. Maybe those six hundred years had given her a backlog of rest. "I want to get back to the garden right away." With that, she bounded out of bed – and, I tried to not pout, out of my arms.

That made the second time that waking up the sleeping princess hadn't gone *quite* as I dreamed. Still, watching her sail across the room on legs ten times more confident than yesterday's filled my heart in an entirely different way.

"I'm coming, I'm coming," I said.

Camellia pointed me to her private bathroom to wash up, and I magicked my skirt and shirt clean too, not having thought to ask Fiona for spares. When I came out, Camellia had retrieved a plain, sturdy dress from somewhere – the servants' quarters, by the look of it – and was pulling on a pair of standard issue District boots that matched mine.

"Are you ready?" She was practically hovering with excitement. "I think I can handle the stairs today." She paused, chewing on her lip. "On the way down, at least."

"The way up is a problem for later," I scoffed. "Come on, then. Let's get back to the garden."

The garden, when we got there, was only slightly less daunting than the day before. I stopped at the edge of the green tangle to survey the mess. Camellia had no such qualms.

First, she picked her way to the camellia bush and kissed the flower good morning. I didn't hide my laugh, and she blushed as she turned back to me.

"You're so soppy," I said.

"We terribly ancient creatures have to stick together, you know." Her smile turned sad. "We're all that's left of my old life."

"We'll get it back to full strength," I said, and *we'll get you back to full strength* echoed in the air between us.

She shook her head as if to clear her thoughts. "Let's get started, then."

* * *

It took nearly two weeks before we could see the paths again. Partly because there was more greenery than I'd ever seen before, weeds wrapped around vines wrapped around something with the deepest, tangliest roots; partly because we had to take a lot of breaks, whenever Camellia's limbs began to shake. Most days we worked an hour at a time, then paused to lie in the sunshine for a while before starting again. When it rained, we holed up in the library and traded history, Camellia offering me things I'd never known about Borealis court life, while I racked my brains for what had happened in the last six centuries.

It was astonishing how happy I felt, with the two of us hidden away in this castle so far from the real world. The more time I spent with the real Camellia – made her laugh with snarky comments about history, offered my shoulder when she cried with frustration at her weakness, brushed dirt from her forehead where she'd pushed her hair back while planting – the more I forgot about that ethereal princess of legend, the one who had no personality but gratitude and curse. This Camellia, the one who made me cackle with laughter as she did impressions of dignitaries long since passed, she was better. She made my heart sing whenever she looked at me – and I'd spent enough time with Fiona to know what that meant.

Was I ridiculous, to be thinking of love after only two weeks? But then, it wasn't two weeks, was it – I'd been dreaming of Camellia for more than twenty-five years, and the reality of her was so much more than the dream.

"What on earth are you thinking about?" she asked, interrupting my reverie. "You've been watering that plant for five solid minutes."

Oops. "Nothing. Just what a nice day it is." I muttered a soak-away spell I usually used for condensation on the library windows, and then an apology to the plant. Camellia's habit of talking to them like they were people was rubbing off on me. "How are you doing?"

"I've almost finished this bed." She waved her trowel proudly at the lumps in front of her where she'd been planting bulbs. "I just hope they grow quickly. The waiting is the worst thing about bulbs."

As she waved, the air shimmered around her hand; the lumps in the soil wiggled, and green shoots emerged, growing swiftly until they were as tall as our boots.

"What the—" Camellia leapt back from the bed, grabbing my arm. "Cora, did you do that?"

I most certainly had *not* done that.

"Camellia," I said carefully, pulling her round to face me. "Before you went to sleep... did you have any magic?"

"I don't— I don't think so?"

"Did you ever do any gardening?"

She twisted her mouth into a wry knot. "Only in the princessy kind of way. I wasn't allowed to do anything hard, or get dirty, of course, but I cut flowers sometimes. I had a little tree in a pot in my study - we all did, but Father was always jealous because he could never get his to grow as nicely... as mine." She trailed off on the last two words, eyes wide. "Was that *magic*?"

"I think so," I chuckled. "Camellia, I think you're a witch."

"Oh," she said, and then, "Oh!" She dropped her trowel and *ran*, faster than I'd seen her yet, to the camellia bush. Falling to her knees, she wrapped her hands around its branches and buried her face in its leaves. I watched, mesmerised, as a fountain of rich pink buds swelled on every twig, bursting open like fireworks, their silky petals the size of my hand.

I ran to Camellia, sinking down into the dirt beside her. She turned to me, her eyes shining with unshed tears. "Cora, *look*. I can fix it."

"You clever, clever thing," I said, grabbing her hands and planting a kiss on the back of each one. "You wonderful, magical woman."

The air shimmered between us for a second, and my breath caught, my gaze captured by the awe in Camellia's eyes. I swayed closer, almost unthinkingly, but felt something stir in my hair; a bit of ivy that had caught in my bun took life and slithered across my head to form a wild crown.

Camellia giggled. "Now I'm the witch and you're the princess," she said.

Damn, but I wanted to kiss her.

The ivy had other ideas, though, still growing, reaching tendrils out to slide down over my face. The moment was broken when it stuck a leaf in my eye. "Ow," I said. "Not that I don't love your magic, Camellia, but could you turn it off?"

Then we were laughing, pulling ivy out in yards from my hair as it grew and grew, breaking down in giggles as it tangled our hands together. Clearly we had some work to do to get this wild magic under control.

\*\*\*

When Camellia woke me the next morning, it wasn't with her usual excitement; instead, it was with the sound of her crumpling to the floor as she tried to get up.

"*Ascolsa, ascolsa, ascolsa betanda!*" She sounded furious.

"You all right down there?" I asked, scooting to the edge of the bed to peer down at her.

"My legs," she moaned. "They're doing it again. And my back. Ow."

I tugged her back up into bed. "I'm not surprised, you know. You did a *lot* yesterday – even if we don't count the magic, which always wore me out when I started, you were digging and running and planting and everything. No wonder it's caught up with you."

"It's stupid," she said.

"I know it's frustrating, but resting isn't stupid."

"But it's a waste of a beautiful day!" she groaned. "I want to be out there *doing* things. Helping."

"Maybe today you have to help yourself, not the garden."

She muttered, almost too low for me to hear, "I don't want to. I feel like I've done enough resting for a lifetime, and it still isn't enough."

"I know," I said, drawing her into a hug. "Listen, the garden needs rainy days, right? It's annoying for us, yes, because we can't do much, but the rain is good for the garden."

"Where are you going with this?" She sounded cross, but she relaxed into my arms.

"I'm trying to say, look at it like spring arriving. You don't get to a point where the weather is just magically sunny every day – there's always a few rainy days mixed in, because it's not a straight line. Neither is you getting better. Think of today like a rainy day: it feels rubbish, but it's needed. It's good for us. You've got so much stronger already, and you've had so many sunny days in a row. Let yourself have a rainy one every so often."

"Fine," she said petulantly, and oh, how I wanted to kiss that frustration from her face. "I know you're making sense, even if I don't want you to."

"It'll be sunny again soon." I nestled my cheek on top of her head as she let it fall back on my chest. "Trust me."

\*\*\*

As it turned out, we had two days of recovery before Camellia broke down and insisted I carry her down into the garden around lunchtime so we could eat in the sunshine. Afterwards, she convinced me she was strong enough to sit on the floor and plant some of the herbs; I agreed, as long she tried not to do any magic and let me do the digging.

We settled down side-by-side, and while I'd very much enjoyed our time stuck in bed – not like that, thank you – swapping stories and enjoying the peace and quiet, a huge sense of contentment filled me at seeing Camellia back in her element.

As I passed her a small rosemary plant, she smiled and tweaked my sunhat so it shaded my face more. I felt my cheeks heat anyway.

"We should let the District know about your magic, I was thinking." I'd sent only barebones reports while we'd been holed up inside; somehow our discoveries seemed too new to share with anyone else. Fiona had accepted my explanation that Camellia was resting the day before with no more fuss than my request for another pot of apricot jam.

Camellia sighed. "Yes, I was thinking about what happens next, too. I can't really be a princess anymore, can I? There's no such thing as Lineria, and if I've got no queendom to rule, what am I going to do - lurk at the back of someone else's court all 'hi, I used to be in charge here'?"

"It would be a little awkward," I said. "You'd make everyone love you within days, though."

She paused in her planting and looked at me with a quizzical tilt to her head and an amused sparkle in her eyes. "Oh really?"

"Of course," I said hurriedly, feigning deep interest in the lavender I was holding. "You know, with your diplomatic training and everything."

"Just that?" Was that a catch in her voice?

"What else did—" Luckily, I was interrupted by the ping of the spell that let me know a letter had appeared in my bag from Fiona. I scrambled up to get it, grateful to have a chance to hide my blush. "I'd better look at that."

"Oh, of course," Camellia chuckled. "It's probably very important."

"Wait, no, it *is*," I said in disbelief. "It's—"

"What?" she cried, trying to leap up to join me in reading, but wobbling back down immediately. "Oh, damn it. Tell me, tell me."

"It's... good news. They've found out why the curse broke after all this time."

"And?"

"Coccinelle retired! She went back to the Faelands – something about falling in love and getting bored of her bad reputation – which was the last straw for her lingering curses. They just gave up when she crossed the border."

Camellia squealed. "So there's no one insisting I have to marry them? I'm free?"

"You're free," I said, falling to my knees and tackling her in a hug that would have stopped a bear in its tracks. "You don't owe anything to anyone."

"No prince?"

"No prince," I said. "No one but you." The air changed between us into something glimmering and charged. I couldn't take my eyes from her face, and she gazed back at me, just as stunned.

"I can go to Alvary. Find out how my parents lived." She laughed. "I can find out if I have great-great-great-relatives."

"You can do anything you want to," I whispered.

She paused for a second, two seconds, a lifetime. *Kiss me,* I thought irrationally, then forced the idea down.

Finally, she spoke, more hesitant than I'd ever seen her. "Do you think... I mean, I'm probably too old to start... But... When I get back, would the Academy take me?"

"You want to be a *District Witch*?" In all the joking and wondering we'd done about Camellia's future, the idea had never occurred to me.

She blushed. "No, of course, it's a ridiculous idea. I just thought—"

"Camellia," I grinned, "it's a fantastic idea."

"Really?"

"Yes!" I grabbed her hands in my excitement. "Listen, I wish I'd thought of it! It's the perfect way to fill in everything you need to know – goodness knows I can't teach you everything they want me to – and you'd get to explore your magic. You'd make a wonderful witch, too. You're so clever, and kind, and determined. Anyone would be lucky to have you on their case."

"And me being an ex-princess won't be a problem?"

"Not if you're willing to muck in and learn like everyone else. There's always a couple of royals in each year, and as long as they're not snooty, they get along fine with everyone else. Just, maybe don't insist everyone calls you "Your Serene Highness"."

"That was one time!" she laughed.

"Everyone will adore you," I said, ignoring the twist in my stomach at the thought of her laughing and sharing secrets with her new witch cohort. I would miss her, miss this easy pattern our days had fallen into, so very much.

"And I'm just checking," she said lightly, "but it *is* the Northern Academy's library you're based at? Not anywhere else?"

"Yes?"

"Good." She gave me a smirk. "I'll apply there, then. I can see I'll be needing to do a lot of research between classes, and I'll need to see my favourite librarian, oh, every couple of hours at least." She turned back to focus on the rosemary she was planting, as if she hadn't just turned my entire world to butterflies. "Turns out you were a thief all along. You might not have stolen any treasure, but you went straight for my heart."

Suddenly, I knew I had to be brave. As brave as the adventurer I'd always dreamed of being. As brave as my beautiful legend of a princess, this soil-smudged, tireless, magical woman. "Camellia."

She didn't look up, but there was humour in her voice. "Yes,

Cora?"

"I'd really like to kiss you now."

"I thought you were never going to ask," she said, and then "Oh, mind the herbs!" as I closed the distance between us, plucked the trowel out of her hands, and planted my entire heart on her smiling lips.

Adie Hart is a lover of stories and the words behind them. With a background in the history and literature of the Ancient World, and an abiding love of classic fairy tales, she writes everything from fun fantasy adventures to dark mythological retellings.

When she's not writing, she can usually be found reading, gardening, or trapped under her large cat! Check out her website at https://adiehart.wordpress.com.

# Season's Keep

R. A. Gerritse

The gates of Season's Keep slammed shut, shaking its foundations, waking Sora from her deepest slumber yet. It couldn't be – had it been three seasons, was Darah's journey already at an end? Well, she was back, it seemed.... So, probably? *Well, fuck me, I guess,* she thought. Reluctant to let go of her warm, comfortable blankets, she cursed the hour either way, for it felt too early – way too early to end her peaceful sleep.

Sora rubbed her eyes and rose, shivering, struggling to adjust to the cold, the muted light, to life itself – flooding back, drawing her out of a blissful, dreamless warmth into a harsh reality. You see, while she slept, frigid and foreboding, Winter's bite had found its way into her room through a crack between the curtains. *So cold.* Sora shivered. *Shadows and frost, every damn time. Why can't my shift, if just for once, start after Denna's?*

For a keeper of the new dawn, she was not much of a morning person. Grumbling, she stepped into her boots, pulled her robes over her head, wound a scarf around her neck, buried her hands inside her pockets, and sauntered – stumbling, yawning, stretching, cursing – over to the frostbitten mirror in the corner near the window.

*Is it colder than usual?* she thought, rubbing the last sleep from her eyes. *Or is it just me getting older, feeling the weight of days?* Whatever it was, something sure felt off, but she couldn't quite tell what. Shaking it off, she cleaned the mirror's surface with the hem of her robe, wiping the frost away – her now damp sleeve only made her feel colder.

"Hello again, darling," said her reflection. "You look worse than ever, but hey, what else is new?" At least there were no new wrinkles today – no visible ones anyway. She swore she felt older, though.

Sora sighed and, with herculean effort, painted on an unfelt cheerful smile. "Rise and shine," she told herself. "It's a brand new day, a brand new lie." And she could sell it too – she knew that well. That is, seemingly, to anyone but herself.

"It will have to do, I guess. Duty calls. Again, it seems," she muttered, hearing Darah's ruckus moving through the halls below like the Winter storm she was. Did she sound louder than usual? Angrier? More frustrated? Again, the foreboding feeling that something was awry crept up on her, sending a shiver down her spine with a creeping sense of urgency. She released a shaking, frosted breath and tried to shake it off. Again. *You're getting paranoid with age,* she mocked herself and turned around to mark the start of a new season. "Have patience a bit longer, dear sister. I'm almost on my way."

Of all her sisters, Sora was the most punctual and the only one of the four who diligently kept track of the cycles – she felt she had to. *If not me, then who'd remember?* Of all the trails of footsteps through the sands of time, it seemed only hers ever remained. The rest simply got erased, only to appear again, rising and falling with the tides of eternity. *If only someone could grant such gifts to me.*

From the paved floors to the high ceilings, the walls of her spacious yet sparsely decorated quarters – carved to match her heart – formed a tapestry of painful memories no longer kept by anyone but her.

Scanning the yellowed, plastered walls for an unmarked spot, Sora found a bare patch near the door still untouched by the tracks of time. Wielding a chisel she grabbed from her dresser, she carved with the utmost care, adding a shallow line with equal width and distance to the maze of countless others, marking yet another beginning. Each of the countless marks on her walls, every journaled start of her perpetual cycle, cast a single shadow, further darkening her grim reality. *Another one, another round. How much longer? How many more before I'm done?* Would that day ever come? She sighed deeply and wondered if she'd soon need to switch rooms, for these walls were almost entirely filled. And why did she feel so down today, so much more than her usual gray?

Shaking her head, she replaced her tool on the dresser, left her room, and locked the door, then made her way through empty hallways – silent but for Denna's snoring next door and the desperate, near-exhausted sounds of Darah's rage down below – and hurried to follow the sounds of her sister's frustration to the main hall, where she found her trembling and panting, leaning against a wall.

*And I thought* I *looked tired,* Sora thought as she paused in the doorway in shock, taking in the sorry state of her sister and the trail of her destruction leading from the kitchen. "Oh, Darah, you poor thing," she said. "You look like hell! Was it that bad again?" And as she said it, she felt it again, the sense that something was so very wrong and out of place.

Darah's frosted eyes, still blazing with an inner deep blue fire – an all too familiar, all-consuming existential hatred for everything fate had made her be – turned Sora's way, met her gaze, and then melted, bursting out in tears. She collapsed, curling up on the floor as if realizing she was home, done for a season, and – perhaps above all – no longer alone.

"Worse," she sobbed with her head buried in her hands. "So much worse. So much death, so much decay. This has to stop – I don't think I'll ever have the strength to go out there again to clean up Jena's damn mess."

Sora watched her wipe her tears. *She looks it,* she thought, swallowing that rising dread – everything felt...worse this season. And was that fear in Darah's eyes? What mess could Jena possibly have left her to clean up might have shaken her usually fearless sister this much? "Are you sure it was Jena's doing, though, sis', and not the fallout of one of Denna's blistering summers again?"

"I don't know, Sora, and honestly, I couldn't care less either way. I'm so tired, sis' – I am done," Darah said, visibly surprised that she actually meant it, and as she spoke those defeated words, Sora saw the last fire leave her.

*And so it becomes my mess to solve again,* Sora thought with an inner sigh she'd never show the world. Honestly, she did not hate her calling, no, not really, as much as it felt like a curse at times. *At least this burden is not solely my own. Not all of it, anyhow – only the lonely parts.*

Burying her bitter thoughts, Sora embraced her sister, placing her two fingers high in Darah's neck, just below the ears, and began whispering her first enchantment of this cycle, drawing forth a luminescent stream of wavering, sparkling orange-tinted energy from her mind, guiding it straight into the vault that was her own heart.

"It's alright, you can let go. It's done – forget. Tomorrow shines a gentler, healing light."

As her last word fell silent, as the last sparks of pain from Darah's recent memories were safely locked within her, Sora felt the fight, with all its tension, leave her sister.

And so Sora's season *always* started – with Darah in her arms, somewhere on the floors of Season's Keep, helping her forget the death she'd seen, gently rocking her – and all her fears – to sleep. It was her thing, her part to play in the workings of the world, and her sister was but the first of many souls in need of soothing. But is the first step of any journey or task not always the hardest? Taking in Darah's memories, pain, and tears as she let go surely felt as hard as it could be for Sora. This time, though, the season's horrors nearly overwhelmed her.

Darah had not exaggerated. The memories Sora freed her from painted a chilling picture of the coldest Winter she had ever seen – blanketing the fallout of a devastating Fall, just not in white; no, all destruction remained in plain sight this year.

Her sister had worked hard to put the mourning world to sleep, kicking and screaming, but it was one of restless nights and nightmare dreams. There was turmoil and unrest. There was fear and uncertainty. There was so much loss and pain – it was a hibernating monster locked in a prison of frost that would consume the world should it ever be released. *And it's up to me to tame it... I hope I even can.*

"I have my work cut out for me – there's no way these poor souls are ready to start anew," she whispered as she put the now-sleeping Darah to bed, finally understanding the foreboding dread she'd been feeling. She could feel it in the very air now that she knew what to look for. It had never before been this bad.

Sora regretfully, enviously eyed Darah's comfortable pillows and blankets – a warmth, it seemed, she'd just left behind and knew she wouldn't feel again for the length of a most probably devastating season. It was the only warmth strong enough to still the screams, mute her dreams, and make even her forget – if but for a few month's blissful sleep.

"Don't worry, sis'," she said. "I'll set it right, I promise." And Sora was determined to pull it off despite her wavering self-confidence. After all, didn't even the most harrowing journeys start with a single, not necessarily confident step?

She let go of her dark thoughts and focused on the mountainous task ahead. "I'll share their woes, dim their pain, and help them forget. Like I'm for you, and you're for me, I'll be their reason to go on. Rest well, my sister dearest, and dream some sweet dreams for me. We'll meet again after next Winter's turn."

Over the frosted lands between the world of life and Season's Keep sounded the hoofs of Promise – Sora's majestic winged mount – to the hopeful rhythm of Spring. She could have soared the starless skies but preferred to stay aground, to hear the echo of their footfalls – a cadence bouncing off the shimmering veil beyond. Maybe it was pure fancy, but to her, it always felt like that sound alone – the drum of hooves announcing her arrival – in some small way, already helped stir the sleeping cycle back in motion.

Sora paused at the edge of forever to take in the devastation – dead lands and bare trees so far the eye could see, not a living soul in sight. All who survived the harrowing Winter were hidden deep within their shelters. The task before her seemed impossible – to breathe life back into this wasteland – but wasn't that the same thing she said every time? Then what was so different this time around?

"Like the grass at Winter's end, I'm not dead yet – only thirsty. Once the sun reclaims its seat to rule the lands, watch me thrive," she sang softly, as was her little ritual here, at the point of no return. Did her pause get longer with every turn, though? Maybe.

*Enough stalling, Sora, let's begin,* she thought, and so she did – casting her second enchantment of the cycle.

She whispered to the frost, the storms, the dark at the edge of seasons changing, "Move on, the world will be alright." Daunting silence to skip a beat, she held her breath, bracing for the merciless encore – standing tall at life's edge, shivering. "Ready or not," she screamed, "here I come," as she galloped through the gates into the world to slam the door shut on Winter once more, as she had done so many times before.

Into the freezing realms of the living drifted the sounds of Sora's song – full of emotion, soothing even the last lingering Winter winds, calming to a breeze.

Tuning up the sun, she returned warmth to all frozen with a promise of rebirth – a chance to start again. She sang it stronger than before. It mattered little; none who heard would remember, but it couldn't hurt. She would need every last bit of hope on this journey – padding even the slightest chance.

*This time, I will give it everything I have.*

With the temperatures adjusted and the hordes of Winter's chaos tamed, it was time to nudge the living – to help them on their feet again. Not her first rodeo; she knew exactly where to start. She'd do this one by the books, for so far chaos could be planned.

First, she woke the flowers, if only to set the scene – putting color back on the canvas to take the edge off all its shading, letting the world know that Spring had come again. And with the color came the scent of what could be, overpowering what was. With the muting of the gray began the great Forgetting of all the darkness that had passed.

*Let's hope I made it bright enough.*

Next, she got the birds to join her song and spread the word. "It's safe – come out, go, mate, lay your eggs. Sora is here, and she brings warmth!" Beak to beak, the song of hope reclaimed the skies, breaking the silence, and the sounds of rebirth opened many sleeping eyes – their minds taken off the darkness, eyes raised to the new Spring's light.

With the world dressed up in color, with the winds tuned to the sound of cheer, the living began to fall back into motion, driven by the winds of change. Sora then visited all those still locked inside, with the outside out of view, to set off their biological clocks and timers. "Rise and shine, sleepyheads! It's time to create new life!" And from their homes, trees, and caves, they rose to populate the Earth again, driven to add the sounds

of tiny wings and feet to the ever-forward marching beat of time –
a brand new verse to help forget the chorus.

Lastly, she saw to it the insects went to pollinate, to clean up,
to bring nourishment and beauty, to keep humming the
forgetting song from Spring well into Summer – as a catalyst to
keep the motion now buzzing through the world. Secretly, they
were her favorites. So resilient, so willing to start from scratch
without needing the slightest nudge – they had her back, even if
she visited them last. There wasn't a season where they weren't
already up and about. "Yeah, I must be doing something right,"
she said, smiling for the first time this cycle.

Hers may be the hardest task of all her Sisters – making the
world forget. Hers may be the most taxing burden – carrying the
weight of memory. *But I get to see all this,* she thought, watching
the world come alive once more, even after the darkest of nights,
laughing and cheering, loving and living – a brand new cycle in
the face of the seasons of death.

*May there be many more.*

*I've made it,* Sora thought, tired and dead-weary but feeling
accomplished and content. She sat on a hill overlooking her
favorite village as it prepared for Summer Solstice. She loved
this quaint little town so much, probably because it seemed time
stood still here for at least the last few decades. *And they're
resilient. Just like me.*

She was still going over the now almost wrapped-up season in
her head – how she had dreaded the cycle at the start and how
well she'd done once she'd simply stepped into its rhythm –
when she felt a soft, warm hand on her shoulder. She smiled. "I
was waiting for you, Denna. Did you sleep well?" Sora looked
up to her sister, who, as usual, looked as glorious as a sunrise.

"Always, dearest sister," Denna said. "Summer dreams, you
know? There's nothing better."

"Is that why you always sleep with the light on?" Sora asked as Denna sat down on the edge next to her, lazily dangling her legs over the ledge, stroking the petals of the dandelion she'd plucked from her hairband.

Denna smiled a dreamy smile, silent, as if momentarily lost in thought. "The world needs all the brightness we can give it," she eventually said, almost whispering as if recalling a fond memory, and then, with care, placed the flower in Sora's hair. "There, that befits your smile. But how was your run? You seem... happier than usual?"

Even with her eternal smile, Denna frowned, taking Sora in as if seeing her for the first time. "You almost glow, sis'! Has my positivity finally started to rub off on you?" She paused for a few heartbeats, sharing Sora's comfortable silence, then shined even brighter. "Good for you!" she said, giving her a playful fist bump on the shoulder.

For a moment, her sister's observations about her threw Sora for a loop. *Am I? Happier? I mean...*

"Well, there's the Sora I know and love again," Denna laughed. "Don't overthink it, dearest sister. Just embrace it. Happiness looks good on you."

Sora considered, if but briefly, telling her sister about her difficult start of the cycle and asking what events could possibly have led to the most brutal Winter season she'd ever seen, but decided firmly against it – she'd never want to dim the shining beacon that was Denna. *And maybe she is right, and I should not overthink these things.*

She *felt* happy, and maybe that was enough. Right then and there, she decided she'd keep the lights on that night and, after a long pause, smiled as she honestly answered Denna's question, setting a new, brighter tone for many cycles yet to come.

"My season was most wonderful."

As a rock journalist for Metal On Loud Magazine, <u>Randy</u> watches the world in search of both rhythms and answers. As an author, host of the Twitter poetry prompt tag #vsspoem, and a lyricist for four different bands, poetry is part of his every day – it even found its way into his novels.

His first self-publication: a collection of micro poetry forged into a single, two act epic poem called The Rhythm of Life, is now available on Amazon.

Randy's first published short stories Rain Must Fall and Days Gone By are now available in the anthologies Of Silver Bells and Chilling Tales and Of Mistletoe And Snow by Jazz House Publications.

# DARKNESS GREEN

Laila Amado

Nightfall in this city smells like votive candles. Houses huddle close to each other down the narrow streets, their pointed roofs scratching at the low clouds. In the gathering shadows, a woman hurries along the cobbled street that stretches all the way from the railway station to the main square with its town hall, cathedral, and perpetually waterless marble fountain.

Her wide red riding hood flaps in the wind like a sail in a storm.

At the corner of two crossing streets, she pauses and looks around, her nostrils flaring slightly as if catching some elusive scent. A small flock of children dressed in pointy black hats run by, giggling. The smallest of the group carries a brightly painted papier-mâché goat head on a wooden stick. The woman watches them run.

In the silence that follows the click-clack of their heels on the cobblestones, she turns and walks in the opposite direction. Her steps carry her uphill, towards the taller buildings and rippling flags of the central quarters of the city.

* * *

*Once upon a time there was a little girl who loved the*

*shadowed forest paths, her grandmother, and sugared plum berries. She hadn't learned yet not to trust the wolves, even those whose pelt is soft to the touch and smells like moonlight.*

\* \* \*

The Grand Hotel shines bright like a lantern. Tall windows spill their golden light on its broad, polished steps and the flagstones of the pavement. Its façade rises upwards, story after story of elegant arches and gleaming glass.

At the receptionist's desk, all oak panels and polished brass, the woman in a red riding hood signs her name in the leather-clad guest registry book. Careful hand spells out letters in an unhurried, rolling cursive. The maître d'hôtel takes back the ledger and his manicured smile falters, eyebrows lifting up.

"Is this really your name?" he asks, incredulous, breaking the proper protocol of welcoming a paying guest.

"It is, indeed," the woman says.

"Darkness Green?" reads out the maître d', as if pronouncing the words out loud will somehow make them more real.

"That is correct."

Good manners set aside, the maître d' blurts out the question tickling the tip of his tongue. "Pardon me, but what did your parents call you?"

"You don't want to know." The woman smiles, showing small white teeth. The smile is as sharp and cold as the blade of a new moon.

Still the maître d' can't bring himself to stop. "What do your friends call you, then?"

"The ones with any sense call me Miss Green," she replies, and the maître d' feels a sudden cold shiver run down his spine.

"Welcome to the Grand Hotel, Ms. Green," he says, struggling to pull his professional mask back on. "Are you here for the celebration of the Hexennacht? Our city is popular with tourists for the Walpurgis Night ball and the burning of the wicker witch."

"I'm here on business," comes the curt reply. The woman's gaze travels over the sofas, lamps, and the decorative panels of the lobby with little interest.

"Enjoy your stay," says the maître d', his composure regained and the manicured smile back in its place.

The woman in the red riding hood gives a generous tip to the bell boy but picks up her small leather suitcase herself. The elevator carries her up to the topmost floor and, for a split second, she feels weightless, like a small bird taking flight.

\* \* \*

*Inside the wolf, there is darkness, and grandmother's bones, and the cloying, sweet smell of the beast, with its notes of blood, sticky fear, and howling rage. After you taste it once, this smell never quite leaves your nostrils.*

\* \* \*

She bypasses the busy main building of the hospital and cuts into the park stretching over its grounds. Lines of neatly trimmed hedges separate the wards from each other. The squat building of the mortuary sits in the back, hidden from view by a cluster of overgrown bushes and a couple of as yet leafless trees. Inside, the corridors are dim. The woman in the red riding hood follows the guidance of faded arrows stamped into the linoleum floor until she finds the room.

"You called for me," she says from the doorway and the doctor gives a startled yelp. He is a small man, balding and slight, fidgeting with the glasses he holds in his hands.

"I wasn't at all sure you'd come," he says in a tone both sad and apologetic. He wants to say something else, but the woman in the red riding hood cuts him off.

"I come when called," she says. "The letter said you needed my help. Is that correct?"

The doctor places the glasses on the bridge of his long nose and carefully considers the woman in front of him. At first. he seems hesitant to speak. "Every year we celebrate the Hexennacht," he says at last. "Do you know the meaning of this word, Miss Green?"

"I know the lore," she answers. "The witch's night precedes the coming of the spring. Before the dawn of May Day, borders between the worlds grows thin, and we must sing and shout to chase away the evil spooks of winter. Or so the tales claim."

"Yes, yes." The doctor nods with unexpected enthusiasm. "We also dance and burn the fires. And when the clocks strike midnight, we burn the effigy of winter, a giant figure of a witch, made of straw and wicker. They're building it even now, just outside the city."

"Come nightfall, the bonfires burn bright. Pretty boys and wild girls dance away the soles of their shoes to the screeching howls of the pipes, spill the ale on glowing timbers, meet the sunrise with sore, parched lips. Flame, smoke, and ash are all sacred." The woman in a red riding hood recites the book she was reading on the train. The doctor looks relieved.

\* \* \*

*A hunter, hired to stop the beast terrorizing the villages, caught it outside the limits of a distant wood. The bullet, forged from high grade silver, caught it straight in the shining amber-yellow eye. When the belly of the wolf was cut open, a little girl emerged from it, unscathed, her face covered in red, red blood.*

\* \* \*

Light from the lamp renders the doctor's glasses white. He pulls a large brown paper envelope from a drawer of his table. Shakes out the photographs. The woman in the red riding hood touches the glossy paper of the prints, spreads the photos out like a dealer spreads a deck of cards.

She sees a white neck splattered with spray of blood, a couple of errant dots marring the crusted, melting snow of early spring; a flurry of pink lace, soaked in burgundy that is unlikely to be wine; the curled fingers of a lifeless hand; hems; bonnets; tangled hair; stockinged feet.

"We find them every year," the doctor says. "Every year, after the Hexennacht is over, a girl is found dead. In the forest, or in a dark alley. Torn up and twisted like a discarded, broken rag doll. I've studied their wounds. Right here, on this table." He gestures towards the marble slab. "And submitted my reports to the constabulary. Each year."

"What do the constables say?"

"A beast of prey." The doctor's lips are pressed together in a thin, white line.

"I gather that you disagree with this assessment," the woman says, her eyes still on the photos on the table.

"There is a method to this killing, atypical of any beast. What beast feasts on one night only and preys on no one but young w-women?" The doctor stutters in the end.

The woman in the red riding hood looks straight at him and, for a split second, the doctor sees green shadows shifting in her eyes. "I'm inclined to agree with your assessment," she says. "These cases warrant an investigation, and I promise to do whatever is in my powers to find the culprit of this carnage." She gathers up the photos with utmost care and places the envelope in the doctor's hands. He seems uneasy.

"Is there something you would like to ask me, Doctor?" she says.

"Is it true what they say about you?" he asks, and two pale pink blotches flower on his cheekbones.

"And what is it that *they* say?" she asks in return, cocking her head.

"That you can find them by scent alone?"

"Find who, good doctor?" A faint smile lingers on the

woman's lips.

"Predators," the Doctor offers. "Hungry beasts disguised in human skin."

She draws the hood of her cloak up and turns to leave, but pauses in the doorway. "Where would you go looking for a predator, my doctor?"

"The Walpurgis Night dance at the city hall," he says without doubt.

As his guest walks away, down the long corridor of the mortuary, the doctor hears her final words. "I know the beast from inside out. The smell forever lingers in my nostrils, and I never miss my mark."

\* \* \*

*The hunter raised the girl as his own, for no family claimed her. He loved her dearly but time and again she sneaked off into the woods, where the hunter would find her sleeping in the crook of a root or in a nest of leaves, her red riding hood splayed out like a pool of blood. He gifted her a silver knife to keep her safe. The first of many.*

\* \* \*

The ballroom glitters with the light of a dozen crystal chandeliers. A whirlpool of plumaged hats, masks, and snapping fans rotates around the dancing floor to the notes of festive music. The band plays. Cascades of champagne pour down the pyramids of glass flutes in rivulets of sparkling frizz.

The woman in the red riding hood enjoys the dance. She glides across the floor on the arm of a sailboat captain, makes a full circle around the room with two young men dressed as peacocks. She waltzes, in succession, with an elderly baronet in a pink tuxedo, a man in a wizard's hat, and a musketeer. A polka tune takes her flying across the dance floor, the soles of her shoes barely touching the polished oak tiles underfoot. Her chest rises high and falls in a rapid rhythm; her nostrils flare. All eyes are upon her flailing red cape.

Hot, she escapes the clutches of her dancing partner and glides towards the French windows, open into the night. Walks out onto the balcony. The cold air still carries notes of winter, and the last errant snowflakes dance in the light of street lanterns. Beyond the glow of the city streets, the forest lies dark. The woman in the red riding hood studies the pointed, blue-green cones of the firs and the black branches of the – so far – bare trees. An effigy of winter, the wicker witch, towers over everything. The pliant branches of an osier have been forced to form its limbs and torso. Here and there, amid the trees, first fires come to life and cast red shadows on the plaited straw.

"The Hexennacht brings out the best in the musicians of this city. The violin is outright inspired," says a voice behind her. He is standing in the doorway, and the light from the ballroom casts him in an umbral shadow.

"I prefer the cello – its dark, majestic undertow," says the woman in the red riding hood.

He takes a step forward, smiling, and she takes the offered flute of champagne. The popping bubbles leave a metallic aftertaste on her tongue.

"Would my lady care for a dance?" He offers his hand. It's warm and firm, and she feels her heart give a little startled flutter in her chest.

Music carries them across the ballroom floor in a passionate embrace. He is a confident partner, his hand at her back calm and assured. She can't help but notice the generous curve of his lips, the rich color of the curls brushing the top of his high white collar. Every pair of eyes is upon them, the most beautiful couple on the dance floor, and, when he leans in to kiss her, his lips taste like honey and bitter, wild berries.

"Let's take a walk in the forest," she whispers, and is almost sad to see a flicker of yellow amber in his soft brown eyes. The red riding hood flows around her shoulders, and the darkness of the wood swallows them whole.

\* \* \*

*The darkness of the forest is neither black nor inky blue. It is the green of fir trees, moss, and ferns, the eyes of wild cats, and the deepest places of hidden lakes. It is the darkness green and hungry.*

\* \* \*

Red fabric has two significant advantages. First, it is the most beautiful of all fabrics. Second, it hides the blood stains well.

Miss Darkness Green steps over the red cape, discarded on the carpet of her hotel room. She wipes down the blades of her silver knives and places them back in the designated holders inside her small leather suitcase.

The small teapot in her room makes a lovely cup of tea. She wraps herself in a warm, cozy blanket and sits at a table by the window. In the distance she can see the fires burning in the forest. The din and music are carried by the wind. Sipping her tea, she watches the effigy of the dark witch catch fire. First, small embers crawl upwards, breaking out into flames on the wicker limbs, and then the whole thing goes up, lighting up the night.

In the morning, they will find charred bones where the effigy of winter stood. There will never be another maiden found ripped up in the melting snow of the first spring morning. The city will buzz for a week and then settle, but by that time the woman in the red riding hood will be long gone, the steam-belching train carrying her away, towards another hunt in the green darkness of the world that is a never-ending forest.

Laila Amado is a vagabond storyteller who writes in her second language and has recently exchanged her fourth country of residence for the fifth. Her stories have been published or are forthcoming in Best Small Fictions 2022, Daily Science Fiction, Cotton Xenomorph, Three Lobed Burning Eye, and other publications. She is on Instagram at Laila Amado and on Bluesky at amadolaila.bsky.social

# The Circus of Forgotten Things

Caroline Logan

James was his mother's favourite child. She had a large brood of them, but, whether it was for his bright blue eyes or the copper curls upon his head, Maw MacIntyre loved Jamie just a wee bit more than the rest. And, inevitably, love like that was noticed.

The adults in town noticed when Jamie's mother would hoist him into her arms at the slightest danger. His brothers and sisters noticed when extra food appeared on his plate. Jamie noticed when, every spring, he wasn't allowed to leave the house.

First, the cherry trees that lined the main street turned the pink of spun sugar. Then the daffodils sprouted proudly from the grass, trumpets raised and ready for song. When the first lamb was born, bleating joyfully as it entered the world, that's when Jamie's home became his cage.

"I'm doing this for your safety, my love," his mother said.

Jamie looked out the kitchen window, watching his siblings play in the daisy-speckled grass. "Why me?" was all he'd ask.

Maw MacIntyre's mouth would twist as she stirred the porridge. "You're special, Jamie. I can't let them have you."

Jamie never worked out *who* exactly his mother was protecting him from, but he knew her fear was inexplicably linked to the season, and what came with it. Because every year, like clockwork, as the sun rose on the first day of spring, the circus would arrive.

He'd never seen it, but the neighbourhood children told him of the wonders as they passed his window. The dancing horses, the strongman, the acrobats. Tents so large they could fit ten houses inside. Mysteries, marvels, death-defying acts. Jamie so badly wanted to go, but even if he'd been allowed out of the house, it wasn't possible. His mother didn't even let his siblings attend.

"Every year they forget," she muttered darkly as the night sky was lit up by crackling fireworks. "Utter fools."

"What have they forgotten?" asked Jamie's brother Liam.

She shook her head. "The same as you, it seems. Trust me when I tell you not to go near the circus and soon you'll see."

When Jamie woke up on the first day of summer that year, his body felt heavy, as if it had been the first sleep he'd had in a while. His eyes were sore like he'd been crying, but he didn't remember what about. Making his way downstairs, he found himself in the kitchen, staring out at the village and thinking something had changed.

"Ah, you're up," said his mother, coming in from the garden through the open door. "It's a lovely day, make sure you don't waste it."

Of course. It was summer; he could leave the house. Still—"Did something happen yesterday? Something sad?"

"Yes," she sighed, gathering him in her arms. "But you've forgotten again. It's all right, everyone is safe. And you're here with me, my Jamie."

He wanted to ask what she was talking about, but the birds called him from outside, beckoning him into the sun after so long cooped up. Jamie squeezed his mother before rushing out, still clad in his sleep shirt and trousers. Soon, his brothers and sisters joined him, playing at pirates and picking bouquets of wildflowers, all under the watchful eye of Maw MacIntyre, who, after months of fear, finally let herself feel relief.

*** 

Jamie unfolded the piece of paper, as he'd done every morning since he'd received it, and traced his finger over the printed words. If anyone else happened upon the parchment he placed under his bed each night, they'd have found an admissions letter. *Congratulations*, it read, *you have been accepted into the College of Social Sciences at the University of Glasgow.* But Jamie saw it as something else: a ticket to a new life.

In only four months, he'd be leaving his village to journey to the city. And while he'd miss his mother and his siblings, he would not miss the walls of their cottage. *This spring,* he vowed, *will be the final time anyone locks me up.*

"Jamie?" his mother called from downstairs. "Breakfast is ready."

Jamie tucked his letter away and swung his legs out of bed, taking the time to pull on his wool trousers and linen shirt. It wasn't as if there was a rush. It was March; he wouldn't be going anywhere.

Maw MacIntyre greeted him with a smacking kiss when he appeared in the kitchen, her wooden spoon dripping porridge on the worktop. "I thought you were going to spend all day in bed."

"What would it matter if I did?" he asked, taking his seat at the table. Through the window, he could see his sisters playing a jumping game, throwing a rock into the boxes they'd drawn in chalk and skipping around it. The wind picked up and his youngest sister, Mairi, almost lost her bonnet. Pushing her hat firmly against her curls, her mouth opened in what he imagined was a shriek. But he couldn't hear it. Inside, there were only the sounds of the porridge bubbling and the tick of the clock on the mantle.

His mother clicked her tongue as she spooned the oats into a bowl for him. "Won't be long now until the summer," was all she said.

Over the years, Maw MacIntyre had hinted she was as unhappy about Jamie's imprisonment as he was. Like it was someone else's will. But Jamie's father wasn't around, and he'd never heard anyone threaten his mother. So why did she keep him inside?

"I'm going down to the market." Maw MacIntyre placed the steaming bowl in front of him, along with the shaker of salt. "I'll see if I can find you a new book to keep you busy. One with the Romans or the Greeks."

"That would be nice," he said, because he had no other option.

"You know to stay inside," she said, grabbing her shawl. "If one of the children comes in with a problem, send them next door to Mrs Baird. They're not to follow me, do you understand?"

"Yes."

"Because the circus is still in town, and you know what that means."

Jamie looked at her blankly. "No, I don't."

Maw MacIntyre regarded him wearily. "No, I don't suppose you do. Just stay inside; I'll be back soon."

She flung open the door and, for a glorious moment, the fresh spring air flooded into the kitchen. Jamie breathed deeply, feeling as if it was blowing away the dust from his lungs. But then, as quickly as it had blasted in, it was gone, as his mother shut the door. And shut out the world beyond.

Jamie ate his porridge carefully, blowing on it so it wouldn't burn his tongue. He'd give anything to be heading down to the market, to smell the rain-soaked air and touch the fresh blooms sprouting from the grass. But his mother was right, he did know better. He wasn't even locked inside, but he knew he still wouldn't dare disobey her. Because something told Jamie that there was a reason Maw MacIntyre kept him inside. If only he could remember it—

The door slammed open, followed by a burst of laughter and a trio of little girls bounding into the room. Jamie was only related to two of them, but that never seemed to matter to Joanna Baird, the youngest of their neighbours' daughters. She peeled her sopping coat off and chucked it in a heap in front of the fire, the fabric slapping wetly against the flagstones.

"Mairi fell over," she told him, gesturing to his sister to sit on one of the chairs. "But at least the boobrie didn't peck her to death."

"The what?" asked Jamie, dropping his spoon to find his mother's medical kit.

His neighbour gave him a look of disdain that only an eight-year-old could muster. "A shapeshifting water bird. It tried to attack Mairi but she fought it off."

"It was part of our game," his other sister, Katie, told him.

Jamie nodded. "I see. Well, Mairi, we'll get you patched up so you can go back and fight some more monsters for us. Where does it hurt?"

"My knee," said Mairi, looking delighted at the attention.

Jamie pushed her skirts back and sure enough, there was a tiny scratch there, just above her long socks. Blood welled in the pinpricks of scraped skin, but it would heal quickly, Jamie thought as he poured a drop of alcohol onto a cloth.

Joanna peered over his shoulder and hummed. "Just as well,

Mairi, or I'd have had to sacrifice you."

"What?" Mairi squeaked, just as Jamie touched the stinging liquid to her cut.

"Your blood is red," said Joanna, pointing. "You're not a faerie."

"What colour is faerie blood?" asked Katie from the sink.

Joanna rolled her eyes. "Everyone knows it's green. That's how you tell someone is a changeling: the child the fairies leave behind when they take a human."

"So we should try stabbing anyone we think is a faerie?" asked Mairi.

Jamie sighed. "Stop putting tales in my sisters' heads, Joanna Baird, or I'll have to start watching my back. No stabbing," he told them all. "Or you're not going back out."

"Well, you can't stop me," said Joanna primly. "I'm going to the circus this afternoon."

Jamie placed a kiss on his sister's newly bandaged knee and fixed her skirts. "Oh really? Who's taking you?"

"I'm taking myself." Joanna pinched a biscuit from the jar on the counter and broke it into three pieces, giving the biggest to Mairi and another bit to Katie. "I've been wanting to go for weeks and I finally have enough money to get in."

"Ooh, can we go?" asked Mairi, her mouth full of crumbs.

"You know we can't," said Jamie with a sigh. "Now if you're all quite done helping yourselves to food, you'd better go back out to play."

The three girls turned to the window to find the rain had picked up since they'd barrelled in. The tree outside waved in the wind as if to beckoning them to join it, but only Joanna seemed keen on the invitation.

"Maybe I'll just go to the circus now, since you two are being wee fearties. I'll come round on my way back to tell you all about what fun I had." And with that, she was scooping up her sodden coat and disappearing out the door.

"Let's play faeries in our room," said Katie with a grin. "We'll set up a faerie ring with our bed sheets and when the others come home, we'll grab them."

Mairi clapped her hands in delight and together they ran off upstairs, little feet pounding against the timber.

Jamie hung his head in his hands, but couldn't help letting out a chuckle. Children were wee devils sometimes, but you had to laugh.

The rest of the day, he pottered around the house, tidying away clothes and old newspapers. His two youngest brothers, Liam and Thomas, arrived home around lunchtime, covered in mud and leaves but grinning from ear to ear. Then came Maw MacIntyre, with the promised book for him and a new pair of boots for Katie. It was just turning to dusk outside the window when the final member of their family, his brother Archie, appeared in the doorway. At first, no one paid him any attention as they helped their mother with dinner. But as he entered the kitchen, the lamplight glowed on his face, showing him pale and drawn, as if he'd seen a ghost.

"What's wrong, Archie?" asked Liam.

"Has anyone seen Joanna Baird today?" he asked.

Katie frowned. "She was here this morning. Left around ten."

"She hasn't been seen for hours," said Archie. "The whole town is out looking for her."

"I'm sure she's fine," Mairi told him. "She said she was going —"

"—nowhere," fibbed Katie, her eyes widening at her sister. "She said she was going out, I think."

"Out where?" asked Maw MacIntyre sharply.

There was a sudden silence in the kitchen, as Katie and Mairi bit their lips. Their brothers looked on with confusion. Only Jamie was willing to tell her.

"Joanna said she was going to the circus."

Maw MacIntyre looked grim. "I see. That's a real shame."

"What do you mean?" asked Thomas.

"I'm afraid Joanna won't be back," replied their mother, scooping mince onto a plate as if they were discussing something mildly troubling, like the rain or wet socks.

Liam's brows knit together. "The circus is only down at the village green. Perhaps she lost track of time."

Their mother slammed her wooden spoon on the countertop. "This is why I forbid you all from going. Every year this happens and every year you forget."

"What happens?" asked Katie with tears in her eyes.

Maw MacIntyre sighed. "Children are stolen, right from under their families' noses. And it's always when the circus is around. It doesn't matter how long we look, they're never found again. Or at least, *our* children aren't. Sometimes, we find a— a *person* who looks like the child, but they aren't the same. Not right. And soon they disappear too."

Jamie had never heard of this before. "What are you talking about?"

"Changelings." Their mother whispered the word like she was afraid of saying it out loud.

"Joanna was telling us about them this morning," piped up Mairi.

"Was she?" She cupped Mairi's cheek with her large hands and gave her a sad smile. "At any rate, she's gone. I'm sorry."

This was absurd. Joanna couldn't have gotten far. "No," croaked Jamie, shaking his head. "You have to go tell someone to search the circus if that's where she went."

"It'll do no good, Jamie. Every year they try, and every year they fail. Don't worry, when summer rolls around, you'll all have forgotten about Joanna."

"I don't want to forget her," sobbed Katie. "She's my friend."

Their mother went back to dishing up the plates, turning her back on her children and the conversation. "I think we've talked about this enough. Time for dinner."

Jamie couldn't believe the fierce, fiery Maw MacIntyre would give up so easily. As if Joanna was gone forever. *Or dead.* "I'm not hungry anymore."

The woman's shoulders slumped but she didn't turn around. "I'll leave yours in the oven," was all she said.

Jamie took one last look at his silently weeping siblings, before climbing the stairs and shutting them out.

\*\*\*

No matter how Jamie tried, he couldn't sleep. Not when his younger siblings crept into their beds, nor when his mother finally retired. He'd left his window open to have a tie to the outside, but the wind was loud, shaking the trees and rattling the gate. What was worse, though, was the shouting. Desperate pleas for Joanna to come out of her hiding place punctuated the cold night. And below all the sounds, off in the distance, the roar of a crowd. The circus was putting on a show, even with a child missing.

Jamie racked his brain for any information he'd learned of the circus. It came every spring. From where, he knew not. And then it was gone again by the first day of summer. He'd heard there were shows and tricks, but hadn't heard of a single person in it. It cost money – though he wasn't sure how much. Joanna had mentioned she'd saved her pennies for it.

The thought of Joanna's gleeful face as she'd stated her plans that morning had him wrenching himself out of bed. There was no way he'd be able to sleep that night.

"We should be out there," whispered Jamie to himself, as he shuffled to the window. "We should all be looking for her."

But they couldn't. Maw MacIntyre had forbidden it.

"In only a few months, you'll be able to go wherever you want," he vowed. Except, that wasn't right, was it? Jamie was seventeen now, a man in anyone else's eyes. What would waiting four months do? He looked out over the chimney tops in their village, towards a warm glow. The big tents were obscured by the houses, but just above the roofs, he could make out a series of flags, flapping merrily in the breeze. It wasn't far, just ten minutes if someone was quick.

*I could be quick,* he thought.

And then he was pushing from the window, pulling on his clothes as quickly as he dared in the sleeping cottage. He tucked his shirt in and clipped his suspenders to the front of the wool trousers, snagging his flat cap from the chair and easing into the hallway.

Jamie had lived in the house all his life, so he knew how to avoid each creak in the stairs and quieten the turning of the heavy key in the lock with a tea towel. Then, with nothing but a deep breath to mark the momentous occasion, he opened the door and stepped into the night.

Reality didn't catch up with him until he was past the front garden. *I'm out, I'm actually out.* Could it be that the air was different? A little fresher than summer, but less sharp than winter? It smelled of burned-out fires and dew from the grass. A giddiness built in his chest, making his footsteps light as he wove between the cottages. Why hadn't he done this before? But as he neared the village green, he remembered. The circus.

The area was illuminated by the glow of artificial bulbs, woven on strings that crisscrossed between poles. They lit up the sides of three huge structures painted gold and red. The flags Jamie had seen from his window each bore a letter, the same ones repeated over and over again across the bunting. C-I-R-C-

U-S. No signage told the visitor who exactly the circus belonged to, nor where it was from.

Jamie crept closer, his boots sticking in the mud. No one was about, but from the laughter and the music, it was clear a show was still on inside the largest tent. Like a siren song, the sounds drew him in until he was right by the ticket booth. It was only then that he realised he'd forgotten something very important: his money.

He raised his face to the window sheepishly, ready to explain, but what he saw inside was not a human. A wooden puppet with painted eyes and lips smiled down at him from the box. Its jaw opened on a hinge, presumably operated by the puppeteer somewhere underneath.

"Here to see the show?" it asked, in a high voice.

Jamie swallowed and shook himself. This was just part of the act.

"Yes, though I've forgotten my change."

The puppet threw its head back in laughter, one of its little gloved hands coming to cover its mouth. "*You* don't need to pay. Go on in. Just don't pet the lions, they bite!"

Jamie blinked. "All right?" He eyed the ticket booth dubiously, waiting for the puppeteer to come out, but the dummy just stared back, waiting. Finally, when it was clear that was all he'd be getting, Jamie shrugged and made his way to the tent's entrance.

It was obvious that the circus was popular from the sheer number of spectators. Rows of timber bleachers rose from the dusty tent floor, with people sitting elbow to elbow, craning their necks to get a look at the performance. How far had all these people come? There were certainly more than Jamie's village held.

The crowd gasped at something particularly thrilling, so Jamie crept towards the performance area to get a look. There, in a ring marked by rope, was a multitude of wonders. Horses with great feathers protruding from their heads pranced around the outside, their hooves in perfect sync with the jolly organ music. Men wearing powdered wigs juggled shining baubles while riding unicycles. Two women in matching leotards took turns balancing on each other's shoulders. And above it all, a masked figure balanced on a tightrope with only an umbrella to steady them.

"Ladies and gentlemen," boomed a moustached man in the centre. "I hope you have enjoyed the show. Be sure to buy some food, explore the booths outside, then join us for the next performance in half an hour, when our resident daredevil, the Flying Dragon, will showcase his acrobatics act."

The person on the tightrope bowed and waved to the cheering crowd as they took their last few steps across the rope, catching the ladder with ease. This seemed to signal the end of the production as the audience streamed down the stairs and out into the night, laughing and gossiping. Jamie hung back, squeezing himself between the rafters. While he'd have loved to sample the circus's food and sideshows, that wasn't why he was there. Joanna was missing, with this her last known location. He had to find her, but where to start?

"Half an hour," barked the man in the centre of the ring, once the crowd had emptied. "And keep your eyes out for anyone young enough."

*Young enough for what?* Jamie wondered. Could it be that the troupe was on the lookout for any children of Joanna's age? Had they been warned of her disappearance?

If the performers were looking for Joanna too, perhaps it would be useful to speak to a few of them. So Jamie followed the bleachers around to the back of the tent, looking for a way backstage.

He didn't have to search long; the rear of the pavilion backed onto several timber huts. *Dressing rooms,* Jamie guessed. This is where the artists would get ready for their shows and take a well-deserved break. None of the doors had names on them, but the closest had a red wyvern painted onto the wood. The Flying Dragon, Jamie thought as he rapped his knuckles on the door.

A movement inside told him that the occupant had heard, so he took a step back and allowed his senses to wander. The backstage was dusty and smelled faintly of horse, but beneath the animal smell was something else, something sweeter. Haunting music diffused through the thick canvas from outside, but he could also hear chattering from the performers still in the centre ring.

"—need to go a beat faster—"

"—lock your legs out—"

"—steal another child—"

The last sentence caught his attention, and he strained to make out the rest of the words. Could they be talking about Joanna? He was so intent on listening that he didn't notice the door in front of him creaking open, until a familiar voice beckoned him from within.

"Ah, Jamie. I thought you'd never come."

Jamie sucked in a breath, attention now fully on the darkened room. Had someone said his name? "Who's there?"

"A very old friend," said the voice. "I'm afraid I have a show in twenty minutes, though, so if you'd like to speak to me, you should come in."

Cold fear trickled down Jamie's spine. Whoever – or whatever – was inside that room knew him and something told him he didn't want to know how.

"You're looking for the little girl, aren't you?" The voice was silky smooth now. "Joanna, she said her name was."

Jamie took a deep breath. So this person had seen her, had spoken to her. "All right, I'll come in. If I have your word I'll be able to leave again once we're done talking."

The stranger chuckled. "Smart boy. Yes, you have my promise."

With a nod, Jamie stepped forward. The room was thick with perfume and smoke from the many candles dotted around. He wondered absently if the inhabitant left them lit during the performances. They provided just enough light to make out a tall figure, wearing the costume of the high-wire performer, seated at a dressing table. He was rubbing something on his cheek, leaning closely to a mirror, but from the angle, Jamie couldn't see his reflection.

"What do you know about Joanna?" he asked, voice shaking.

The man gave a low laugh. "I'm surprised you don't have more questions about me. But I'll forgive you, I'm sure you're sick with worry for your lost friend. Don't you know who I am?"

"I might if I could see you," said Jamie, fighting the urge to run out the way he came.

"Do you even need to? Don't you recognise my voice?"

Jamie bit his lip. He did, but he couldn't place it. "Just turn around and speak to me or I'll leave. I'm sure other people know where she is."

"You're right about that. *I'm* not her captor."

So something *had* stolen her. Jamie clenched his fists, but before he could demand who, the man spoke again.

"I'll turn on this lamp beside me and then you can see for yourself who I am. But you must promise you won't scream or run. I do truly wish to help you, but there are others here who will hurt you."

"I promise not to scream," said Jamie, leaving the last part out. If this stranger with the familiar voice was lying, he wasn't sticking around.

"Alright," the man conceded. And then, with a scrape, he struck a match, using it to light the oil map at his side. With deft hands, he lifted it into the air and turned in his seat so his face was fully visible.

Jamie stumbled backwards, his hip colliding with the door frame. Was this some sort of trick? He'd heard of funhouse mirror mazes, surely this was one of them?

"No, you aren't seeing things," said the man.

"I must be," said Jamie. "You're wearing my face."

Same blue eyes, same hooked nose, same thin lips, same copper hair. Jamie had seen those features plenty of times staring back at him through looking glasses, in window reflections, in the pond near their house. The stranger didn't just look similar to him, he was identical. Jamie knew even his mother wouldn't be able to tell the difference. But when the man smiled, it was an expression Jamie had never seen on his own face. It was sharp and inhuman. And then he knew.

"You're a changeling."

The stranger snorted. "So you've heard the stories? What else have you learned about this circus?"

"That you've been stealing children and leaving fae in their place. Is that what you'll do to Joanna?"

The man – *Not-Jamie*, his mind supplied – placed the lantern down beside him. "I haven't stolen anyone. If it were up to me, we'd leave this place and we wouldn't be back. But the ringmaster insists on coming, year after year, taking human children as servants."

"Can't you stop him?" Jamie asked desperately.

"I've tried, but he holds all the power," said Not-Jamie, leaning back in his chair. "No one can break the curse of this circus, unless they can control the ringmaster." He drummed his fingers on his knee. "With you here, though... Maybe I finally have a chance."

"What do you mean?"

Not-Jamie waved to himself. "We're identical, so if you were to go out into the ring wearing my clothes, no one would suspect you weren't me. While you're out there, I could sneak into the ringmaster's chambers and steal something very powerful. All fae have... a token that controls them. If any are smart, they'll bury it somewhere for safekeeping, but the ringmaster likes to keep his close."

Jamie couldn't even begin to imagine what that token could be. A ring? A book? "Do you know what it is?"

"I do," confirmed Not-Jamie without elaborating. "And, if I have it, the ringmaster must do what I say. I could order him to have the circus leave and never return. But I can't let the others know I have it until I'm rid of him fully. Then I can be the next ringmaster."

*What if that's worse?* Jamie wondered. He didn't know this stranger any more than he knew the ringmaster. "And if I help you?"

"I'll find Joanna and bring her to you. You can both leave."

Jamie resisted the urge to wring his hands, shoving them into his pockets instead. Wasn't this why he'd come? But something about it seemed too good to be true, too easy. "What if the other performers notice I'm not one of them?"

"They mustn't," said Not-Jamie firmly. "I'll only need five minutes. Pretend that you're me, and then I'll cause a distraction so you can get away."

He studied Not-Jamie, looking for any hint he could be lying. But the other boy held his gaze, jutting his chin out. *It's this, or I go home empty-handed and Joanna is lost forever.* Finally, Jamie nodded, sealing his fate. "All right," he said, all the while feeling as if he'd made a deal with the devil.

\*\*\*

The thing about being confined to your house all spring and wrapped in cotton wool your whole life is that it doesn't prepare you for trapeze acts.

As soon as Jamie entered the ring, his eyes were immediately drawn to the high-wire, up in the dome of the tent. Before, he hadn't appreciated just how tall the ladders were, or how exposed the rope was, suspended pin-straight way above the cheering crowd's heads. Now, he was very aware. *Please don't take long,* he thought at Not-Jamie, wherever he was.

"Welcome, ladies and gentlemen, boys and girls," boomed the ringmaster. "This is our final show of the night, and by far our best. You'll be treated to comedy from our clowns, the beauty of our equestrian acrobats, and death-defying stunts from the Flying Dragon!"

At this, the audience roared. Jamie remembered at the last moment to raise his clammy hand in greeting.

"My act is the last," Not-Jamie had told him backstage. "Just stand to the side and pretend like you're waiting. I'll cause a distraction before it's your turn."

Jamie hoped that would be soon. Already he was attracting peculiar looks from the other performers. The problem was, now that he knew they weren't human, he couldn't help noticing their strangeness. He hadn't been aware, for example, of the lion-tamer's long canines jutting over his lip. Or that the juggler's skin shone with a pearlescent hue. Or even that the stilt-walker wasn't walking on stilts at all; their limbs were unnaturally long, as if something had stretched them out.

Jamie shivered. *Just stand here and soon you'll have Joanna. You'll never have to meet a faerie again.*

The ringmaster observed each performance with glee, twirling his moustache to the delight of the audience. Jamie watched him out of the corner of his eye, trying to find his tell, the feature which marked him as non-human. But everything about him was average. His height, his weight, even his age. *Perhaps he's the leader because he's the best at disguise,* thought Jamie as the ringmaster clapped his white-gloved hands. Though

Not-Jamie had been just as good. If he wasn't an exact copy of Jamie, there would be nothing to set him apart from a human.

*He'll make a good ringmaster, then,* Jamie decided.

The first set of entertainers finished with a bow and with a nod from their commander, they were replaced by a new wave. Jamie shifted his feet. It wouldn't be long until the Flying Dragon was expected to perform.

*He'll get here.*

They were replaced by a knife-thrower, who had no shadow. His assistant, strapped to a wheel, grinned with serrated teeth as the blades embedded themselves into the wood. One of them nicked the skin of her arm, sending blood trickling across her pale skin. It would have been impossible for the audience to notice, but Jamie could clearly see it was green like emeralds.

*Just like Joanna said,* Jamie thought. *Only two acts to go.*

Next were the fire breathers. Jamie gaped as they blew their flames without a source of fuel in sight. The crowd didn't notice that the fire came straight from their mouths as it roared high over their heads.

*Come on.*

Soon, the second-last performance of the night was up: a couple of contortionists whose ears were long and pointed and whose heads spun all the way round.

"You're next," said a voice beside his ear.

Jamie spun around to find the ringmaster smirking down at him. "I–"

"Unless there's something wrong?"

With a gulp, Jamie looked up to where the trapeze bar was lowering from the ceiling. "No– no, of course I can–"

"Excellent," said the ringmaster, clapping him on the back with such force that Jamie almost lost his footing. "Up you go." Then he turned and raised his arms wide, addressing the audience again. "And finally, it's time for the main event. Please, a round of applause for the Flying Dragon."

The beam came to a stop right in front of Jamie's face. Oh lord, he was actually going to have to do this. With shaking hands, he gripped the cool metal. Already his palms were sweaty, making the bar slick. How was he supposed to hold on, let alone swing and jump to the other ropes? In desperation, he hooked it under his armpits instead, grabbing the ropes in a vice-like grip.

The cheering swelled and Jamie plastered a smile to his face, under his mask. He could at least pretend he knew what he was doing, even if his heart was hammering in his chest. *Or I could make a run for it; tell the other villagers that the circus had kidnapped Joanna, along with other children.* Because there was no way he'd survive this performance. Either he'd plummet back to the ground or he'd freeze, and the faeries would know he wasn't one of them. But then the trapeze bar began to rise, pulling him off his feet. *Too late,* he realised, as he looked down.

*I'm going to die.*

Jamie thought of his mother as he rose into the air. She'd only ever wanted to protect him, he could see that now. All those years being locked up for nothing.

Ten feet off the ground. Twenty feet. Thirty feet. And still so far to go. The ceiling was higher than any of the houses in the village. When he hit forty feet, Jamie closed his eyes. He didn't have a say in where he was going but at least he could control how much he saw. The crowd clapped far below, oblivious to his fear and the disaster they were about to witness.

The trapeze bar rose to what must have been halfway to the top – and stopped.

Jamie swung in mid-air for a heart-dropping moment, his arms aching from holding him up. *Is this the part where I'm meant to jump?* But then he felt a whoosh as the trapeze was lowered, much faster than he'd ascended. His eyes were open before he could stop them, just in time to see the pavilion's floor rushing to meet him.

The rest happened as if in slow motion.

"The tent! It's collapsing!" someone shouted from the audience. And then all hell broke loose as the crowd scrambled to rise from their seats, entertainment forgotten. All around, ropes were snapping and canvas was sagging while performers ran from the ring.

And all the while, Jamie was falling.

Until he wasn't.

His descent slowed just as he reached the sand-covered ground. Controlled. Measured. Calculated. As soon as he was close enough, he let go of the bar, landing on the floor in a trembling heap.

"Come on, you can't just lie there or you'll be buried," said a voice, then a palm was cupping his elbow, pushing him up and towards an exit.

Half the canopy had now caved in, crushing the wooden bleachers and sending debris flying. Jamie dodged between people grappling for an exit as screams filled the air. Horses bolted, knocking bystanders to the side, shouting in pain. At one point, a beam fell from the ceiling and the hand on Jamie's elbow disappeared. He looked over his shoulder for his saviour, but a moment later, he heard Not-Jamie's voice from his other side, "Just keep going!"

Pumping his legs for a final burst of speed, Jamie at last emerged into the cold, night air with relief. *We did it*, he thought, looking around for his saviour.

"Not here," he said, steering Jamie away from the panicking crowd. He nudged him out of the circus, past the ticket office, round the fence, where he finally collapsed, doubling over with his hands on his knees.

"I thought you were a goner," Not-Jamie panted.

"I wouldn't have been if you'd been quicker," said Jamie.

"It took me a while to find what I was looking for."

*That's right, the token.* "But you did find it?"

Not-Jamie tossed his head back to rest against the fence, revealing a blackened eye. *He must have been injured as we were running.* Dark blood trickled under his nose and one sleeve of his shirt was ripped.

"Do you want to know what it is?" asked Not-Jamie, giving him a sly look despite his injuries. He reached into his pocket, producing a piece of paper with a flourish. "I have the ringmaster's name. His true name."

Jamie blinked. "That's it?"

"Don't underestimate the power of a true name." The faerie boy sniffed, hiding it away again. "If you knew mine, it would change my life. And yours."

"I'll just stick to Not-Jamie then." Jamie pulled the mask off his face and dropped it on the grass. "Where will I find Joanna?"

"The next field over. She might be a little hungry, but fine apart from that."

He felt a surge of relief but didn't turn to go. Something about Not-Jamie's slumped figure made him look so breakable. "What's next for you?"

"We leave and never come back. Perhaps I'll order the ringmaster to take us south." He spread his arms wide. "The world is mine. Or it will be, once I'm fully in control."

He should go find Joanna. But there was one question that had been bothering him. "Were you never tempted? To steal me away? To live my life?"

The faerie's face became unreadable. "Once, it was all I ever thought about. Every spring when the circus came to town, I would watch out for you. But I'm not made for that, not anymore. My place is among the faeries and on the tightrope."

*Thank God.* He gave a tight-lipped smile. "Good luck, Not-Jamie."

"And to you, Jamie. I hope Joanna is alright. Give my best to Maw MacIntyre."

*Odd,* thought Jamie as he walked away. If his family had never visited the circus, how did Not-Jamie know his mother's name?

The sun was rising, casting the village green in golden light and buoying his spirit. Soon he'd deliver Joanna back to her mother and he'd have an adventure to tell his siblings. What could have been the most dangerous night of his life had ended in a triumph. And all because he'd met his changeling.

All of a sudden, the need to see Not-Jamie's face one last time, surged through him. He raised his hand in goodbye before he'd even turned and was glad to see the other boy had remained, watching him leave with a wistful expression on his face. Now, in the daylight, it was easy to see their resemblance, even from so far away. Jamie smiled again, gave a salute, and continued on his way.

Later, he wouldn't be able to pinpoint the exact moment he knew. The realisation came upon him gradually, slowing his steps and sending cold dread through him. Even when he finally collected Joanna, shivering but whole, from the field, he felt no joy. When he arrived back at the cottage, he could only stare at his feet as a freshly-awoken Maw MacIntyre scolded him for leaving, before retreating wordlessly to his bedroom, the adventures that had caused such excitement silenced upon his tongue forever.

Because, while the likeness of Not-Jamie was unmistakable, so was something else.

The crimson-red blood trickling from his nose.

Caroline Logan is a writer of Young Adult Fantasy. Her Scottish fantasy series, the Four Treasures, was published by Cranachan Books and is available online and in all good bookshops. Caroline is a high school biology teacher who lives in the Cairngorms National Park in Scotland, with her husband and dogs, Ranger and Scout. She graduated from The University of Glasgow with a bachelor's degree in Marine and Freshwater Biology. In her spare time she likes to ski, paddleboard and play Dungeons and Dragons, though she is happiest with a good book and a cup of tea.

# SHE VANISHES

Josie Jaffrey

In the spring, she vanishes.

It's not a gradual thing. Aïdes doesn't see her planning her route, or writing the dates on their shared calendar, or even packing her bags. It is simply that one day she is there, falling asleep in his arms in the bed they share, and the next day he wakes to find her gone without a trace.

He looks for her, of course. The underworld is a big place, but there are limited hiding spots, realistically speaking. She won't be in any of the grim bits – no one goes for a casual stroll along the River of Misery or takes a picnic out to the River of Fire – but she's not in any of her usual haunts either. The palace is empty, the square is bare and the meadows of Elysium are teeming with heroes but devoid of his wife.

She's left him. She can't have left him. She wouldn't leave him. And anyway, she hasn't even taken her sandals, which are still lined up neatly by the bed.

She's just not there anymore.

He looks again, checking all the same places in case he missed her the first time, and some extra ones besides, but he still comes back with empty arms to her abandoned sandals.

She's gone. Vanished. Poof.

He drops to his knees and moans.

If a heart makes a sound when it breaks, that was it.

* * *

The moon waxes and wanes. Aïdes is not himself without his wife. She was a levelling influence on him, mitigating the worst of his rages and magnifying the heights of his joy. Without her, he is mercurial and dark. Perhaps he'd feel better if he talked about it, but by now the inhabitants of his realm know better than to broach the subject of her disappearance. In fact, they try not to talk to him at all, but then something happens that begs an exception. Something that they can't manage on their own. It's only happened twice before, and on those occasions the eruption of temper from their landlord rivalled the sulphur-spewing, bird-felling mouth of Aornos itself.

An incursion.

How Aïdes hates loiterers. It doesn't seem to matter how many *no trespassing* signs he posts; without fail, some idiot who wants to prove how big his sword is or how deep his love goes will come striding up to his gates and upset the guard dog, and then he has to deal with the noise complaints. There's none of that this time, though. This time, the bastard got in.

"Is Berry okay?" he asks as he hurries to the guard post.

"He's fine," the guard replies, making soothing gestures with his hands. Everyone knows how much Aïdes loves that damned dog. "A bit drowsy, but nothing that a good rest won't fix."

"You're sure?"

"Chiron's with him now. He'll be fine, sir. I promise. About the intruder–"

"Where is he?" All the careful concern Aïdes displayed a moment ago has been wiped from his face by his sudden rage. The transformation is so startling that the two versions of him might be mistaken for different people. "To think that I might have lost Berry as well, on top of everything else, just because some little shit-"

"This little shit," the guard says, hauling a man up from the floor. He's bound at the wrists and ankles, but despite his obvious physical inferiority, he's glaring defiance at Aïdes. "What do you want me to do with him?" the guard asks.

Aïdes sniffs the man. "Mostly mortal," he says, his lip curling. "Chuck him out."

"I would speak with you, Lord Aïdes!" the man proclaims in a voice more steady than it has any right to be.

"Piss off." Aïdes is already walking away.

"I *will* speak with you, Lord Aïdes!" the man says, trying to shoulder past the guard.

"No, you won't, sunshine," says the guard, but he's already lost his grip and before he can regain it, the man has thrown himself to his knees at Aïdes's feet.

"I appeal to you, Lord Aïdes, in the name of true love! My wife has been taken from me, and I will have her back, or die trying! Have you not loved, my Lord? Have you not felt adoration in your soul, like the thudding press of blood in your veins? I have walked through the land of the dead to lay myself supplicant before you and beg for the return of my love, my heart, the light of my life, and I will not be denied!"

"He's a rather dramatic gentleman, isn't he, sir?" the guard comments, but Aïdes's eyes are shining with sympathy.

The guard sighs and thinks, *Here we go.*

"I have," Aïdes whispers, like his heart is breaking all over again. "I have loved."

Which is how Orpheus ends up leading his poor dead wife out of the underworld, while Aïdes curls up in his palace and weeps into Berry's fur.

\* \* \*

The next day – to the extent that there are days down here – Aïdes contemplates just staying in bed. But there's divine correspondence to deal with, and the ferryman's takings to count, plus Berry gets grumpy if he doesn't have a decent walk before lunchtime. Aïdes decides to deal with the last task first, shoving a coat on over his pyjamas to venture out into the fields with his faithful hound. He isn't expecting to see anyone, least of all the woman he released from the underworld yesterday, and certainly not in the mood she's in.

"Hello," he says. "Are you... all right?"

She glares at him.

"My husband," she says sharply, "is an idiot. One instruction: don't look back. *One* instruction, and he's so soppy he can't even manage that."

"I'm sorry," Aïdes says, pulling pointlessly on Berry's lead. The creature never learned to heel and, after three millennia of disobedience, he's not going to change his spots now. "There are rules," he adds.

"And really," she goes on as though she hasn't heard him, "did anyone ask me what I wanted? It's quite nice here, with all the meadows and fruit and whatnot. I was rather happy, thank you very much, relaxing, snoozing, catching up with old friends. But did anyone ask me? Oh, no. Gods forbid that anyone ask the *woman* what she–"

"It was my fault," Aïdes says.

She pulls up short in mid-rant. "What?"

"I lost my wife, you see," he says, feeling his eyes well up for the third time today. "So when your husband forged a path through the hazards of the underworld to rescue you from death so you could spend the rest of his mortal life together..." Aïdes shrugs. "It struck a chord. I thought we should help."

"Oh." She deflates a little. "It's not that I don't appreciate–"

"We had such a deep love," Aïdes continues, "my wife and I. It burned so bright, so fiercely, with such purity that I wondered sometimes whether it might consume me whole." He looks off into the distance as he speaks, letting his gaze trail over the horizon towards the memory-erasing waters of the River Lethe. "And I wonder, sometimes, if it might be better just to let myself forget her and move on, but... Our love burned so *very* brightly."

"I see," she murmurs. "The poetry is catching."

"Excuse me?" Aïdes says, bringing his attention back to her. "I'm sorry. I was lost in... *the remembering.*"

"Oh, nothing," she says quickly. "So, you're in charge here, are you?"

"That's right."

"I thought you must be, given the way the other guards were behaving around you. And you're, what, head guard? Guard dog handler?" she adds, nodding at Berry.

Who chooses that moment to slip his leash. He barrels right into the woman, hitting her with such force that she falls to the ground. The two of them end up in a giggling, barking mess of skirts, slobber and oversized puppy.

"Berry!" Aïdes yells, but the dog ignores him. He's having too much fun. "Berry, get back here this instant!" In the end, Aïdes has to drag him away. "I'm so sorry. He has no manners."

"That's all right," she says, grinning as she wipes the grass and dirt from her dress. "He's a lovely boy."

She gets to her feet, thinking perhaps the dog has managed to break the dark mood they were both in, but then Aïdes says, "He's been a great comfort. It's lonely, the desolation of her loss. Without Berry, I think I might very well have expired."

"Well, you're in the right place for that," the woman says cheerfully. The joke does not land. She tries a different tack. "Have you tried searching for her? I know the underworld is vast, and I know some of the barriers between lands are difficult or impossible to cross, but she must be here somewhere, and I'm sure if we looked hard enough–"

"No," Aïdes insists. "It's hopeless." He flops down crosslegged onto the grass with his head in his hands. Then Berry muscles his way under Aïdes's arms and onto his lap, rather spoiling the effect.

"Well, let's look anyway," the woman says. "I'm Eurydice, by the way."

"I'm A–" Aïdes realises, belatedly, that she doesn't know who he is. He raises his head from his hands and looks at her.

Does she really not know?

"A... what?" she asks.

She really doesn't know.

"Ajax," he says quickly. "I'm Ajax."

"Nice to meet you, Ajax." She shakes his hand, then uses their grip to pull him to his feet. "Come on. Let's see if we can't find your wife."

* * *

Eurydice tries to follow an exhaustive route around all the parts of the underworld she knows, but in truth Berry is the one who leads the way.

"He misses her," Ajax comments as Berry drags him by the lead to the riverside. "This was where they used to go together in the mornings. She planted these bulbs, all for her love of springtime, and now she's not even here to see them f-f-flower." Ajax tries, and fails, to stifle his tears.

"They're beautiful," Eurydice says, casting an appreciative eye over the snowdrops, hyacinths, narcissi, aconites and bluebells that litter the riverside. His wife must have spent weeks, or maybe months, sinking them all into the soil, because they spread out in a sea of pastel perfection in every direction. "She liked to be in the fields?"

"She lived out here," he says.

Eurydice follows his gaze, looking up at a blue roof that is not the sky, and feeling the warmth from a glowing light that is not the sun. Ajax, on the other hand, looks as though he's feeling nothing at all; there's a blueish ring around his lips and the rest of his face is bleached white, as though by the cold. She wonders when he last ate, and how well he's been taking care of himself since he lost his wife. He looks like he's wasting away.

"Do you mind if I ask how long ago you... lost her?" she asks.

"A month ago," he says. "Perhaps two."

Eurydice nods. Time is strange in this place, and it's easy to lose track. She herself is unsure how long she's been here beneath the earth, living through days that are not days at all, but change from day to night depending on which part of the underworld you step into.

"It feels like years," he continues. "It might as well be decades, or centuries, because without her there is no light in the world, no solace to be found in the comforts of living, and no rest from the constant pain of her absence. I might as well lie down here and let the flowers that she planted mark my grave."

"Tell me more about her," Eurydice says. It's clear that her companion is slipping into a maudlin mood, and she's well enough acquainted with extravagant personalities to know this is something to be avoided at all costs. Perhaps if she can get him to focus on happy memories, he might pull through his moping and out the other side. "Tell me what she looked like, what she liked doing, how she spent her time."

"What's the point?" he says, staring into the slow-moving water of the black river. "She's gone."

"Well," Eurydice says, improvising furiously, "if you tell me about her then we might find a clue as to how we could find her."

"It won't do any good."

"Well, tell me anyway."

So he does, at length, and as they walk along the river through the land of the dead, day after day, Eurydice begins to understand the scale of the loss he feels. She also begins to understand that their simple search party will achieve nothing. He has looked everywhere, farther than Eurydice has ever been in the underworld. He has asked everyone. His wife is not here, and there is nothing Eurydice can do to change that.

It seems so unfair. She knows her own husband will join her here eventually, and she can't understand why that shouldn't be the case for everyone, whether they're regular residents or guards.

But the fact remains that she cannot fix Ajax, she can only listen to his grief and hope that, over time, he might find a way to make peace with it. So that's what she does, day after day, for this man who is fast becoming a friend.

After all, they both have time to spare.

* * *

One day, some indeterminate period later, there's a surprise for Eurydice waiting in the Elysian Fields when she returns from their latest walk.

"Yours, I believe," the guard says as he ushers a man towards her.

"Orpheus?" she says, open-mouthed. "What are you doing back here so soon?"

"They murdered me, my love!" he says, flinging himself into her arms and showering her with kisses. "Without you beside me, I could make only music that was as discordant as the feelings raging within me, a soul in torment strumming tuneless noise to rend the air, just like the heart was rent within my breast! They begged me to stop, but I played on until the maenads – those most decadent followers of the most decadent

Bacchus – silenced me, sending me back into your arms where I longed to be, just as I had yearned that they would!"

"You *what?*"

"As if I could ever live without you!" he exclaims. "Though they wrenched my body limb from limb, the pain was as nothing when compared with the anguish I felt at your absence, at the agonising fracture of the bond between us, two joined souls ripped up from the roots and torn asunder, until their very *being* screamed with the unbearable torture of separation!"

"Yes, all right," she says. "Why don't you have a lie down in the grass while I talk to this gentleman?"

"Ah, to soothe my fevered brow in the cool meadows of the Elysian Fields!" he says, reclining on the ground with his limbs stretched elegantly like he's posing for a sculpture. "Now that you are near, my love, my restless spirit shall be in repose until the end of all our endless days!"

'Yes, good.' Eurydice says. It's not that she isn't delighted to see him – she loves the dramatic fool to a degree she would never have thought possible, even if she doesn't show it – but her mind has caught on a distraction, and she can't concentrate until it's resolved. 'You just stay there and rest,' she says, then she leaves Orpheus snoozing in the grass and steps away a few paces, guiding the guard along with her. 'It's as easy as that?' she asks him.

"As easy as what?" the guard asks.

"You just deliver spouses to each other and reunite them in the underworld? It's that straightforward?"

"No," the guard says, a little affronted to have his role explained away in such simple terms. "Obviously, only the couples who actually want to be together. The ones who don't... Well, we don't do it."

"I see."

She thinks for a little while, glancing back at Orpheus, who's now snoring peacefully. No wonder he's exhausted, given all he's been through. The rending, and suchlike.

"You look like you have something on your mind," the guard says.

"Yes."

"About your husband?"

"No, about my friend," she says. "You know, we've been walking Berry together."

"Yes, and we're grateful for that, ma'am. It keeps his mind off things. You know."

"I do," she says. "I do. The thing is... What happened to her, if you don't mind me asking?"

"To whom?"

"To his wife. It seems so strange that you can present my husband to me as soon as he dies, and yet you can't reunite the two of them. From everything he's said, it sounds like she would want to be with him as much as he wants to be with her, but maybe it has something to do with the specific circumstances? How did she, you know... die?" Eurydice asks, whispering the last word.

"*His* wife?" The guard blinks. "Dead? Who told you that?"

Eurydice squints back at him. "You mean she isn't?"

"No. Gods, no," the guard says, laughing. "She's visiting her mother. She leaves every spring for six months, and thus begins the Grand Mope. She'll be back in the autumn."

"*What?*"

"Wait, you really thought she was dead?"

"Of *course* I thought she was dead."

"Well, yes," the guard concedes. "I suppose I can understand why you'd think that."

Eurydice is silent for a moment as she absorbs the enormity of this revelation. And it's true: Ajax never said his wife was dead, not exactly, just that he'd lost her. Eurydice had simply assumed – not unreasonably, to her mind, given where they were – that he meant...

"So, not dead?" she asks the guard, just to be sure.

"No."

"Just away for half the year, sort of like Lord Aïdes and Lady Persephone?"

"Yes," the guard says, confused. "Exactly like them, in fact." He pauses for a moment, then adds, "You do know that he *is* Lord Aïdes, right?"

Eurydice's eyebrows shoot up.

She scowls.

She pouts furiously with her arms crossed for a few long seconds, says, "Right," then uncrosses her arms and strides away across the fields towards the palace.

The guard watches her go for a dozen paces, then watches her stride back just as quickly.

"Keep an eye on him for me, would you?" she asks, gesturing towards her slumbering husband.

"As you wish. He'll probably sleep for a while now anyway. Exhausting, you know. Dying, crossing the river, collapsing dramatically."

"Thanks," she says. "I won't be long."

Long enough to scream and yell, then stomp off in righteous fury, and no longer.

* * *

Eurydice has never been inside the palace before. She's walked around it with Berry and Ajax – *Aïdes* – on many occasions over the past however long, enjoying the gorgeous gardens and the lush landscaping, all of which make a lot more sense now that she knows his green-fingered wife lives there, because she's the *queen*.

And, you know, the literal goddess of spring.

There are no doors on the building, just columned corridors that lead to empty, curtained rooms that smell of dust and unwashed cloth. Despite her attempts to cheer Aïdes out of his doldrums, it's clear she's made little impact, because the place is a mess.

"You," she says, pointing a finger at him when she finally tracks him down in the atrium, "I have a bone to pick with you."

Aïdes looks around, his eyes widening as he sees Eurydice.

"Oh," he says.

"Yes, *oh*. You are ridiculous. Do you know that I thought your wife was dead? *Dead*. Not just off on her holidays for six months, but dead, *Ajax*, which isn't even your real name and, now we're on the subject, I find out you're the *god* of the *underworld* and you. Never. Told. Me." She punctuates each word with a prod to his chest.

"Oh."

"Is that all you're going to say?"

"I didn't mean to mislead you," he says, looking at his feet. "Not about Persephone, at least."

Eurydice seethes. "You told me her name was Penelope."

"Because you didn't know who I was and I didn't want you to find out," he says, shamefacedly. "I'm sorry. I should have told you that first day, but when I realised... It's just that it was nice to talk to someone without all the baggage that comes with being me."

"A god."

"Yes."

"Who's moping around his palace because his wife is visiting her mother."

Aïdes turns around, looks up and pretends to scan the shelves, though it's clear that what he's really doing is holding back tears. "You don't understand," he says. "The love that we share is so profound, so indefinably vital and urgent–"

Eurydice has been indulging his elegies up until now, mostly because she thought they were eulogies, but now she's had enough.

"You do realise that my idiot husband has just gone and gotten himself killed because of this kind of nonsense?" she says. "He could have enjoyed the rest of his mortal life – perhaps even remarried, had some children, left a legacy behind him – but instead he committed suicide by maenad. And you're here doing exactly the same thing, *wasting* your life, and your wife isn't even dead."

Aïdes pulls his chin back, affronted.

"I wear my pain in tribute to her," he says. His bottom lip is sticking out a little more than it should, like that of a recalcitrant child.

"It's not disrespectful for you to enjoy yourself while she's away. Do you think she wants you to be sitting around here moping for half the year, when you could be doing helpful or enjoyable things instead? Or at least cleaning the place up a bit," she says, nudging a pile of miscellaneous detritus with her sandalled toe. "I'm sure she'd be happier if *you* were happier."

"You don't know that," he mumbles.

"If she loves you, why would she want you to be miserable? Look, it might be easier for you to sit around here wallowing, but that doesn't make it right. If you really want to do something in tribute to her, then you can do better."

"Like what?"

"Like... I don't know. Something she'd like. Something to

show that you were thinking about her, and that you missed her, without making her feel guilty that she's been away. Because that's all this is," Eurydice says, taking in the state of the beautiful building that surrounds them. "You're letting the squalor build up so you can show her how miserable she made you by leaving, which she can't help, because it's not her fault that she's needed above ground during the growing seasons. Is it?"

"No," Aïdes mumbles. "I suppose not."

"So isn't it just a tiny bit selfish for you to make her feel like it is?"

"I didn't mean to–"

"But I bet she feels that way anyway."

Aïdes has never really thought about it. He should have, but there's a certain amount of solipsism that comes with being immortal and all-powerful, and he's embraced it. Now that he thinks about it, it's true that Persephone tends to come home each autumn carrying an air of weary apology about her, as though she has no energy to argue any more about whose fault this time-share arrangement is. And, now that he thinks about it, when the spring approaches there is a kind of nervous excitement that she can't hide, however much she tries, and for the first time it occurs to Aïdes that, as the goddess of spring, she probably rather enjoys going up to the mortal world to make it bloom.

He's made her hide that part of herself from him.

Worse, he's made her feel guilty for the things in which she finds joy.

And he's confined her to this pale imitation of the world, where she has planted bulbs so she can share the spring with him, even when they are not together.

In return, he has been so very selfish.

"I'm sorry," Aïdes says to Eurydice. "You're right. But I think I have an idea of how I can do better, and I'm going to need your help."

"No," says Eurydice, crossing her arms. "You're not. You're going to do this on your own."

"But I-"

"You are the *god* of the *underworld*, and you are perfectly capable of doing whatever you have planned alone. I, on the other hand, am a mere ex-mortal whose idiot - but wonderful and dearly-loved - husband is passed out in the Elysian Fields and will doubtless be waking up soon and wondering what to do with himself. I need to be there when he does."

He has been so *very* selfish.

"You're right, of course," Aïdes says. "You should be with your husband. I'm sorry. Please forgive me."

Eurydice nods sharply, turns to leave, then stops and turns back for two last words: "Good luck."

"I don't need luck," Aïdes says with a smile. "I just need a bit of time."

\* \* \*

When Persephone returns at the harvest, the Elysian Fields are a kaleidoscope of purples and blues, reds and oranges, pinks and yellows, bursting with spring flowers of every kind. She stops at the edge of the black-mirror river and stares, letting the startling colours rush into her soul with the freshness of a breeze after rain.

"Do you like it?" Aïdes asks, coming to stand at her side. Berry's there too, licking her hand in enthusiastic greeting.

"But... it's autumn."

"Up there," Aïdes replies. "Down here, it can be any season I like, and I want it to be your season, always, for as long as you like. So I did some planting, and I can do more next year, and the year after, until the whole underworld is flowers, if that's what you'd like."

"You sentimental fool,' Persephone laughs, but there are tears in her eyes.

"I missed you," he says, kissing her cheek. "Did you have a nice time with your mother?"

Persephone smiles, bewildered. He's never asked her this before.

"I did," she says. "Thank you. Did you have a nice time while I was away?"

"Yes," he replies, surprised to find that it's true. "I made a friend. And I enjoyed making life for once, instead of taking it. I think I understand the appeal."

"Oh, do you?" Persephone smiles, and it's a smile Aïdes hasn't seen for a long time. Maybe not since that very first year, when they couldn't seem to stay out of each other's arms, and when they'd both assumed children would follow very swiftly from their marriage. Now, the future they envisaged together feels like it's been on hold too long.

"I do," Aïdes replies, smiling back.

Then he takes his wife in his arms and shows her just how much she has been missed.

For the first time in a long time, there is no guilt in their reunion. For the first time in a long time, the joy outweighs the pain. And for the first time in the underworld, as it does everywhere else, spring comes when the goddess of spring returns.

Josie Jaffrey is a fantasy and historical fiction author who writes about lost worlds, dystopian societies and paranormal monsters (vampires are her favourite). She has eleven novels published so far, along with lots of short stories. Most of those are set in the Silverse, an apocalyptic world filled with vampires and zombies. She's currently working on vampire murder mysteries (the Seekers series) and a YA series about the lost civilisations of the Mediterranean (the Deluge series). Researching the latter is the first time she's used her Classics degree since university.

Josie lives in Oxford with her husband and two cats (Sparky and Gussie), who graciously permit human cohabitation in return for regular feeding and cuddles. The resulting cat fluff makes it difficult for Josie to wear black, which is largely why she gave up being a goth. Although the cats are definitely worth it, she still misses her old wardrobe.

# Be Careful What You Wish For

S. Markem

*...But it's not true that I would rather write than read. I would rather read than write. To be honest, I would rather hang upside down in a bucket than write.*

Douglas Adams

It was a gorgeous, eleventh-century spring morning – truly lovely. It was the kind of morning that makes pigeons frisky, gets songbirds singing, and even persuades normally nocturnal hedgehogs to come and take a peek.

It was so nice, in fact, that this author has once again broken the unwritten rule: *never* start a story with the weather.

And on this fine morning, we find Bill the Gnome making his way to the solar of Blagre's Manse armed with a tray of biscuits and beer – the customary morning snack during this period.

As gnomes go, Bill was what you'd call an archetype: the originator of a look that spawned a million garden-ornament-imitations. But, back in the day, gnomes were something of a rarity and highly prized for their administrative talents. Your chances of ever having seen one were vanishingly small, and therefore, Bill was entirely unaware of his clichéd existence.

Talking of clichés...

Bill knocked on the door to the solar. He entered to find his employer, Blagre, the wizard, sitting at his desk thumbing through an old book, showing little interest.

Blagre was, in almost every respect, what you'd expect from a wizard. You're probably not far off if you're thinking of a pointy hat, big nose and long beard. Tropes make a writer's life easier.

If, however, you have *not* read one of my stories before, you may not know that Blagre had a somewhat peculiar philosophy: he believed he was a character in a novel – and so was everyone else. Absurd, no?

(I apologise for all this lazy exposition at the start of this tale; we are forced to take the most direct route; this is a short story.)

"What's up, Blagre?" said Bill. "It's such a lovely day. Why so glum?"

"Why must *all* your conversations begin with the weather?"

"My, my – you are grumpy today. Don't blame me; blame your author."

"I am not 'grumpy', my good gnome. It is *far* worse than that. I am at an existential crossroads. I don't even feel like drinking beer!"

"No beer? My goodness, what witchcraft is this?" Bill chuckled to himself.

"Bah! Do not make fun of me. My soul is adrift. My life has lost its meaning. I can see no future – nothing. It's all just so empty."

"And when, exactly, did you realise this?"

"About ten minutes ago. It just came over me in a wave of hopelessness. I dare not think it, but perhaps.... no, it cannot be.

It's too terrible to even contemplate for a moment."

"What is?"

"I just said I didn't want to contemplate it, didn't I?"

Bill put down the tray, removed his little red hat and scratched his balding head. "Very well then, don't contemplate it; just tell me specifically what we're *not* contemplating so I can avoid contemplating it by mistake."

"Oh Bill, dearest Bill... what if... what if.... what if our author has run out of ideas? Or alcohol? Or worse, is dead?"

\* \* \*

Sam looked up from his laptop screen. It was ten in the morning, and the weather outside was dreadful. It couldn't have been less spring-like if you lived in Scotland - bitterly cold, howling rain, and so dark you'd think the sun needed a bulb changing.

The only positive side to this freakish weather was that the Starbucks he was currently frequenting was mostly empty.

Ahh Starbucks. Could one imagine a more soulless environment? Office workers (who, of course, have no souls), unpaid writers (who are trying to sell theirs) and groups of mothers with prams (because it's too early to start drinking alcohol).

Dreadful places, but for one saving grace: they are the same the world over. Everyone knows what they look like, how they smell, and how awful the coffee is. It is a boon for a short fiction writer whose primary concern is always the word count.

Well, it would have been handy had I not wasted two paragraphs explaining the concept. Is this bathos? I hope so - I've always wanted to use that word.

Anyway, the coffee cavern was mostly empty except for a handful of staff and the beautiful young woman who had just walked in (*she* was the reason Sam had looked up from his laptop). He knew she was beautiful even *before* he'd looked up – that's how beautiful she was. Knockout!

Tall, elegant (even in jeans and a T-shirt), flawless china skin, unimaginably blonde, short-cropped hair, and aquiline features with bright sapphire-blue eyes.

Make no mistake about it; this was the kind of beauty that set artists on the road to madness, had Kings losing kingdoms, and was the kind of thing that, after a lifetime of many other experiences, one remembers just before one dies.

Obviously, I have never died (at the time of writing), but I suspect it's that sort of thing that crops up – or at least, I hope it is.

She walked in, grabbed a coffee (which was already waiting for her) and made a beeline for Sam's table.

"May I sit here?" she said. She sat in the chair opposite without waiting for any approval.

"Urm – hullo." He said – not a great conversationalist; commonplace amongst authors, I'm told.

"I'm Daisy. What's your name?"

Sam pointed to the takeaway cup on which the staff had scrawled his name.

"Marvin?" she said/

"No. It's Sam... they always write Marvin, though."

Daisy laughed, the kind of laugh that reminded you of music. "That's adorable."

"It is?"

"Yes, of course. How sweet. You have a nickname – they must like you. You must come here a lot?"

"Well, yes, I do – to work."

"You're working now?" She said, nodding toward his laptop.

"Er – can you call it work if you don't get paid?"

"Ah ha! You're a *writer*!"

Sam puffed his cheeks. "I guess so, although I used to be an accountant – until recently."

"An accountant? How interesting."

"It is?"

"No, I was being polite – but being a writer *is* interesting. What do you write? Let me guess. Murder mysteries? Everyone is churning those things out these days."

"No, nothing like that. I write absurdist fiction – I guess you'd call it that."

"Ah, comedy. Funny stories?"

"Not really... well, sort of... I mean, I don't know. Absurd. I'm not sure if it's funny – that's subjective."

"What's this one about?" she said, again nodding toward the laptop.

"It's about a wizard. He thinks he's in a novel – which is absurd, you see? It's probably a metaphor for religion, although perhaps I retrofitted that to make it sound more important?"

Daisy smiled a sympathetic sort of smile. "You're right then."

"About what?"

"It isn't funny."

"Oh," he said, slumping his shoulders.

She burst out laughing – a symphony of laughter. "Don't look so glum. For someone writing funny stories, where's your sense of humour?"

"I'm sorry. I'm not feeling myself. It's just I've lost my way a bit."

"Writer's block? Very common, I'm told."

"No, it's more than that. I mean, writing *itself* – it's absurd when you think about it. Dreaming up fanciful stories and then expecting people to read that nonsense (wizards, faerie-folk, trolls) and *believe* it when it's *clearly* made up. And people *do*, which is itself quite absurd. I'm stuck in an absurdity paradox. I can't take it remotely seriously. And I don't even make any money at it – and that's beyond absurd – it's *ridiculous.*"

Daisy smiled – the sort of smile that could signal a key plot point was coming – and placed a reassuring hand on Sam's.

"Don't be such a capitalist. Money is not a true measure of worth. All art is intrinsically valuable. I'm sure yours is too."

"If all art is valuable, then no art is valuable. It's all the same. You may as well call anything art."

"That's absurd."

"I know. You see? I can't help it." Sam laughed. He hadn't felt like laughing for weeks.

"Perhaps you should get back to it?" she said. "I'm interrupting you."

"No, no. I wasn't really writing much today anyway. In fact, I'm so desperate for inspiration; I'm actually looking at one of those A.I. websites – the ones that write stuff for you."

Daisy looked shocked. "No – tell me, you *didn't?* That's cheating."

"Oh, no. I haven't used it. But that's how desperate I am right now."

"Well, look – it just so happens I know a bit about the creative process. I can help if you'll let me.

"Help?"

"Yes, help. Here... I have something for you."

Daisy reached into her clutch bag, rummaged momentarily, and then placed a small object on the table.

"What is it?" said Sam. "A jellybean?"

"Uh-huh. It's a mango-flavoured one. You like mango?"

"I guess. I prefer lime, but sure."

"Well, you see, it's not just any ordinary jellybean. It's a *magic* jellybean."

"Mango flavoured?" said Sam, laughing.

"That's right, a magical mango-flavoured jellybean. It will inspire you if you want it. I promise."

Sam smiled. It was a sweet gesture. Frankly, she was so pretty he'd have eaten a Brussel sprout if she'd offered it.

"Thanks," he said, popping the jellybean in his mouth.

"Good, good. I have to go now. Will you be here tomorrow? Because I will. You can tell me if the jellybean helped."

"Probably," said Sam.

Daisy left. Sam stared at this laptop screen... and then it hit him.

* * *

Blagre had been melancholy and obsessed over his fate for nearly a week. Things rarely held his attention for more than an hour, and so Bill the Gnome was getting worried. Blagre wasn't eating and had locked his door – refusing all company.

But, as usual for this time of day, Bill carried a tray of wine and biscuits (Blagre had gone off beer entirely) up to the solar and knocked on the door. "Shall I leave it outside?"

"No, no! Come in, come in, Bill. Refreshments, quickly!"

Bill entered the room to find Blagre sitting on the floor, parchments strewn everywhere, quill in hand and looking – well – overstimulated. Coffee hadn't been discovered yet, but he looked like he'd had too much of it.

"Are you feeling better?" said Bill.

"Much, much better, dearest Bill. I have figured it all out. I have found a way to break the spell, so to speak."

"You have? I mean, that's wonderful. May I ask how? And what all this mess is for?"

"It came to me out of nowhere. A flash of inspiration. I am going to be a *writer!*"

"A what?"

"A writer, Bill. An author. A scribe of the imagination. A weaver of literary spells."

Bill considered the revelation for a moment, then said, "But – and forgive me if this is an impertinent question – I thought you – er *we* – were in a novel *already?*"

"I am. I am the main character – you, Bill, are a significant but *supporting* cast member. So?"

"Well now, I may only be a gnome, and I may not possess your – er – intellect, but aren't you in danger of creating a paradox?"

"I don't see how."

"Very well, let's see what you've got so far before I get worried. What's the story about?"

Blagre stood up, parchment in hand, and cleared his throat. "Once upon a time, there were two cave trolls. They were bored of eating children and decided they wanted to be highwaymen."

He paused.

"Go on," said Bill.

"That's it. That's what I have so far."

"Oh."

"For goodness' sake, Bill, I've only been at it for a week. But – what do you think? Be honest."

Bill put down the tray, took the parchment from Blagre's hand and re-read it.

"Well?" said the wizard.

"I'm not an expert, but if you ask me, 'Once upon a time' is a cliché, even for this century – don't use it. Also, cave trolls barely do more than grunt – the opportunities for dialogue are limited. And also, if they wanted to be highwaymen, wouldn't they have to go out in the day? No one travels at night. Cave trolls turn to stone in sunlight. And also..."

"Bah! Everyone's a critic," said Blagre. "Look here, don't you have some important beans to go and count? *Begone.* Leave me to my work. I do not want to be disturbed for a week. You hear me?"

One week later...

Timidly, Bill the Gnome poked his head around the door to the solar. Inside, he saw Blagre sitting in a rocking chair, feet up on the table, snoozing. In the far corner of the room, a small goblin-like creature was perched on a stool amongst a great pile of books. He was holding one, flicking through its pages at an alarming rate. When he reached the end of the book, he picked up another one and began to do the same thing.

Bill put a hand on Blagre's shoulder and shook him gently. "Are you all right?"

"Ah, what's that? Oh Bill, hello. Sorry, I was taking a well-deserved nap. I have been so busy. Did you bring beer?"

"The writing is going well then?"

"Ah yes, the writing. You know, I have learned a great deal about writing in this past week."

"You have?"

"Yes indeed. Firstly, I have learned it is very, very, *very* boring – I'd rather pull teeth. And secondly, that I am no good at it."

"That took you a week? *I* could have told you that."

"Very droll, Bill. No, it did not take me a week, but *that* did," he said, pointing to the goblin in the corner.

"May I ask what, precisely, *that* is?"

"You see, this is the brilliant part. It is painfully obvious I have no talent for writing, but it seems rather unfair that this should be a barrier to creating a marvellous story. After all, I suspect our own author has limited ability."

"It would be hard to argue with *that*, all things considered."

"Precisely, and so I got to thinking, what am I good at?"

"Nothing springs to mind," Bill said, smiling.

"Pah. *Magic*, Bill. I'm good at magic. And so, I have created a magical solution. See yonder goblin there? That is Gippity, and he is going to help me."

"Geepeetee?"

"Yes, Gippity – spelled with 'i' not 'e'. You see, goblins are not adept at using their brains; nevertheless, they are rather sponge-like and have a larger-than-expected capacity to take stuff in. They are also easy to manipulate. I have enchanted Gippity so he can absorb all these books in my library."

"He's reading all these? I didn't know goblins could read."

"Not reading, Bill, *absorbing*. I have thousands of books, and he's going to *absorb* them all. He hasn't got the faintest idea what they all mean."

"But why? I mean, I don't understand."

Blagre got to his feet and stretched. "It is hard for a gnome to understand magic, but by absorbing all these books, Gippity will contain the essence of everything there is to know about writing currently. And then, when he's finished – which should be next Tuesday – I will be able to ask him to write a story for me! Brilliant, no?"

Bill thought for a moment, scratching his chin. "I have a question," he said.

"Ask away."

"Isn't that... I mean, surely that is plagiarism?"

"Nonsense! *Nonsense*! Suppose *I* had read all those books. Would that not inspire my own writing?"

"But you haven't read them."

"A technicality."

"I'm not sure it is."

"What you are missing, Bill, is that the original idea will still be mine – I will just ask Gippity to do the boring work of writing. I mean, who cares about the words? Who could tell the difference? And if you can't tell the difference, then clearly, it doesn't matter. It is merely a labour-saving device. One should not fear progress, Bill. Gippity here might make writers of us all! *Imagine that*."

"And what are you going to ask him to write?"

"I am inventing a whole new genre: *Scientia Ficta*."

"What is that in English? My Latin is conversational at best."

"I think it translates to Science Fiction, Bill. Stories about the future."

"*Science*? What is that?"

"I'm not sure, and I fear it may be anachronistic, but nevertheless, it will be a story about the future, when people think there is no such thing as magic or fairies or trolls or anything of the sort."

"That's absurd. How would the world work without magic?"

Blagre smiled and patted his stomach. "Absurd indeed. But no matter – Gippity will fill in the details. How about some lunch?"

\* \* \*

The next morning, Sam arrived at the coffee shop early. His

laptop was closed, and he gazed at the door. Starbucks was busy that day – that annoyed him; however, the weather was much better, you'll be pleased to know.

Eventually, Daisy arrived, looking much the same as she did the day before (my word count is already past the halfway mark).

"Hullo again, Marvin," she said, smiling at Sam.

"I was hoping you'd be back," he said as she approached the table.

"Oh, I'm flattered," she replied.

"No, I don't mean like *that*... oh... I mean... well, yes, but no. I know this sounds silly, and I know it was just a placebo effect. But that jellybean... it *worked*. I mean, I knew what to write. "

"Really?" She laughed.

"Yes, yes... and I know this sounds even more ridiculous, absurd even..."

"Go on."

"Do you have another one?"

"Hmmm, let me check." She rummaged in her clutch bag. "Alas," she said at length.

"What?"

"I only have an orange one," and she placed it on the table with a smile. "But I told you, these are *magic* jellybeans. Do you know what that means? Are you sure you want it?"

Sam smiled. "Yes, yes, of course. I write about wizards; I am as qualified as anyone else regarding magic."

"Very well, but after today, I won't be coming back to this coffee shop. Frankly, it's an awful place; I don't know why you like it."

"But... what about the jellybeans?" The thought of not seeing her again created a strange and unpleasant sensation in his stomach – even worse than the cappuccino.

"I have plenty of those, but only if you are *absolutely* sure you want them. Here's my address," she said with a wink and handed Sam a business card. "There's a GPS location on there. My cottage is off the beaten track. It's quite a walk from the main road. Why not visit me? Tomorrow if you like. Shall we say ten am?"

Sam watched as she left, then popped the orange jellybean in his mouth.

* * *

The next morning (which was also warm and sunny, although why that matters is beyond me), Sam found himself pushing through bracken, brambles, and all manner of other things Mother Nature creates to irritate us. He looked at his phone, checking he was still going in the right direction.

"She wasn't kidding about it being hard to get to," he muttered.

Let's skip past the boring stuff about travelling many miles...

The undergrowth relented, and he saw a picturesque little cottage ahead of him. It was the sort of thing that wouldn't look out of place in a Constable, with one exception. There were no windows on the front of the building.

Relieved to finally be free of the brambles, he walked up the short gravel path to a big, red wooden door and knocked.

The door opened so quickly that he nearly fell forward. There was Daisy, looking even more attractive than the almost impossible standards she had already set. Today, however, she was dressed in a long flowing dress of sky blue, barefoot and wearing a small tiara that glinted in the sunlight. An other-worldly presence surrounded her (I have no idea what that specifically looks like, but we'll assume it's a pretty obvious sort of effect.)

*Bit overdressed for this time of the day,* he thought, happily oblivious to the ham-fisted foreboding I had just employed.

"Ah, Marvin, my dearest Marvin. I am so glad you decided to join us. Do come in."

"Us?" he said.

"Why yes. Me... and my other writers."

"Other writers?" he said.

"Marvin, dearest, are you going to repeat everything I say?" She laughed her musical laugh and ushered Sam into the cottage. "There are many writers here. I told you I know a lot about the creative process. You might think of this as a commune: a community of writers."

"Oh," was all he could think of, unable to hide his disappointment.

"Oh, Marvin, don't look so glum. Silly me, where are my manners?" Next to the doorway was a small table, and on the table was a glass bowl filled with jellybeans. "Flavour?" she asked.

"Oh, er – lime?"

She plucked a green jellybean from the bowl and handed it to Sam, who dutifully ate it.

"Now, follow me, won't you."

Sam could now see that the inside of the cottage was more like a long corridor, doors lining its sides, almost further than he could see. Daisy took him by the hand and led him along the aforementioned corridor. She occasionally pointed to a door and mentioned someone's name, but Sam wasn't paying attention. He drifted along in a dream-like state; his gaze fixed firmly on Daisy as she gently pulled him along.

At length, they reached a door on their left that was open.

"Please, please," she said, motioning for him to enter.

Inside, the room was small yet cosy and comfortable. A small fire burned in the hearth. There was a wooden bed covered in many blankets and a small antique desk upon which somebody had placed an old-fashioned fountain pen, a bottle of ink and a stack of paper.

"This is nice," he said.

"Oh, I'm so glad you think so," she replied. She pointed to a recess in the wall, just beside the desk. "The dumb waiter," she said. Sam looked perplexed. "For food," she replied to his unasked question. "Once every evening. You wouldn't want to be distracted during the day. And there are your jellybeans," she said, pointing to a jar on the bedside table. "Nine thousand, one hundred and thirty-one, exactly."

"There's no window," said Sam, walking over to where the jar of jellybeans stood.

"No distractions," she replied in the most whimsical tone.

"Distractions from what?"

At that moment, she left the room, closing the door behind her, and Sam heard the mechanical clunk of the lock.

"Distraction from writing, my dearest Marvin. Nothing will bother you now. I will see you again in twenty-five years."

\* \* \*

The following Tuesday (in our historical timeline)...

Bill the Gnome awoke to a loud cry of "Eureka!"

It was still early, and the sun had barely come up. He rubbed his eyes, swung his legs out of bed, straightened his nightgown, popped on his slippers and headed for the solar.

Within, he found Blagre jigging around the room in delight. Gippity was also doing some goblin equivalent of dancing, although quite clearly, with no idea why.

"What's all the commotion?" asked Bill.

"Success, success, Bill. And here it is," said Blagre, waving about a few pieces of parchment.

"Here's what?"

"The *story*, Bill, the story. I have to say, I have surpassed myself this time. Gippity here is nothing short of a miracle worker."

"It doesn't look like a very long story. There's barely three pieces of parchment."

"Bill, you are a delightfully illiterate gnome. The length of the piece is no indication of the quality. It's a masterpiece, written in the style of Beowulf – a poem as much as a story."

"I believe the correct term is 'epic'," said Bill grumpily. "So, what's it about then?"

Blagre stopped dancing and slumped into his chair with sweat running from his forehead.

"You see, Bill, I only meant to give Gippity here a test run, so to speak. I didn't expect his first attempt to be a masterpiece. I just asked him to write a story about *our author*, who must presumably live in the future. Lo and behold, he'd completed the task within minutes – barely any spelling mistakes either, although the grammar could use some work - but when has that ever stopped a great writer?!*?"

"If we put the *obvious* paradox here to one side," said Bill, "I suppose that's good news then. I'm delighted for you. What will Gippity – er – *you* write next?"

Blagre beamed. "That is *not* the good news, Bill."

"It isn't?"

"No. The *good* news is my melancholy has completely lifted. I feel my old self again, and what's more, I'm done with writing – what an absurd profession it is."

Blagre paused for a moment so that I could break up the paragraph for dramatic purposes.

"The future is bright and filled with possibility. And what's more, I can't help feeling there are adventures aplenty ahead of us – for many, *many* years to come."

S. Markem is an accidental writer of fiction. You cannot find him anywhere.

# FORGET-ME-NOT JONES

Jake Curran-Pipe

Many moons ago, I lived in a chilly riverside cottage cocooned by the rushes and cattails of a Welsh marshland. Despite my parents' best effort of nurturing the cottage's ancient hearth, a damp bitterness lingered on the walls of this brightly painted house.

Mister and Mrs Jones had never expected children; every attempt had ended in heartbreak and after a while they surrendered to a baby-free existence. Until one day, in their mid-forties, my sister and I were brought forth in a bundle of excitement and worry.

Finally Willowsett had tiny hands to muck up its walls and carpets in double-time; my parents couldn't be happier with their corner of marshy paradise. My fire-blooded sister, Aster, with her red hair and comet-tails of mess, had the same adoration for nature and magic as my parents. But me, Forget-Me-Not, with my raven locks and timorous spirit, much preferred a corner to read my textbooks whilst they all trudged through the sticky land looking for pixies.

Our parents tried to make the damp little cottage as child friendly as possible but that constant chill in the walls meant me or my sister would sneak out of each other's rooms in the middle of the night to cosy up to each other. Making sure to be back in our own beds before our parents noticed. We didn't want them to feel bad or, even worse, move us out of this marshland haven.

Many moons ago, I used to live in a chilly riverside cottage with my parents and my sister. And now, here I am, back in my childhood bed for the first time in over a decade.

* * *

The late morning March sunlight is blocked by black-out curtains. The outside determined to come in. Aster always wanted to be outdoors, exposed to the world in an attempt to uncover its preternatural secrets. I never want to be exposed though; I want to be entombed. The windowless walls of libraries and laboratories are what caught my imagination.

Today's sunlight is purely for Aster in the garden right now. I have no interest in stepping foot out in the sunny cold and I have no idea if spring has even started to kiss the flower buds awake yet.

The itching anxiety of leaving my room is starting to draw blood. Under the dusty covers, I bring a hesitant finger on my right hand to the corner between my left thumb and index; there's a tacky gild of raw skin there that, if I could muster up any form of emotion, would repulse me to the point of nausea. I pick between my nails and remove the layers of skin that had bunged up in the nailbed. I don't bother to try and stop the gentle ooze of blood from my new wound. Let it bleed, I think. It's not like it'll kill me. The faint sting is the only thing I can feel right now.

A crack of persistent sunlight tries to eke its way into my bedroom. Huh, *my* bedroom. Is it really my bedroom though? It belonged to a little girl called Forget-Me-Not Jones and, yeah, that's me, but the Forget-Me-Not Jones-who-was is never coming back. So whose room is it now? Certainly not mine. I turn my head slightly to the window, the tensed muscles in my neck twinging in protest, and marvel at the unabashed determination the sun has to bathe me in light. *Piss off*, I curse. Can't it see I'm trying to wallow? What does it think I've been doing all week?

Dust swirls in the channel of sunlight like snowflakes. Oh, how I wish it was winter: it's a lot easier to stay inside guilt-free then. The particles dance by the navy wallpaper that's festooned with golden suns, moons and stars, all etched with insolently content faces smirking at me, knowing and smug about my lack of desire to exist. A haunting, taunting memory of the girl I used to be. The girl who used to love her celestial wallpaper and wonky bookshelf.

I avert my eyes to keep them from glazing over in a state of the almost-crying I've been doing a lot lately. They wander over to the ceiling in the far-right corner of the room and catch on a pathetic glow-in-the-dark crescent moon sticker. *Stupid moon.* I scrunch my eyes and try to fall back to sleep. The moon used to bring me such peace. Not anymore.

Not for a while.

*** 

Growing up I often felt like the outcast, the Scully in a family of Mulders. Lost and confused and in perpetual melancholy. Not caused by some maelstrom of pubescent confusion, but from Aster and our parents' adoration for anything... spooky. Sprites, pixies, goblins and ghouls lurked in the marshland around our cottage – according to them – and every so often they'd venture out with field-books and nets and torches desperate for a glimpse of the netherworld's inhabitants. Oblivious to the dispassionate plane of constant mental drizzle that I lived on. Every day I was faced with a smiling, positivity-enforcing trio that were convinced we were to worship the gods of the 'old country'. Now that I'm older I know my parents' sudden bout of paganism came from a trip to San Francisco. That trip led to Willowsett getting transmogrified from a clean-cut, conservative farmer's house to a patchouli-scented dwelling that celebrated gods with names like Arianrhod, Rhiannon and

Taranis.

I didn't have the words for it then, but their enlightened behaviour is probably what made me live in that state of ennui. Seeing Aster thrive and be the perfect carbon copy of Mr and Mrs Jones made me feel constricted and controlled. I never felt anything. It was as if Aster had absorbed all of my vigour and vibrancy in the womb. I was the lesser version of the golden child. Nothing in this world would excite me.

That was until I visited Bronwyn Maguire's house for the first time.

Aster and my parents had come down with some kind of flu in the spring of 1978, no doubt caused by trying to find a pooka: a hobgoblin that enjoyed shapeshifting into perfectly normal animals. They thought they lived by the fens but really they could have seen any old creature and claimed they saw one.

Having no aunts, uncles, nor living grandparents amplified my loneliness in times like this. And so I was sent off to the house of an old colleague of my father's in the town of Llangefni, where I would stay until the flu had passed. Llangefni was only a nearby town but being homeschooled and hardly leaving the cottage, I may as well have been shipped off to Shanghai for all I knew. Before then, I had only known my parents, Aster, Willowsett and the marshland.

If my family hadn't been struck by this illness, I never would have gone to the Maguire household to realise why I had felt so out-of-sorts my whole childhood. I wasn't depressed and I wasn't uninterested in life. It turns out I was just bored shitless.

Mister Maguire drove me to their two-up two-down and showed me into the spare room where his children, Rhys and Bronwyn, were waiting for me, their hands full of sweet things called fruit pastilles and black jacks. I had never tasted anything like them before in my life; I had never eaten things so *sticky* before. That evening I gorged on my first ever fish, chips, mushy peas, and gravy. My body was warm and full and satisfied for the first time ever. Not that my parents starved us: we ate lots of homegrown vegetables in stew and tray bake form. But having grease and batter line my insides was a satiation I could never have previously comprehended.

In Bronwyn's room, there was a poster filled with the moons and planets of the solar system. Only these didn't have coy smiles etched on to them like the bronze statuettes in Willowsett's living room. I knew the planets existed but my mum never really touched on them after the lesson she had given me with text books that didn't even have any images. The swirling oranges and blues of the planets and the argent stoicism of the moons lit my eyes up like fireflies in a hazy spring meadow.

"Me and my dad take the telescope out to the beach sometimes," said Bronwyn, pointing to the cylinder of discovery that perched by her window. "Sometimes you can see clearly here but the light pollution makes it difficult."

*Light pollution.* I pored the words over in my mind.

"Is it true we can go to the moon now?" I asked.

"Well, not everyone. But some men have gone. Have you not seen it?"

"Seen what?"

"They recorded it. The moon landings!" She smirked at my befuddled face. "You must be the only person in the world who hasn't seen it. Do your parents not have a TV?"

Before I could answer, Bronwyn had grabbed me by the wrist and taken me down into the living room where Mrs Maguire was listening to disco records whilst fixing Rhys' shoes.

"Mummy, mummy! Forget-Me-Not hasn't seen the moon landings!"

"What?" said Mrs Maguire, looking up from her cobbling work.

"Can we show her? Pleeease," said Bronwyn as she rummaged through the drawer underneath the television.

"Go on then," said Mrs Maguire, taking the needle off the disco record. I was in half a mind to ask her to keep it on. I had never heard music so infectious before.

Bronwyn pulled out a video cassette. I asked what it was, blushing from embarrassment.

"They're new. You can tape things from the television. They had a rerun of the moon landings earlier this year and daddy taped it."

*All these new words.*

What I saw next I could never have prepared for. The grainy footage of men bouncing across a rocky landscape gave me a hope I never knew I needed. The hope that one day I, too, could escape. One day I would leave that damp riverside cottage that was jam-packed with potpourri and shrines to moon goddesses. I could leave my boring parents, my annoying sister, and I could travel the universe learning everything that there was to learn. My whole life I thought I had nothing to offer the world; that Aster was the one that would make my parents happy with her love of everything earthy. I thought I had nothing. But on that drizzly spring day I realised I had a lot. I had curiosity. In front of me were the moon landings but ahead of me was a life free from dormice running across my bed and mould spreading across the shower curtain. It was a sterile, studious life of telescopes and experiments.

For the next few days I devoured Rhys and Bronwyn's books about space, biology, dinosaurs and chemistry. I had always enjoyed homeschooling with my mum but there was a difference between procuring basic knowledge and the stomach-knotting excitement of discovery that I had started to experience in that tiny box room in Llangefni.

When the house was asleep, I sat by the window and watched the radiant moon glow beams of wonder across the sleepy grey town. Out in the marshland, I had always seen clear night skies dotted with stars and thought nothing of them. Aster had once told me it was our ancestors looking down on us but I didn't quite believe that. Now, I felt that one day I could be up in those stars looking back at the Earth in that glimmering sky.

"What do you want to be when you grow up?" said Bronwyn at our last breakfast together. My parents and Aster had gotten over their flu and Mr Maguire was due to take me home that evening. I could have cried all day. I could have cried so much that the fenlands would flood.

"I want to be a moonologist" I replied. A made up word that I liked. Lunar scientist sounded boring and I was *over* life being boring. I nibbled at my marmalade toast to distract myself. "Can we still be friends when I go home?"

Missus Maguire overheard our conversation. "Of course, darling. Here, I'll write down our landline. Give us a call whenever you want to play out with Bronwyn. Maybe one day we could take you to a museum? Would you like that?"

The rest of the spring consisted of me helping Aster build and paint a giant silver wheel that she said would be an altar for her favourite goddess Arianrhod. A willowy figure in Welsh folklore that represented all things birth, life, and death. Aster believed that if we gave her offerings throughout spring then we'd have a fruitful summer and substantial harvest for autumn and winter.

Sometimes I didn't know if my parents were in on some kind of joke with Aster; if my parents only pretended to believe to appease my sister; or if all three of them really did believe a woman up in the clouds had the power to decide if we ate well that year. Whatever the case, I grew even more restless at the idea of magic beings controlling my life when a world of science and discovery was waiting for me to escape into it.

Occasionally I would be able to speak to Bronwyn on the phone. We hadn't managed to organise a time for me to get back to Llangefni but I was just grateful for the temporary escape during these calls. Bronwyn would read from her science books and tell me the most interesting facts I could find. My heart would sing as it learnt about quarks, steroid belts, and the craters of the moon.

I probably make it seem like living in Willowsett was dire. It wasn't. My parents were kind, if odd, and Aster, whilst boisterous, was a good sister to me. Though we didn't enjoy the same things, or even share the same beliefs, the one thing I could bond with Aster on was our adoration for strawberries.

Once a fortnight throughout spring and summer, our dad would take us to a farm nearby where we would run riot through its land, our knees grubby and our mouths sticky with a sweet, red glaze. Punnets were filled to the brim on those every-other-Sundays with scarlet jewels to spend an afternoon making jam and tarts. Cooking time was the only time Aster and I could align our interests: logic and order met passion and intuition.

"Mummy, can I learn more about science?" I said whilst measuring the baking ingredients; Aster was next to me at the table making a witch-like concoction of strawberry, rhubarb, sugar and goodness knows what else.

My mum sighed.

"Darling, I love how much you love to learn. But I think, and your father thinks, that science strips the world of its magic and wonder. It distances us from nature. We were never supposed to rip it apart and probe it; we are supposed to worship it."

What she meant was that me becoming a scientist would make me realise how ridiculous their devotion to Celtic gods and pixies was. I paused my measuring and stole a strawberry from Aster's pile, who gasped like a diva, and popped it in my mouth whilst I thought over my retort.

"But science *is* magic!"

How naive I was.

*\*\*\**

The dust swirls in the ever-insistent sunbeams were starting to annoy me. Everything in this bedroom was annoying me. I wanted the duvet to swallow me whole and send me to a place of eternal darkness and softness. Free from the mind-numbing depression that is still not getting any better as I stagnate in a childhood bedroom that hasn't been updated since 1986. Back to the place where my dreams were born, and now those dreams are dead.

*\*\*\**

Throughout my teenage years, I was having secret science tuition from a girl that the Maguires knew. One day my mum caught me with one of the books my science tutor had supplied me with. Rather than berate me, like I thought she would, about being a liar and a sneak, she seemed to finally realise what my true love was.

When I was sixteen, I went to the local sixth form college to study physics, chemistry, geography and maths. And when I was eighteen, I moved out of Willowsett for good to study astronomy in South Wales. Aster and my parents cried non-stop on the drive down. I tried to be the composed one but as soon as the final box was unpacked in my halls of residence, and my family made their journey north, I cried all evening and didn't come out of my room. I eventually perked up and thought if those men can go to the moon, then I can certainly do this.

Despite the initial hope and excitement, it turned out being a woman-in-science in the early 1990s wasn't the best time to be alive, what with the misogyny minefield to navigate on top of the nihilism and apathy of American grunge music I had become hooked on. Being the only woman in my astronomy classes, I struggled with making friends. I had hardly ever been around other boys in my life apart from sweet Rhys Maguire. And now I was the only woman in labs filled with over thirty men. Thirty leering, greasy, sweaty men that thought I had stumbled into the classes by accident. I swear one of them patronisingly explained what a zenith was to me whilst trying to peek down my top. I felt like throwing hydrochloric acid in his face but unfortunately we weren't studying chemistry.

I was devastated there were no other women in my year. My whole life I had been around such positive feminine energy. To be in an environment where that not only was uncelebrated, but despised, was disturbing. It made me realise the hell that the women in science before me had been through.

\*\*\*

There's a pang in my stomach that reminds me of those days in my lonely uni flat where I would have spaghetti hoops on toast for four days straight. The bed around me is freezing from having not moved my body in what could be over twelve hours. Aster has given up on trying to look after me. I'm surprised she even wanted to help in the first place.

\*\*\*

When I was down in South Wales studying my lifelong love, the loneliness set in at an alarming rate. At first, Aster called me every other day and I'd lie to her about how lovely my course-mates were and all the crazy, studenty things I was up to.

It wasn't long before I started screening her calls.

Every week I spiralled more, closed myself off more, and I no longer had the strength to lie. I didn't want to be confronted with telling the truth.

When I went home for Christmas and for our birthday in May, I masked my sadness from my family. It was like slipping into my previous self, the girl before the moon, just letting the motions guide her through the day.

I was ashamed and embarrassed that this new life of mine wasn't all it was cracked up to be. But I couldn't let them know that. They would make me come home to Willowsett and there I would remain a failure. Growing vegetables with my sister and praying to rain gods during heatwaves, laughing about the girl I thought I could have been.

When I wasn't in class, I was listening to depressing shoegaze on my boombox. If I left the flat, it was to food shop or to go drinking with people I guess I would call acquaintances. Sometimes I would even go to the pub alone, and wait for someone to try and hit on me.

Someone I had got speaking to in a pub had recommended reading books about conspiracy, the collapse of society, and the curse of technology. That I had to know the 'truth'. So I visited the fringe bookshop on the outskirts of town. These tomes of despair under the charade of veracity led me to spiral about my own career path: when I was younger, science and technology symbolised hope for the progression of humanity. We had gone to the moon, were curing diseases, and becoming more connected with each other. But as science progressed, more and more it was being used for evil and greed. It scared me. A world growing with science and technology scared me. What once had made my eyes open to the world had made me so insular I could barely exist.

Science definitely was not magic.

And that's when the only plinth that was keeping me up, working hard at my studies, started to crumble. One night, Aster called me and I answered it without thinking, immediately regretting the decision. She told me all about the new silver wheel altar she had built for Arianrhod back at Willowsett. A crazed sensation fell over me and I blurted out to her I was depressed. Her response?

"I'll pray to the moon for you. You can get through this."

"I don't need your fairy tales right now," I snapped back, and hung up.

She wasn't to know, but the moon had become a symbol of false hope and disappointment to me. Something I spent my childhood admiring had led me down a path of isolation. I didn't want her or her stupid beliefs praying to the moon for me.

And so there I remained, in my damp seaside flat, quietly devastated by the state of my life and the world until one day I stopped going to class altogether. I soon moved out of my university flat, half wanting to accidentally leave my address book and forget Willowsett's landline number. I wanted to disappear, afraid I'd be immolated by burning shame.

It was with the universe's impeccable timing, and what felt like the only bone it would ever throw at me, that my family were going on a voyage to the fairy pools of Skye the week when my graduation should have been. I was able to slink away from university without a single prying eye. I told them my graduation picture and degree got destroyed in a leak.

I had grown exhausted and ill from the entanglement of lies I had found myself in. At first I used them as quick fixes for a deeper problem. I didn't realise I would start losing myself in my own false reality. I had to get out of Wales. I had to start anew again.

When I was young, I adored being alone. Devouring books and listening to music was my solace. You'd think being alone at university would have been great for me, a blissfully isolated existence. But no, I found out quite aggressively that there was a strong difference between being alone and being lonely.

With no false community of university, starting anew was harder than ever without the scholarly safety net. The 1990s were spent working cafés, video shops and bars whilst I ventured between cities in England and Scotland. I'd go home for birthdays and Christmas, just like I did at university, and I would continue the tales of my new life in astronomy.

There were boyfriends with beards that got me into electronica and girlfriends with interesting piercings that gave me the freedom to experiment with my body. I was starting to feel secure in my insecurity. In 1995, I broke my leg in Dundee and during autumn 1996 I ended up running a bookshop for several months in Horwich. The closest time I ever came to returning to science and technology was being a receptionist for a video game developer in Derby, 1997. I had developed the bohemian habit of quitting a job as soon as I started to feel trapped; perhaps I was more like my sister than I thought.

I wasn't necessarily happy, but I felt freer in myself. It was just those two visits to Willowsett every year where I was confronted with the carelessness of my existence.

Every day I thought about telling Aster the truth. Deep down I knew I could never feel right if I didn't tell her. Every day I wanted to find the strength to tell her the truth.

I couldn't even bring myself to tell her the truth the day of our parents' funeral. Late 1998, they were camping in Yorkshire and were drowned by a flash flood. It took ages for Aster to find me. I was in Nottingham at the time. It broke us both, naturally, and I stayed at Willowsett for three weeks. But even then I quelled any thoughts of honesty: it didn't feel like the right time. It was already a horrendous December. To find out your twin is a depressed, lying, apathetic nihilist that regrets every choice she has ever made isn't exactly uplifting.

There was an eclipse in summer 1999 and it was the most excited I had been in a while for something. I remember watching the moon entomb the sun in its shadow for those few seconds, and my inner child begged for me to return to science. But I knew I couldn't. If I failed in that field it would devastate me. After being so excited to be a scientist, the misogyny and unethical morals that infected the field had put me off for life. And yet that young Forget-Me-Not Jones would still sometimes yearn for the moon.

It was Bristol, autumn 1999. People had started to get mobile phones; computers with internet were appearing in living rooms across the nation; Hallowe'en that year was scattered with folk dressed in black leather, shades, and talking about different coloured pills. I was scared. Humans shouldn't be so *connected*. Many vodka-induced conversations in the fug of cigarettes at the pub I worked in were debating the social ethics of humanity being so integrated with technology. That fear I felt back at university reading those cynical books about the exploitation of science and technology for evil had started gripping at my chest again.

Science wasn't magic, it was tearing this world apart.

Time to move on. To a bigger city with more distractions.

"Forget-Me-Not?" said a voice in the corner of the café several months later. I was working in the Earth Café in Manchester, March 2000, spending my days shovelling mushroom wellingtons, roast potatoes, and gravy onto the plates of urban vegetarians who enjoyed eating their lunch in a mist of patchouli and spa music.

My stomach twinged with the recognition of the voice.

"Aster..." I said in the midst of clearing a table. She looked back at me, her curly red hair incandescent with the café's mood lighting. I saw her eyes trying not to judge the purple streaks in my raven hair. My black choker and sleeve of gothic tattoos were worlds away from that young girl of moons and stars in Willowsett.

"It was... It was Bronwyn Maguire. She told me she saw you here."

"Bronwyn was here?" I smiled. My body rang with guilt for the elation I felt hearing that sweet girl's name. I could barely remember her face now. Funnily enough, I had thought of Aster this morning when one of the cook's was showing off her new recipe for strawberry fool. I couldn't remember the last time I had eaten a strawberry; they reminded me too much of home.

Aster's eyes could never hide her emotions. In them I could see a storm of anger, sadness and happiness, as if she was working out what to be first. Eventually, her eyebrows dropped and her face relaxed of all tension. It was then that I realised that I had never, ever seen her outside the grounds of Willowsett apart from that day us Joneses drove down to move me into halls.

She had caught me. Last time we spoke I told her I was working at the University of St Andrews in the astronomy department.

"How are you?" she said.

And with that simple question, the weakening pillars holding up my pretence of happiness cracked. I broke down.

***

An owl is pecking at the bedroom. The sun set a few hours ago. Aster had knocked on the door wanting to feed me. I didn't answer, which was an answer for her. I know it's an owl because its hooting woke me from my sleep. My bird-watching father would have been able to identify which species it was but I have no idea. My best guess would be a tawny: they have the classic twit-twoo. It definitely wasn't a barn owl with their ghostly, primordial shrieks.

I want to move over to the curtains and peek through to see the curious owl perching on a branch, but I don't. Instead I wonder, once more, if my life would have been better if I never left Willowsett. I could have spent my life in an ignorant bliss identifying owl calls and going out looking for will-o'-the-wisps. Instead I burdened myself with curiosity.

Maybe Mother Nature is teasing me. Owls are the symbol of wisdom, after all. Something I used to chase. Huh, maybe the Cherokee folk were right, and owls *are* a symbol of evil.

I wonder how long I could go without eating before I starve to death.

Would Aster let me? Is she counting down the days until I definitely need food rammed down my throat? She witnessed my breakdown right there in the Earth Café and her first instinct was to take me back to Willowsett. I wanted to protest and kick and scream but the tears surrendered me to returning. I want to purge myself of the memory of my blabbering confession to Aster on the drive home. I told her what a complete and utter sham I was, expecting her to throw me out in disgust, but she was silent. Which made me feel worse.

My bladder pangs in desperation for a wee but I ignore it. I've ignored my body a lot since the day Aster brought me back here. I wasn't too sure if I wanted it to continue existing. But I knew I didn't have the ambition to end my life. No, that would require planning and effort: two things I'm really not that into these days.

Springtime used to be my favourite season before I stopped having 'favourite' things. If someone asked me what my favourite season was now, I'd shrug and mumble. But before I would have said spring. Precocious spring with its pastel pink blossoms of hope and excitement for the new. A meteorological tabula rasa for the soul.

I drift back into my limbolike non-sleep where my body stops trying to make me do things like urinate and eat. This ephemeral dreamscape is the only way I can find some sort of peace.

Later in the night, my eyes flutter with the sharp brightness of light spilling into the room. The rail of my curtains had slipped off its hooks somehow and had exposed me and my bedroom to the outside world. Moonbeams were illuminating me as if I were a pop star ready for a performance. My body rises for the first time in a day as I scramble to fix the curtains. My eyes, still adjusting to the light, catch the moon in the starless sky. A silvery orb in a sea of navy satin. It's a waning gibbous.

Release. Gratitude. Introspection.

During my time at the Earth Café in Manchester, my eyes wandered to the spiritual books that were left in the mini-library. I was drawn to a book that was called *Moonology* and caught myself smiling at the title. For the first time in years, there was a shimmer of happiness when thinking back to my childhood. I gave the book's pages a quick flick and ended up on a chapter that described the various phases of the moon and their meaning. It struck me that the waning moon, a moon that is disappearing, is said to be the time to reevaluate your life. Surely a waxing gibbous, a moon *leading* to a full moon, would be more suitable? Before I can stop myself, I am standing by the curtainless window looking up at the brightly shining moon. I look down into the garden to see where its glow has been cast. I can see the tutti-frutti early spring flowers peeping out of the dark. The petite, powder blue petals of forget-me-nots look back at me.

I prop the curtains back on to their rail and block out the moon's light. My body hums with uneasiness as I take in the image of forget-me-nots flooded in that satellite brilliance. The glow-in-the-dark celestial stickers on the walls seem brighter as if enveloping my bedroom in childlike wonder again.

I hear a creak from downstairs that snaps me out of my trance. My joints ache in the newness of their movement and I start to notice the numbness in my back caused from being stubbornly horizontal. I look back at the bed and pity the dreary, dusty covers I had been hiding under ever since I returned to Willowsett. I am very aware of my body and my being. I don't want to move because a creaking floorboard will indicate my rising to Aster. I still don't want to speak to her. I don't want to speak about or acknowledge anything right now. I just want to not exist. I look down at the shiny wound on my hand. My own bloody metaphor of guilt picking away at me.

Before I can contemplate any further, I find my body moving towards the bedroom door. I unlock it and step out into the warm landing; a shock from the frigid room I had been hiding in these past days. My bare feet step in something squidgy but I'm so hyper-focused on what I am about to do, I don't even look down to see what it was I stood in. I pass down the carpeted landing and move so quickly down the stairs, I wonder if I flew. The back door opens and my feet cry in pain at the sharpness of the gravel they've just stepped on to. It's chilly but I don't care.

In the corner of my eye, I see the moon standing tall among the velvet night. Not a single cloud obscures her eminence. *Fuck off*, I think. *You're the cause of all this. You made me dream, made me hope, made me explore. I could have been happy reading my books, disconnected from the world, learning to live with my eccentric family. But you had to draw me out from my room; hypnotise me with the allure of discovery and mystery and knowledge. You ostracised me from my family, made me think I was better than them just because I had the insane notion to try and be a scientist. You're the reason I'm so alone. Bullied and harassed by cruel, male classmates. Purposeless and drifting across the country. All because of you. My obsession with you made my life worse. You threw me out into that cold, vicious world when I could have been safe and ignorantly blissful. You did this.*

Wooden fencing separates the flowerbeds from the fenland. Where the tall grass can shroud me from the world; where the salty brine of peat stings my nose; and the sludgy, seizing marsh can drag me into a watery tomb. My heart is pounding like the fists of a March hare. The moon's argent shimmer bewitches the fenland into a sanctuary I want to disappear into. I just want to free myself from shame and guilt. Surely the water from the fens can cleanse me of my sins? I know I'm not thinking straight but I can't think of anything saner right now than throwing myself into that marsh purely to feel something different. Something exciting.

A silver glow grows bright behind me, effulgent and encroaching. A light so bright, the dark night begins to feel like day.

I don't want to look in case it distracts me from this primal urge to throw myself to the earth. I don't want to look...

And yet, I turn around.

Curiosity always did get the better of me.

I don't know if it's the brightness of the light or if my eyes aren't used to such brilliance after days in my bedroom cave, but it feels as though the sun is glaring directly into my pupils. I wince and squint as I let my eyes adjust to what I'm seeing. In the bed of forget-me-nots where the wishing well and toadstool statuettes sit, little lights dance in the moonbeams like will-o'-the-wisps bewitching a traveller. The lights fuse and shimmer and disappear. And there is a woman.

Taller than me, her face angular yet soft, she stands with a confidence and solemnity that makes me almost want to bow. My body liberates itself from the tension and pain it had become riddled with; my bones feel airy, my chest weightless, my nerves calmed. I think I can feel myself start to smile.

Her statuesque frame is draped with silver, satin-like robes. Her hair is platinum and striking, her skin glossy and bronze. A vibration pulses through me in a way that reminds of the time I tried to change a lightbulb when the electrics were still running. A deep, shuddering shock resonates deep within me and I fall to my knees in the cold, March-time mud.

"Do not be afraid," purrs a silken voice.

Isn't that what the angels say? I'm not sure how to react. As a woman of science, everything I'm seeing right now must surely be explained with logic. But a woman formed in the moonbeams, her bare feet tickled by my namesake flower, and emanating a preternatural aura that brought me to my knees suddenly has me open to the mystic.

"Let go of what doesn't serve you. Be grateful for what you have received," she says.

The waning gibbous.

"Wh-" my voice cracks for its lack of use. "Who..."

"I have many names, for I have been here eternally. I have been worshipped, and painted, and studied. I guide sailors, nurture the lonely." Something ribbits from the rushes behind me. A smile forms in the corner of her mouth. "The frogs know me but not my name."

"Are you..." I start to say before I catch myself at the lunacy of the idea. I glance up at the moon above. So slight in its crescent appearance yet the brightest I have ever seen it.

"Not technically. Space rock has no sapiency. I am the idea of her. Her Earthbound servant. The spirit of the moon."

Her eye contact is piercing. I want to panic, and scream, and protest at the notion of her existence. Yet all I can feel is tranquillity. An ecstasy of peace I may have never experienced before.

"I do have a name here. You may know of it. In these ancient Celtic lands they call me–"

"Arianrhod," I gasp.

She smiles in return and gently bows her head.

"But why are you here? Why me?" I ask.

Arianrhod continues her fixed gaze on me. She smirks and clicks her fingers. The shimmering moonbeams fizzle out and she steps off her plinth of forget-me-nots. She walks towards me, her ornate fabrics trailing behind her like wisps of cloud. She offers me a hand and I rise from my grovelling.

"Listen, love, I'm gonna drop the deity act and just get real. I can tell you're not going to listen to me if I'm gonna be all majestic," the goddess says. Her voice has changed from poised and chocolatey, to a husky North Wales twang. "To be honest, I thought you were a lost cause. But looking in your eyes just now, I could see it. The smallest glint. You wouldn't even know it was there."

Somehow I'm more taken aback by this, than her celestial apparition in the moonbeams.

"What do you mean?" I can barely process this conversation, let alone the implications of gods and goddesses actually existing.

"The glimmer of hope, as they say, my love."

I laugh. "I gave up on hope a long time ago."

"That you did, and you've been a right misery guts ever since. Don't get me wrong, I love a good mope every now and then, but honestly this has just gotten ridiculous-"

"If you've really been watching me this whole time, then you'd know how *shit* my life ended up being after I decided to dedicate my life to studying *you*." I take my eyes off her and look back up to the moon. "What do you mean, you're the *idea* of the moon anyway?"

Arianrhod puts her icy fingers on my chin and brings my gaze back to her. "Listen, I'm not about to get into a philosophical debate about my own existence when *you* are the reason for me being here. Stop thinking for once and just feel. You're depressed. Have been for a while now, which you know. You've lost your drive and your purpose. You lied your way into an oozing pit of toxicity-"

I can feel the heat of annoyance and embarrassment flickering in my body.

"Who are you to-" I start.

"I'm here to help you. It's why I was summoned. By revealing your secret, you are ready to move on. You just can't see it."

Summoned? I didn't do any summoning. She puts her hands gently on my upper arms. I want to squirm away but I can feel her aura calming me down again. I'm washed in docility.

"You have lost sight of the wonder around you. The excitement of discovery that was your lifeblood when you were younger. The universe is full of mystery and beauty, but of course you know that. You just need to reopen your heart and mind to it. I know you've faced hardship ever since you left this little island. But your purpose is not here."

Tears start to sodden my eyelashes. A flood of regret forming in my eyes.

"Everything turned out so wrong," I stutter. "Everything I used to love I destroyed. My studies, my family... I fucked it all up."

I've never vocalised that before. It's terrifying and liberating.

"Listen, love, it's not your fault. Life hardly ever goes in the direction people plan."

"And what do you know? Floating around in your gowns and moonlight? As if you know anything about being mortal and stupid."

"Again, this isn't about me, is it?

"So what are you going to do?" I ask. I want to weep into the arms of this otherworldly woman but I pull away from her. "How are you going to help me? Tell me it's okay to not be okay, that everything gets better? That being sad, confused, and lonely is a part of life I have to get over and move on? That I was right in leaving my family to pursue my own dreams because I don't owe them anything? That lying to them was the right thing to do? Are you going to tell me my parents loved me no matter what? Are you going to tell me my sister doesn't hate my guts–"

"Shut up, hurry up and come here," she snaps. "I don't have much time left on this plane so we need to be quick. Also, I've got an itchy bum." I move forward and Arianrhod's icy fingers touch my temples. Her silver gaze calms me once more. "I'm not here to tell you anything. I'm here to show you."

As those words leave her lips, her fingers press firmly on my temples and a jolt surges through my brain, knocking my head back and lurching my eyes to the back of my skull.

Before me a spectacle of galaxies and shapes beyond the bounds of my mortal comprehension lifts me from the ground. A sudden giddiness swells in the pit of my stomach as the cosmos unfolds before me like an intricate tapestry woven with threads of light, time, and stars. I fall through this cosmic reverie, my body tingling and surging like it would on a rollercoaster – and yet I know I am still. My body is firmly in the Willowsett garden but my mind is lightyears away.

Despite the perceived descent through space, there is a calmness embracing me as sticky and close as the air after an April shower. Something serene whispers assurances of my safety. Even though I feel myself cascading through the universe, I'm not afraid.

Colours swirl around me, some I've never even seen before, vibrant hues painting the fabric of space-time. A kaleidoscope of wonder and discovery formed of branches that await exploration. I can feel myself grinning as I start to understand the interconnectedness of all things.

As my body is gently pushed and pulled through wormholes and showers of diamond, Arianrhod's voice echoes through the expanse. I can't make out what she is saying but her mesmeric tones give me a great sense of comfort. In the heart of this celestial odyssey, I am starting to feel a profound sense of purpose. As stars and whirls of galaxies unseen dance in my eyes like blossoms swirling in the wind, I start to reach out. My hand stretches. I have to touch something. My fingers are strained and longing, trying to grab on to –

Nothing.

Darkness.

Willowsett.

My flimsy pyjama-covered body and bare feet are suddenly aware of the bitterness of the night. The moonlight that washed the garden in its glow is now obscured by cloud. Storm clouds. I feel panic in my chest rising, my breaths are getting shorter, tears prick in my eyes and I ready my mouth to let out the most awful wail. But it doesn't come.

Instead, I am laughing.

My body, so unused to this sensation, has no idea how to

react. But I am laughing. Laughing alone in the garden as droplets of rain speckle my skin.

I glance over to the forget-me-not patch. There's been some disturbance, as if somebody has been stood there. I laugh even louder. I want to look up to the moon but she has been obscured by the thunderous dark clouds that have enclosed the island. I run toward the house.

The moon has known me all my life. Has watched me laugh and cry and dream. It has and always will know me. It will know my children and my children's children. The cycle never ends. The vision Arianrhod gave me made me realise that.

To not only dream of the stars, but to reach out and grab them. To unravel their secrets and weave my own discoveries into the tapestry of human exploration.

Stepping into the kitchen, I linger by the table. My whole body is fizzing and whirling, feeling like I could be pulled in any direction. I need just a moment to realign myself into this reality. I try to take in what just happened.

Arianrhod visited me. I was ready to disappear but she came to me. A bridge between the arcane mysticism of the past and the boundless potential of science. I was ready to give up; unable to cope with what the universe had dealt me. My own hope and drive had been worn away by society but that... whatever it was... reignited that flame in me. The fire to discover. I know my purpose now.

The next generation of women in science are my new inspirations. I want to encourage girls to be fearless in their scientific journeys and make sure they know to never let anyone make them feel unwelcome at the frontier of discovery. This is what I'm here to do. New beginnings from the new millennium. Those things I saw out there... I'll never see them again in my lifetime. But if I work to encourage the next generation, and they inspire the generation after them, then who knows where we can go? The cycle must never end. My little-girl self was right all those years ago.

Science *is* magic.

I move across the kitchen and a dim flickering catches my eye in the living room, by the rain-splattered window where Aster keeps all her candles, crystals, and offerings. I see a tiny candle flame jittering in the early morning air. A few more minutes and it will be gone. I wonder who Aster had been worshipping and take a further look.

It's an altar. My heart flourishes when I see the name of the goddess beautifully engrained on a stone tablet. I bend over, smiling, and blow out the candle.

Jake Curran-Pipe is a horror and fantasy writer from Manchester. He enjoys writing scary, exciting, and intriguing fiction about underrepresented people and communities. Jake currently lives in Glasgow where he is the assistant producer of a theatre that used to be a Neo-Gothic church!

# Lady of the Flame

A. J. Van Belle

**Brig**

The lace of branches parted for me, making a path through the woods where there was none before. My breath frosted on the air, and something about that felt wrong, unseasonable, but I could not recall why.

My feet crunched a layer of frost, though I took care not to tread on the prettier patterns of frost illuminated by a cold, round moon. When I touched a bare branch in passing, a pale green leaf sprang forth.

How odd. I had the feeling this was not the first time such a thing had happened, not the first event of leafing at my touch. But I did not know when or where or how I remembered this from.

All I knew of being me was that I had walked a long, long time, my walking stick by my side. That the tendrils of hair sometimes blown by the wind across my vision were a blonde so pale they were almost white. I knew I was seeking higher ground, because the kind and giving people in the village in the valley swore the others who lived high on the hill were grasping and cruel. I had never witnessed such a thing, and so I came uphill to see for myself.

The forest's understory glowed, telling me its secrets in light. Under ferns in luminous green lived whole villages of plant spirits. Rocks glowed in brilliant blue light, a sign of the ancient rock spirits that inhabited them. I thought of the lights that glowed through all things as the underlayer of the world. In the low-lying village, I'd learned no one else besides me could see these lights or feel these dwellers of the forest floor, so sometimes, on winter nights, I'd entertained the children with tales of the spirits that made the woods alive.

I continued striding forward, moving ever uphill. Thick branches crossed my way ahead, like arms barring the way – and yet when I touched them they leapt aside, buds bursting forth on their twig-ends. In the space revealed was a cottage, a home made of wood and wattle, smoke drifting from its chimney and freezing against the moon.

I smiled to myself, not knowing why I felt pleasure at the prospect of entering this home. Only that these would be my first hill-dwellers, and I would be glad to meet them.

## Hid

The wind blew the door against the wall with a clap like a falling tree, and the woman who stood in the door looked carved of pure ice.

The dolly I was fashioning for my adopted niece dropped from my hands. Old Frid in her chair by the fire, Ned with his red beard and clay pipe, and wren-haired Aila next to him with her embroidery, all stared too. We had never seen such a person.

Almost as tall as the doorway, her hair a blonde as white as the frost on the bushes, the woman turned her head slowly, taking us in. She wore flowing garments in several shades of green and gold and carried a staff cut from alder wood with golden wires wrapped around its head.

"A wizardess!" five-year-old Rae said in awe.

"Close the door, lass," Frid advised the woman. "You're freezing us all right out of our knickers."

The woman jumped at the words, as if she'd hardly realized she was in the presence of other humans.

"Don't say 'knickers,' Granny," Rae admonished. Ned and Aila laughed.

The stranger closed the door, came forward, and crouched by the fire. She placed her staff carefully on the floor in front of her and held her hands out to warm them. Even with orange light flickering over her features, she looked unnaturally pale.

"What brings you all the way out here?" Frid asked, kinder and warmer now that the door was shut and we were protected from the cold wind.

The woman shook her head without looking at Frid or anyone. "I don't know."

Ned set his pipe aside and leaned forward with concern, elbows on knees. "Do you mean you don't remember?"

For the first time, the stranger smiled. "It's a long story, but there's not much to it. I've been wandering the countryside for many months, and I remember all *that*, but I don't remember how or why I started."

"That sounds like our Hid," Aila said, nodding toward me. "She lived in a cave in the woods when we found her, and she didn't know how she got there."

I blushed. "Aila. That was months ago." The people in our small village all spoke fondly of how they'd found me in the cave, a young woman living alone in a home made weather-tight and cozy, perfectly content, or so it seemed. And my adoptive family still liked to tease me about not knowing what my earlier years were like or how I came to my solitary abode.

"Sorry," Aila said. "We've all always loved you from the time we found you there – that's the only reason I talk about that time." That only made me blush harder. I wanted to be normal here with my family, and sometimes I almost was except for the dreams, so I didn't know why Aila had the need to remind me I was like a creature sprung full grown out of the soil.

"Would you like some porridge?" Frid asked the newcomer. "It's thin – we're running low on everything, with this winter weather lasting so long past the spring equinox. But we'll gladly share with you."

The ice-blonde woman looked confused by the question. Her brow furrowed, and she stared into the fire as if seeking an answer there.

Aila got up. "I'll get some." She returned with a wooden bowl filled with the watery concoction we'd made of oats, split peas, and our last few withering carrots. She put the bowl in the hands of the stranger, who stared into the murky contents. "My mother's right, it isn't much," Aila admitted apologetically.

"My name is Brig," said the stranger. No one had asked her, but I was glad we had a name now to put with the face.

"Pleased to meet you, Brig," I said. "I'm Hid. Aila is my adoptive sister, and that's her husband Ned, and my adoptive mother Frid."

"I'm Rae!" Rae said before I could add her.

Brig smiled. She seemed pleasant, even if she didn't understand much – about our ways, or about herself. Even about whether she would like something to eat.

She continued staring into the bowl, not taking up the spoon Aila had given her with it. "I feel so strange eating in front of you. I shouldn't take your food."

Frid rocked her chair gently. "Everyone has to eat, lass."

Brig held the bowl out toward me. "Would *you* like some?"

"We've all had our suppers already," Ned assured her.

I knew why Brig chose to offer the bowl to me in particular. Everyone else looked healthier. Ned's face glowed a burnished tan in the firelight. Aila's hair gleamed gold, her cheeks rosy. Frid was robust, with hands thick and strong from work. And Rae was a round-faced, sanguine child. I must look positively ghostly next to the rest of them: wan face, too-thin limbs, lank hair the color of the night sky. I looked into Brig's ice-blue eyes and felt the need to tell her the truth. "I don't eat."

My adoptive family collectively gasped. No one outside our household knew. Some of the people of our hillside village would have feared me if they knew. They would have thought I was a changeling, or worse, a banshee incarnate. I knew I was none of those things, as did my family. But to say it to someone we didn't know, someone who'd barged into our home unasked and unannounced, was pure recklessness.

"Oh!" Brig said. "Of course not. Silly of me." She shook her head as if to clear it. "I do eat, but of course you wouldn't."

We all stared at her. Hair like filaments of ice, a face as blank and white as the unseasonable snow – and she knew this thing about me, as if it were normal. As if it were common knowledge.

Frid leaned forward in her chair so her face was close to Brig's. "How do you know that, lass?" she asked in a soft voice. Over Brig's head, she pierced me with a look that said, *And what made you say it aloud?*

Brig didn't answer her question. Instead, she pinned her pale-blue gaze on me. "I eat only fruits and nuts. The things I find on the forest floor, freely given to me by the Earth." She put her bowl down on a hearthstone. "Forgive me. That's why I can't accept this. In the village in the valley, everywhere I went, everyone was so kind. Just like you. They all offered me food. And that surprised me, somehow. I remember... I remember... there was something about someone not offering kindness, not sharing the bounty that they had... but I *don't* remember."

"Doesn't sound like the people in the valley *I'm* familiar with," Frid muttered under her breath.

"That's the moral of the story about the Man in the Mountain!" Rae piped up. "The people wouldn't share what they had with him, so he was turned to stone as a reminder."

I had not heard this story. "That's silly – how would turning a man to stone remind anyone of anything?" I asked.

Aila chuckled. "I don't know. We haven't caught you up on all our fairy tales, Hid, it's true. Rae's just recounted all I know of that one. Maybe it has a longer version?"

Frid shook her head. "Not that I recall."

"Is the story about the Man in the Mountain on our hillside?" I asked. The name was familiar, because I'd heard a particular rock formation called by that name. It was a curl of stone that jutted above the fast-flowing stream where we fetched our water.

"Aye," Ned said, "that's the one."

I stood. "I'll show her."

Frid, Ned, and Aila all exchanged glances. I could read them as well as if they'd spoken aloud: *This newcomer Brig is strange and doesn't even know where she comes from. Can she be trusted alone with our equally strange and small, fragile little Hid?*

Rae jumped to her feet, too. "I'll go with them!"

I saw the indecision on their faces. Frid put a hand on Brig's shoulder and closed her eyes. I could almost see something happening between the two women, but the perception was like a half-forgotten memory, a hairsbreadth out of reach.

Brig looked at Frid's hand on her shoulder. "What's that blue smoke that rises when you touch me?" she asked.

"What blue smoke?" Aila asked, looking confused.

"I don't see anything," said Ned.

Frid removed her hand from Brig's shoulder. "The three of you may go. But don't be long. Once the moon sets, it will be hard to see your way back from the stream, and it's cold enough to freeze the marrow of your bones out there."

"Don't forget your cloak, Rae!" Aila said.

Rae reached for her little wool cloak hanging from its peg on the wall, but Brig got up and put herself between my little niece and her garment. "I have something better." From the many waves of cloth surrounding her shoulders, she whipped off a warm-looking length of wool, dyed a rich umber. Her many layers seemed wholly undiminished by its removal, yet it enveloped little Rae completely, fitting her from shoulders to ankles and forming one of its edges into a snug hood that hugged her head. "There!" said Brig. "You'll never feel the cold."

## Brig

Outside, the child led the way. Hid and I walked behind her, our breaths making wreaths and curls in the air, describing the runes of the ancients in crystalline fog. Where our breaths mingled, they glowed gold and arced into intricate curlicues, a filigree alive with moonlight.

"I feel I know you from somewhere," I said to Hid as we followed the sure footsteps of the child, who skipped and skittered ahead on a well-worn path leading upward.

"I don't think we've ever met," Hid replied, shivering in her cloak. I touched her arm, and her shivering stopped. She looked up at me sharply. "How did you do that?"

I trailed my fingers along the twigs of a dry bush, and buds sprouted where there had only been dormant branches. "I don't know how I do anything. I wonder sometimes, whether, if I could remember what I did before I wandered into the valley, I would know who and what I used to be."

Rae did another skip ahead of us. "We're almost there! Don't be scared, follow me!"

Hid giggled. "Don't worry, Rae! I'm never scared when I'm with you." Letting Rae draw farther ahead, she spoke to me in a quieter voice. "I don't remember life before I was in the cave in the woods, which was a few weeks before my adoptive family took me in. But I do have dreams. And sometimes I think they're dreams about the time before. Do you have dreams?"

"No," I said, feeling a sense of loss for these dreams of which people spoke, a thing I'd never experienced. "I hear dreams can be beautiful. But I don't have any."

## Hid

"Don't go near the water!" I called out to Rae as she rounded a bend in the path ahead of us. "If you fall in, you'll freeze before we can get you home."

Brig frowned, looking thoughtful. "I don't think she can freeze when she's wearing my cloak. But I can't remember why. Anyway, I *would* like to know what it's like to have dreams. Do you think you could tell me?"

"I can try. I dream sometimes that the world is glowing. I dream I can feel underground streams below us, and that I can change the direction in which they flow with a word. It's like there's a language I almost know but I've forgotten, and if I could remember it, I could be part of all the life around us. I could heal the sick and help plants grow." I ducked my head, afraid I was saying too much, that my dreams were too ridiculous for words. I'd never told the details to my adoptive family. "I'm sorry. I know that sounds silly."

"It doesn't," Brig said, a note of wonder in her voice. She looked up toward the cold, clear night sky as she spoke. "That feeling, about almost knowing another language? I think I have it too. Except for me, it comes when I touch trees and their spring leaves pop out, or when I touch *you* and you're warm again. I almost have the words to describe what I'm doing, but not quite. If I ever had them, I lost them somewhere along the way."

We rounded the bend and caught up to Rae, who stood beside the stream, where small webs of ice formed nets over some of the shallow places. She pointed excitedly, not at the rock formation we called the Man in the Mountain, the knobby structure on the far side of the water, but at something that glinted gold in the depths of the stream. "Look! It's so pretty. Can I pick it up, Auntie Hid?"

"The water's too cold," I said. That had been our family's mantra for months. It should be high springtime by now, yet we were nothing but cold every day and every night. "Besides, that's only a bit of fool's gold. Just a shiny rock."

Rae crouched next to the stream and hiked her sleeve up over her elbow. "I *like* rocks. Don't worry! I won't get my clothes wet."

Brig crouched next to the child. "That may have the outer form of a chunk of fool's gold, but its underlayer is a key."

"Underlayer?" I asked.

"The *underlayer* is what I call the light that makes up all things," she explained. All things have an underlayer. It's a glow I see in and around everything. I didn't know at first that others don't see it. That bright thing in the water is a key, and it wants us to pick it up." She pulled up her own sleeve and dipped her hand into the water, but she came away empty-handed. "It's wedged into a narrow space between those two rocks. I can't reach it."

"My hand is smaller!" Rae said. "I'll get it for you." She gave Brig a serious look over her shoulder. "And when I get it, it will belong to you. Even though I *really* like rocks."

She was not exaggerating her fondness for them. She had a collection of favorite stones in the corner of the cottage.

If she managed to keep her sleeve dry, I didn't see how I could object further. Besides, I was curious about this glow Brig described. I wanted to know if I could see this rock's resemblance to a key once it was above the surface.

Rae held up the shiny rock in the moonlight. "Here it is!"

Disappointment clouded my chest. It was only a piece of fool's gold, as I'd thought. There was nothing of a golden key about it.

But Brig seemed delighted - with the stone and with Rae. "Here it is indeed," she said. "You don't have to give it to me, Rae. You may keep it."

Rae shook her head vigorously. "It's a present. For both of you." She grasped my hand and put it in Brig's so her larger hand cupped mine. Rae placed the rock in my palm and closed both my and Brig's fingers around it. "There. You can share it."

I blinked, and in that instant I was in one of my dreams, fully and completely. I felt a thousand rivers running under the surface of the land, near and far, in every direction. I knew the wordless song that would make the springtime come. I could feel the life force in all the plants around us, struggling to break free of the frost that held them in their wintry sleep. And I could feel the life force in the humans everywhere across the land, near and far, and I knew the enchantments that would heal them if they fell ill, and that would make their babies grow up strong.

**Brig**

I remembered.

**Brighid**

I opened my eyes and found myself looking into the baby browns of a young child who wore a pleasantly sardonic grin. She crossed her arms firmly across her small chest. "I think you have some explaining to do."

I laughed. Rae always *was* wise beyond her years. Instead of panicking when she found one woman standing in front of her when a moment ago there were two, she – of course – merely wanted me to explain.

"And explain I shall." I knelt before her on the warming ground so we would be eye to eye. The webs of ice in the stream cracked and were swept away. Leaves burst forth on nearby branches, the rebirth so long in coming. "I am, and always have been, *one* being. This time last year, I visited the villages in the valley and on the hill and learned that neither would share their fruits with the other. The people of each village thought the others were unkind, unworthy. Foes instead of friends."

Rae seemed to be taking that in, so I gave her a moment to absorb. She fingered the ends of my wild mane of hair, the color of a sunrise in the springtime. "One of you had blonde hair. And the other one had black hair. Now you have red hair. Did you get bored with the other colors?"

I laughed again. "No, Rae. When I saw that the people wouldn't trust each other and wouldn't share what they had, I split myself. I became Brig, the half that was my strong physical form and held my magic. And I became Hid, the half that held the knowledge of how and why to wield the magic. Neither of us remembered our origins. We couldn't, if we were to accomplish our mission. So I made myself forget. Brig wandered the valley, and Hid found herself in a cave on the hill. When the valley people met Brig with kindness and shared what they had, and when a hillside family embraced Hid and made her one of their own, we – I – knew firsthand that both villages could be kind to strangers and share what they had. They only need to learn not to fear each other. When you, Rae, shared your sparkling find with us instead of keeping it for yourself, it was the final key that allowed us to become one again."

Rae bounced on the balls of her feet. "I made you happy!" she crowed in pure, innocent delight.

I gave her a hug. "You did indeed." Lush greenery now grew all around us. A few blossoms burst forth on the trees. "I won't be able to live with you anymore."

Rae's face fell and her lips trembled. "Why not?"

I cupped her chin in my hand. "Partly because you don't need me, and partly because I have a lot of work to do. I have to make up for lost time and bring these leaves and blossoms to every part of the woods and fields. But I'll visit you every year at the spring equinox. Can you light a fire for me each year so I'll know you're ready for me to visit?"

She nodded seriously.

I stood and took her hand. "Good. I'll walk you home to your door, and then you go inside and tell your family you rescued the goddess Brighid and brought spring to the land."

## Rae

### Many Years Later

We sat gathered around the hearth in the house of my family, the house I grew up in. Everyone was there to celebrate the equinox: my children, and their children, and their children's children. Some of us had taken our spouses from the valley, so some years, we had our celebrations in the lowland village. But this year, we'd chosen my home for our gathering.

It was a warm night, so we'd let the hearth fire dwindle to coals. But the sacred fire of Brighid burned on in our clay bowl, the one we kept alight every spring until the goddess came to call.

When a knock sounded at the door, the littlest ones, my great-grandchildren, looked startled, as if they weren't expecting anyone. All the rest of us knew who our visitor would be.

The door swung open with a bang. There stood Brighid, an ageless woman almost as tall as the doorframe, with sunrise-colored hair blowing in the warm night wind. Her wooden staff bloomed with spring flowers. We offered her ripe fruits and nuts from our gardens. We always had more than enough to go around.

When the goddess had kissed all the children and swept out the door leaving flowers in her wake, I told them all one of their favorite stories: the tale of Hid who lived with us when I was a child, and Brig who came to our door, and how the two became one.

A. J. Van Belle is a nonbinary writer and scientist, living on Vancouver Island with their husband and two dogs. A Best of the Net nominee, they've penned short fiction and essays that have appeared in journals and anthologies from 2004 to the present. Lauren Bieker of FinePrint Literary represents their novels. They're on Instagram at [ajvanbelle](ajvanbelle) and Bluesky at ajvanbelle.bsky.social.

# PERENNIAL

Katherine Shaw

*Beauty.*

*Strange how those who crave it will do anything to obtain it, while those who already hold it oft find it more of a curse than a gift.*

*For, you see, beauty imparts desire, the being of beauty coveted like a jewel, a trinket to own and polish and display for admirers, a bauble devoid of volition.*

*Why do we act surprised, then, when beautiful things seek solitude, when they hide away in places free from prying eyes and grasping hands?*

*When beauty is in the eye of the beholder, it oft pays well to remain unseen.*

\* \* \*

Springtime.

Each year it begins differently, choosing an entrance that is either late and long-anticipated, or hurried and unexpected, the first blooms emerging while winter's frost is still in recent memory. Snowdrops give way to daffodils and bluebells, bare branches erupt into fragrant blossom. The sun graces the land in ever-increasing spells, warming the bones and driving away the chill.

It was a fine spring day when the disturbances began. The forest floor was abuzz with life, flora and fauna alike responding to the change in season with great enthusiasm.

Nahciss dozed in the growing morning sun, the low hum of passing bumblebees lulling them into deep dreams of flight and fancy. They lay stretched out on a bed of daffodils, their golden skin lost in a sea of oranges, yellows and whites. The sweet scent had always been Nahciss' favourite. There, in their tranquil grove, away from the other fae and creatures of the forest, they could live in peaceful solitude. There were no meddlesome court politics, no romantic entanglements, no humans vying for their favour or seeking to capture their magic. In the grove, Nahciss could simply *exist*.

That was, until Ameno came across the grove, and everything changed.

Where Nahciss was graceful and golden, a being of extraordinary beauty and charm, Ameno was brash and bold, a handsome, broad-shouldered young fae who cared more for his own pursuits of glory than the sights and sounds of the nature around him. He tramped through the forest, forgoing the light-footedness usually associated with his kind, seeking confrontation where others would go to great pains to avoid it.

Where Ameno did excel, however, was in his keen vision. Carefully woven spells of camouflage which no mortal could spot – nor even the average fae – caught Ameno's eye, and he would plunge through the veil to whatever party or plunder lay beyond.

It was this skill which brought Ameno to Nahciss' grove, unbidden and unwelcomed into their life.

Nahciss' ears twitched. They extended their senses, reaching out beyond their body, into the ground around them and through the roots of the flowers and trees which inhabited their private sanctum.

*Crunch. Crunch. Crunch.*

Someone – or some*thing* – was trampling flowers. In *their* grove! It would not stand.

Nahciss rose to their full height, golden hair spilling down their lithe naked body. They tilted their head, listening. The intruder was coming from the west. Nahciss would need to strengthen their protective spells.

They strode delicately but with purpose, bare feet instinctively taking the path of least destruction through the foliage. A rainbow of tulips brushed their heads against Nahciss' lean legs, the soft petals providing both comfort and a reminder of what must be protected.

Nahciss neared the western edge of the grove, the snap of each broken stem tearing through them. Narrow honey-coloured eyes scanned the kaleidoscope of flora, swiftly settling on the intruder. With his dark leather clothing and cropped ice-white curls, he made a stark contrast to his surroundings.

Nahciss remained silent for a moment, observing the stranger's movements with irritation as he stomped through their grove, too brash and arrogant to have even noticed the other fae in his vicinity.

"Who are you?" Their voice was smooth as silk, caressing the intruder's face and turning it towards them. "Why are you here?"

Ameno turned, his emerald eyes widening as he beheld Nahciss' resplendent form. His stance shifted, the traveller becoming the suitor in an instant.

"You may call me Ameno, sweet beauty. An explorer of the land, and lover of all things blessed and wondrous." Ameno dropped to one knee in a flourish of misplaced charisma. "And I see I have discovered the most wondrous being of them all."

He reached to take Nahciss' hand, but they drew back. "You say you love that which is blessed," they said, "and yet you destroy the treasures of nature under your graceless feet."

Nahciss gestured to the ground around Ameno, where a patch of vibrant bluebells lay crushed under his boots. He plucked a flower, making a great show of holding it up to his eyes and inspecting it as he rolled the stem between two fingers.

"You call this a treasure, and yet when compared to your beauty, it is nothing."

Nahciss pursed their lips, irritation fluttering in their chest. "If you do not respect that which lives in this grove, you are not welcome here."

Ameno's vibrant eyes flashed in the sunlight, but his smile never slipped. "But I do offer respect, sweet one, and much more besides." He shuffled closer to Nahciss, clasping his gloved hands together as he gazed up at their face. "I bring reverence, and adoration, and a pledge of my soul to yours, should you accept it."

A bubble of laughter escaped Nahciss' lips. "You pledge yourself to me? How so? You know nothing of me, other than what you see."

Ameno rose swiftly to his feet, grasping Nahciss' hands in his own before they had the chance to withdraw. "And what I see is *perfection*." His gaze swept over their form, lips parted as if ravaged with hunger. "I must make you mine."

Nahciss' blood grew cold. "I think,' they said coolly, peeling Ameno's fingers away from their own. "You need to leave this place."

Ameno's face darkened, his fine fae features seeming to sharpen under Nahciss' gaze. His eyes narrowed, glittering emerald shifting to tumultuous stormy seas. When he spoke, though there was no explicit malice, his voice was stone.

"If that is your wish..."

"It is." Nahciss met his gaze, fire against ice. "Go."

"I see." A devilish smile twisted Ameno's face. "Great reward requires great effort, and treasure only comes to those who dare to seek it." He stepped back, receding towards the shadowed treeline from whence he had first emerged. "Until next time, beautiful one. I shall win your heart, I vow to that."

Not waiting for a response, Ameno turned on his heel and strode out of the grove, his clumsy feet leaving an array of crushed blooms in their wake.

Nahciss watched, arms crossed and shaking their head, hoping they never laid eyes on that insufferable fae again.

\* \* \*

It was three days before Ameno returned to the grove.

Nahciss was admiring the newly-opened hyacinth flowers -- breathing in their intoxicating verdant, sweet-but-spicy scent – when a familiar *crunch* caught their attention. They stood upright, irritation stirring in their chest, and scanned the grove for signs of the intruder.

They reached out, extending their senses through the flora, searching for signs of distress. There, by the hawthorn.

Nahciss glided through the grasses and wildflowers, supple feet barely making an imprint in the soft ground. They cocked their head and listened, wincing as another *crunch* sounded out through the grove. It was him, they were certain of it.

"Why are you here?" There was an edge to the sereneness of their voice, a splash of vinegar in the honey. "You are not welcome."

"Ah," came a voice from within the trees. "That was before... this!" Ameno leapt into the grassy clearing, dressed resplendently in black and silver. Tossing his shining velvet cape over his shoulder with a flourish, he fell to one knee at Nahciss' feet and held an ornately-carved wooden box up as an offering. "For you, sweet one. A token of my love."

Love, after only having met once? It was absurd.

"This was not necessary," they began, stilling their frayed nerves and regarding Ameno with as much patience as they could muster.

"Now, don't be modest," Ameno broke in. "A beauty such as yourself deserves only the finest treasures, although compared to you, they are nothing."

He lifted the box higher, his face beaming up at Nahciss. They hesitated, but at a loss for any other option, they took it and removed the lid. Nestled in a bed of rose petals was a large, finely-cut ruby pendant. It sat in an elaborate setting of pure gold, an array of cherubs and roses worked into the metal's surface, and hung from a fine golden chain.

"It is rather beautiful," Nahciss said slowly, choosing their next words carefully so as to not offend the smitten fae, "and I am grateful. But it is too much. I cannot accept this. I have nothing to offer in return."

"Nonsense!" Ameno jumped to his feet. "Just to gaze upon your splendour is reward enough. Please, put it on, let me see it hanging from your slender neck."

"I couldn't possibly—"

"I insist!"

Before Nahciss could protest further, Ameno plucked the necklace from the box, and began fastening it around their neck. The close proximity to this stranger was unsettling, and their chest tightened. They breathed in his unusual scent: a cool, harsh musk completely at odds with their lush surroundings. Their heart raced, something akin to fear churning within them, until finally Ameno stepped away, and they could breathe again.

The ruby pendant hung heavy around Nahciss' neck, the cold metal burning against their golden skin. It felt out of place. Alien.

"What do you think?" Ameno asked, beaming at them. "A gem almost as radiant as the one who wears it."

Nahciss opened their mouth to respond, but was immediately spoken over.

"No! Save your comments until you have seen the rest."

Nahciss' heart plummeted to their feet. "The rest?"

Ameno's eyes sparkled in the soft spring sunlight. "Darling, do you think I sought to woo you with *one* trinket?"

Embers stirred in Nahciss' chest, but they swallowed them down. Aggression was not the answer. Ameno brought this gift in earnest; they needed to select their response carefully.

"This is a very fine gift." They spoke slowly, hoping to imbue their voice with sufficient neutrality so as to not appear too enthusiastic, but not disappoint their visitor too greatly. Ameno was irritating, yes, but not wicked. Nahciss could offer some patience. "But I do not wish for more. This is quite enough."

The silvery fae stepped forward, slender fingers reaching for Nahciss, who deftly avoided his touch. A white eyebrow twitched at the slight, but the broad smile remained on his sharp pale face.

"Tell me, beautiful one," he asked, his lusty gaze sweeping over Nahciss from head to toe in a way that made their stomach clench. "Have I won your love?"

A crease of confusion marred Nahciss' brow. "No, of course not, but—"

"In that case," Ameno interjected, "I will return tomorrow, and the following day, and the day following that, until your heart is mine."

There was something in those verdigris eyes, something beyond mere bodily desire: determination.

This hunter would not rest until he had caught his prey, and that realisation turned Nahciss' blood cold.

\* \* \*

True to his promise, Ameno returned the next day, and each

day following that. By the fifth day, Nahciss' patience had run out.

Before their peace was disturbed once more, Nahciss tended to the daffodils that surrounded their grove, delicate fingers coaxing them back to full strength following Ameno's latest trample through the flowers. It was infuriating.

Long white clouds drifted overhead, bathing the grove in dappled sunlight. A light breeze caressed Nahciss' golden skin, sending a shiver down their spine. It should have been a perfect spring day, but Ameno had destroyed it before it had even begun.

As if summoned, Ameno's brash voice pierced the air, shattering what remained of the grove's quiet serenity.

"Love of my life, I have returned!"

Nahciss shuddered. All they wanted was a peaceful, solitary existence, and this insufferable fae was determined to make that impossible. It had to end.

Drawing themselves up to their full height, Nahciss set their jaw and strode towards the source of their discontentment. Ameno stood in a small clearing, plucking milky blossoms from a cherry plum and letting them flutter to the ground around his feet.

"Ah, what a vision!" the emerald-eyed fae exclaimed upon catching sight of Nahciss, turning to face them and sweeping into a flamboyant bow. "I think you'll be delighted with what I offer you today."

Nahciss held up their hands. "No."

Ameno's eyes narrowed slightly, but his enthusiasm didn't falter. "Oh, just wait, beautiful one. Today's gift is a real treasure, and one of a kind, very much like you."

His smile broadened, and he stepped towards Nahciss, boots scraping through a patch of particularly fine tulips.

"Stop!" Nahciss called out, their usual velvety lilt strained with annoyance. "Don't you see what you are doing?"

They gestured to the crushed stems beneath Ameno's boots, but if he understood, he didn't seem to care. "I am presenting you with another gift, my love—"

"I am *not* your love," Nahciss interrupted, an unfamiliar sharpness edging their voice. "I am not your *anything*, and it is very presumptuous of you to think otherwise."

A dark flash passed across the fae's eyes, but he proceeded to reach into his fine silver coat and pull out a long item bundled in silk. "Perhaps," he said slowly, "once you see what I offer you today, you will be inclined to change your mind."

He began to untie the parcel's bindings, but Nahciss reached out a hand and stopped him. "Please, don't." They placed a firm hand on the fae's arm, pushing it away from his latest offering. "As I have been trying to tell you, these gifts are not necessary. I am content here, with no treasures or riches, *alone*."

"Ah, you say that now," Ameno insisted, stepping closer, "but a beauty such as yours cannot be forgotten. I swear, once I have presented you with—"

"That is enough!" Nahciss' voice grew louder, drawing on a power they never wished to use as their annoyance stoked the flames in their chest. "I have tried to be polite, but it seems I must speak plainly. Your gifts are not wanted. Your attention is not wanted. Your unwarranted infatuation is not wanted. Now, leave."

Ameno's grin disappeared, his lips twisting into a hideous scowl. Fae were selfish and prideful creatures, and usually got what they desired, one way or another. His hand grasped at Nahciss, fingers locking around their arm with an iron grip. His fingers were painfully cold, and his razor-sharp nails threatened to break through Nahciss' golden skin.

"You *will* be mine," he sneered through gritted teeth.

Nahciss' rage grew white hot, searing through their veins like molten bronze. When they spoke, each word was pure fire. "DO NOT TOUCH ME."

Ameno snatched his hand back as if burned, eyes widening as the ground below them trembled and shook.

"YOU WILL LEAVE THIS PLACE, AND NEVER RETURN." Nahciss' voice reverberated across the grove, shaking trees and sending birds erupting into the sky above. Their gaze seared into Ameno, who stumbled backwards, his own eyes wild with terror as the parcel in his hands slipped from his quivering fingers. "NOW."

The frightened fae turned tail and fled. As quickly as it had come, the heat left Nahciss, dissipating into the earth and air around them. Serenity settled on their shoulders, and they turned, gliding back into the spring flora and the peace it promised.

Buried behind them in the grass, already forgotten, lay Ameno's final gift. A cool breeze stirred the wrapping, revealing the glint of a golden hilt.

* * *

As his steps slowed and air filled his gasping lungs, Ameno's terror transformed. It twisted and turned, merging with his shame and humiliation until it solidified into cold, hard rage.

He stomped through the forest, crushing plant and insect life indiscriminately, and swiping at tree branches with a dagger. A slim bough bent and snapped back at him, his sharp senses allowing him to dodge the blow just in time. Angered, he reached up and broke the branch with his hands instead, and cursed himself for leaving the sword behind with that wretched creature.

A fresh wave of fury washed over him. That monster had lured him in with a tempting visage until they had amassed enough treasure to satiate themself, and then tossed Ameno aside like a fool. It had been a scheme all along, a trick so simple he should have seen through it sooner.

Ameno kicked a stone hard and watched it ricochet off a nearby stump. No. He couldn't have seen it. That devil had enchanted him, blinded him with unnatural beauty until he was under their spell.

And they would pay.

* * *

Once Ameno's mind was fixed on a task, nothing could distract him from it.

Unlike Nahciss, who thrived in solitude, the silvery explorer had a grand network of fae, spirits and supernatural creatures. One by one, he weaved his own magical charm until they revealed the information he sought, and before long, he had a plan.

Ameno set out without delay. He hiked for days without slowing, fuelled by an icy hatred that barely smothered the burning humiliation beneath. As the ground became steeper and the lush forest floor gave way to rocky mountain terrain, the cool spring breeze biting into his pale skin, anticipation stirred in Ameno's chest. He was close.

A mere mortal would have missed the hidden cave, its opening perfectly camouflaged amongst the stones and scrub, but Ameno's keen eyes picked it out easily. He carefully made his way along precarious ledges and deftly avoided falling rocks and debris, eyes always focused on his destination.

As Ameno approached the cave's mouth, a cold despondency suddenly stirred within his chest. His steps slowed, but he persevered, forcing his feet to move as an ever-growing dread bloomed in his gut. He had never before been fearful, and this witch's enchantments would not break him. With each movement, his limbs felt heavier, and when he finally passed through the dark entrance into the inky blackness beyond, a deep chill shivered down his spine. An urge to flee rushed over him, but he resisted, clenching his fists and drawing on the rage that had brought him here.

Ignoring his every instinct, Ameno stepped forward. He took a deep breath, and with all the force he could manage, shouted into the impermeable darkness. "Hear me! I call on the power within, seeking retribution and justice from one who can see it done."

For a moment, there was silence. Then, a voice sounded out, a high, yet powerful voice, reverberating through the space around Ameno such that it seemed to come from all directions at once.

"Who comes before me, with courage enough to enter my domain?"

Terror rocked Ameno, but he pushed it back. He had come too far to succumb to the dark magic fraying his nerves.

"I am Ameno Keen-Eye of the Boeon fae," he said into the gloom, "although your power is such that even my great eyesight is unable to make sense of this place."

A dark chuckle echoed around him, making his silvery skin crawl. "Of course. Your powers must be balanced, as is only fair."

Ameno bristled at having his only advantage foiled by a more powerful being, but he said nothing. He needed the witch's favour if he was going to have his revenge.

"Now," the witch continued, her voice everywhere and nowhere at once, "what justice is it you seek, young fae?"

Fear threatened to crawl up Ameno's throat, but he swallowed it down. Shadows, opaque and multilayered, danced across his gaze. Being unable to focus on any point ahead of him unnerved Ameno greatly, and rendered any attempt at depth perception impossible. He had no means of knowing whether he stood in a great cavern or a narrow crevice.

Forcing as much conviction into his voice as he could muster, he spoke into the blackness. "There is a golden being of great beauty, who dwells not far from here. In the forest, concealed within a flower-filled grove not many can see." He listened for a response, but none came, so he continued. "They are bewitching in their comeliness, and I am not proud to admit that I fell under their powerful spell. I was charmed by this creature, compelled to bring them gifts of great treasure, of gold and gemstones, so overwhelming was their influence. For days I sought out and brought these offerings, unable to eat, unable to sleep, so consumed was I by their magic."

For a moment, the silence continued. Then, whispers echoed around him, thousands of indecipherable words spoken at once, growing in volume until Ameno had to fight the urge to cover his ears. They merged into a crescendo of agonising hisses and collapsed into a single, harsh voice.

"And what," the witch began, their words so sharp they were almost painful, "did you ask for in return?"

"Nothing. I made no request of them."

It was a half-truth, Ameno knew, but he silently prayed the witch believed it.

"And where are these treasures now?"

Ameno resisted the urge to smile. This line of questioning was encouraging. "With the creature," he said to the shadows. "They hoard them like a dragon, their powers of concealment keeping them well hidden. Meanwhile, I have nothing."

The words hung in the air, tension growing around them while Ameno awaited the witch's verdict. He felt his pulse quicken, the fear creeping up the back of his neck. Patience was not a skill Ameno possessed, and the suspense was agonising, each second crawling by slower than the one before.

At last, the witch spoke, and Ameno's heart leapt into his throat.

"Justice will be done." The witch's voice grew louder, thrumming through every fibre in the fae's body. "Your tormentor will be punished. They shall suffer an enchantment much like their own. It will be all-consuming, draining them completely. Once their body succumbs and crumbles to dust, their powers shall become yours."

Ameno's eyes widened and his heart swelled with delight. This outcome was far beyond what he had hoped for.

"But," the witch continued with a firmness that turned Ameno's stomach, "for this to come to pass, you must pledge yourself to my service. You will no longer be a creature of the forest. When I call, you will come, and enact vengeance as I demand."

A cruel smirk twisted Ameno's thin lips and he dropped to one knee, head bowed. "It shall be done, my mistress."

* * *

Nahciss lay once more among their bed of daffodils, their once-restful sleep tortured and unsettling. Flashes of sharp teeth and wild eyes, vicious whispers and bone-chilling screams. They awoke with a start, their breathing heavy, the dappled sunlight that bathed them unable to warm the cold sweat erupting from their skin. They had never before had nightmares. Something was wrong.

Nahciss rose, their breath shallow and their pulse rapid, golden eyes scanning the grove for the source of their unease. At first glance, all was as it should be, then an unfamiliar glimmer caught their attention. They stepped quietly towards it on the balls of their feet, subconsciously avoiding each bluebell and tulip, their gaze fixed ahead.

Anxiety transformed into confusion as Nahciss spotted a shimmering blue pool they were certain had not been there before. They eyed the surrounding foliage – freshly blossomed yellow and white magnolia, vibrant green laburnum, dusky pink lilacs – and found every last stem was in its place, yet that sparkling pool had somehow materialised between the familiar blooms.

Nahciss closed their eyes and pushed their power into the ground, sending it snaking through the soil, betwixt roots and around bulbs, until it reached the water's edge.

And dissipated.

A frown creased Nahciss' brow. Everything in the natural world embraced their magic; for it to be halted in such a manner was unheard of. The pool should not have been there – perhaps it was not of natural origin. The notion felt sinister, and yet Nahciss found themselves drawn to the water.

They had no memory of walking to the pool when they found themselves peering over its edge, eyes transfixed on the golden creature staring back at them.

They were beautiful.

Nahciss stared, unable to move, unable to think, hypnotised by the figure in the water. Their long fingers twitched. They wanted to reach out, to touch the wondrous creature lurking under the crystalline blue surface, but they could not. Try as they might, they could not move their limbs. They were fixed in place, kneeling in the grass, spellbound.

Hours slid by, and still Nahciss stared. The sun dipped behind the trees, taking the day's warmth with it, and plunging the grove into cold darkness, but their gaze never shifted.

When dawn broke, sending streaks of coral and vermillion across the sky, Nahciss appeared as if they were a statue, stone-cold and glistening with the morning's dew.

And still, they stared.

Hours became days, and days morphed into weeks. Nahciss remained at their lonely, immovable vigil, their body weakening, their once vibrant, golden skin turning a sickly yellow.

As they felt their strength ebbing, Nahciss attempted to once more connect with the grove around them, to draw on its magic. Their power stirred, but what had once been a roaring fire was now a barely glowing ember, the heat dissipating more with every passing moment.

Icy horror bloomed in Nahciss' chest, grasping their heart tight. A single, hot tear rolled down their frozen cheek as realisation truly struck: their end was coming, and they were powerless to stop it.

A lifetime of memories flashed within their mind. They smelled the sweetness of opening rosebuds, felt fresh grass springing beneath their bare feet. One image continued to surface: stars of sunshine yellow, dotted in the centre with vivid amber. A complex scent of sweet and spice filled their nostrils, heady and intoxicating. It was a comfort amidst their despair, and Nahciss clung to it, diverting all of their consciousness to this one, perfect thought.

A new heat ignited in Nahciss then, flooding their veins with gold. Shimmering light clouded their vision as what remained of their power came to life, focused on those perfect, sunlit stars. Joy mingled with wonder as Nahciss withdrew from the pool, their body twisting and flowing into something new, but wonderfully familiar.

A single, flawless daffodil.

And so, Nahciss persisted, their spark of magic contained and thriving in this beautiful, springtime bloom. Whenever the seasons shifted, and the heat of summer or the bite of winter threatened their delicate form, they withdrew into the ground.

There, they lie dormant, remaining in peaceful slumber, until spring comes again, and the sun's gentle warmth beckons them back into the light.

Katherine Shaw is a multi-genre writer and self-confessed nerd from Yorkshire in the United Kingdom, spending most of her time dreaming up new characters or playing D&D. She has a passion for telling stories of injustice and battles against oppression, often with a focus on female protagonists. She has published her debut novel Gloria, a contemporary domestic thriller, and has work appearing in multiple anthology collections.

You can find out more at her website www.katherineshawwrites.com

# I Like Quiet Places

Fiona Simpson

The Spring Queen died on a warm night in May, under the Flower Moon.

The town of Gravestaff lay spread out in the valley, grey and black and two-dimensional in the bright moonlight's glow. Like a picture, printed in the local newspaper of a small, insignificant town.

On a barely-there B-road, winding up out of the town and into the darkness, a single car climbed. This car was pink, but like the town, it appeared grey in the monochrome, moonlit landscape. The car's four windows were rolled down, allowing the warm night air to stream in. It had rained that morning, and the plants of the night drank deeply of the moist earth.

Near the edge of the town there was a graveyard. Later that same night, a sleeping bag would nestle unnoticed between the graves. Tonight, a member of the living would take his rest among the dead of Gravestaff.

But not yet.

The road ran between sheep and cattle fields that spread silver in the moonlight. Sleek night creatures, transformed by moonlight to gleaming pewter, stalked over the grass, leaving mysterious trails in the heavy dew. These trails would be gone by morning, unnoticed by the sheep and their new lambs. By morning, these silver fields would be studded gold with daisies and buttercups in the spring sun.

Michael Pike leaned across to the driver's seat and brought his lips to his girlfriend's light pink hair. Irresistible. It was the colour of candyfloss, and he always half-expected it to taste sweet, too. He let his eyes close as he inhaled something better than sugar – just Ellis.

"Do you hear that?" Ellis touched the brakes and her pink Mini crawled to a stop. The silver -birch trees flanking the road glowed stark white in the moonlight. Ellis turned to Michael, her hands gripping the pink furry steering wheel. The amethyst around her neck flashed pale in the moonlight.

"Yeah. I hear it," murmured Michael grimly. A tension throbbed in his jaw and temple. He found he was clenching the edge of his seat, and he relaxed his grip. *Be cool. Be a dude.*

But what the hell was that noise, seriously? Like a screaming, wailing. It was some...person, the worst singer in the world, but it wasn't funny. This person sounded unhinged. High, then low, then fast, then slow, the voice went on – rising and falling and *screaming.*

"Michael?"

The note of fear in Ellis's voice brought him out of his frozen state. He found her hand, cool in the darkness. Squeezing her fingers, he tried to peer through the moonlit trees.

"It's okay, Ellis. Maybe it's, like foxes, fighting? Maybe they caught one of the lambs? I think we should just keep driving and –"

Michael's breath and heart seemed to stop as a shadow moved out from the darkness.

*A fox? Let it be a–*

It wasn't a fox. It was a man. His dark clothes seemed to

absorb all light, while the black and white stripes on his top beamed in the moonlight. He walked slowly into the middle of the road until he was five metres from the Mini's headlights, and he lifted his gaze.

Ellis gasped.

Michael opened the door and climbed out of the car. This kid was around their age, not much older than a teenager.

"Hey, man. Are you okay?"

The man blinked and turned to Michael, his eyes bleary, unfocused. *Drugs,* guessed Michael, feeling almost relieved. *Dude's just a wandering junkie.*

He took a breath to say as much to Ellis, but before he could speak the man spoke, his voice as soft and delicate as the white bluebells lining the roadside. The words were quiet, but Michael heard them perfectly.

"Turn back."

"Dude!" shouted Michael, spooked, annoyed with himself for being spooked, trying to ignore the chilled feeling at odds with the warm spring air. "You're in the middle of the damn road. You hurt? Do you need help?"

The man shifted his blank gaze to Ellis.

"Turn back," he murmured sadly, again.

Enough. This guy was probably freaking Ellis out, and as much as he'd prefer not to admit it, he was freaking Michael out, too. Michael threw himself back into the Mini and slammed the door- hard.

"Drive around him."

"Is he okay? Maybe we should take him back into town."

"No." Michael thumbed the 'lock' button. "We're late enough for Davey's party. He's just a weirdo, Ellis. He's a freaky hitchhiker and I don't like the look of his – of him." He had been going to say 'eyes'. Those weird, anxious eyes had spooked him more than he cared to admit.

"Just drive, Ellis. C'mon."

Ellis steered the car slowly around the hitchhiker and moved on up the road. In the rear view, he quickly became a dark smudge, only the white stripes on his top visible in the moonlight. Then he was gone.

Ellis shuddered. "That was very weird."

Michael slid his hand around her neck, gently pulled her towards him and brought his lips to her temple.

"Baby. Forget him," he murmured into her hair.

On the other side of the silver birch line, hidden from the road, was an open field, a loch of pure silver. A herd of deer burnished with the lustre of the stark moonlight. And in the pure silver night, an uneven keening began, rising to a howling shriek to quicken the heart and freeze the blood of any creature who heard it.

* * *

"I like quiet places."

That was the first thing he said to me, that morning in May.

In some ways, the pale man haunting the poetry section was typical of the hikers that came into my library every day. After all, libraries are free and warm, and we had a tea machine charging just 50p a cup. It was a nice place near the start of several hillwalking trails out of Gravestaff, so it had become an unofficial meeting point for hikers to read maps, drink tea, and gear up.

Like all the hikers that stop by, this one had a big backpack. It was on the floor of the poetry section, leaning up against my personal favourite shelf, Horror Poetry.

But unlike your average hiker, this man was sprawled on his back on the floor between the stacks, his eyes closed, snoring gently.

At that time, I was nineteen. I had been working in

Gravestaff's library as an assistant since leaving school. For someone who liked reading poetry, and doing virtually nothing else, it seemed like a good idea.

To everyone in town, I was just 'that Goth librarian kid'. They were used to me, used to my hair, my long black coat, my skull jewellery. I didn't have any friends outside my job, didn't have a life, in fact. I realise, now that I was waiting for something to happen. And on that morning in May, something did.

I stood behind my desk watching the sleeping man, trying to decide whether to wake him. I was always an easy-going librarian, recognising the importance of the place as a refuge, not just a place of words. So, I wasn't about to throw someone out for napping.

But my boss, Alex? He *would* throw him out in a heartbeat. I also knew Alex wouldn't do it gently.

So, I walked over. The library was so quiet that day. All I could hear was my boots on the floor, the buzz from the fluorescent strip lighting, and the hiker's deep, sleepy breathing.

I stood over him, my black nail-varnished fingers resting on the 'Horror' Poetry shelf.

What a strange-looking guy he was, and that's coming from me. He lay on his back on the carpet, arms crossed under his head. He looked about the same age as myself, around twenty. He had longish dark hair, and his pale complexion looked washed-out under the strip lights. His dress sense wasn't typical for a hiker: black and white striped top, black kilt, though he did have extremely well-worn black hiking boots, flaking dried mud all over the carpet.

I hesitated, wondering how to wake him gently... and at that moment, he opened his eyes.

*His eyes.*

They were nearly black, flecked with bits of green and purple, like *aurora borealis,* the northern lights. At the time, that first time I saw him, I put it down to a trick of the light, some reflection from the fluorescence above him. He blinked those eyes, looking dazed.

"Hey, sorry to wake you up. Are you okay?"

He sat up, rubbing his eyes. Looked at me funny, but I was well used to that.

"Why are you lying there?"

"I... like quiet places." In the silence of the library, his voice sounded low and deep. He sat up, and I noticed a few poetry books beside him. "Sorry," he mumbled, sweeping them into a messy pile. "I fell asleep reading."

I felt a bit sorry for him, so I vended him some tea, and we got talking. He said his name was Afton, and he was just passing through. A drifter.

"You know," I told him, "it's a small town, but there *are* a few homelessness services."    I plucked a leaflet from the pinboard and offered it to him, but he just smiled and shook his head. I paused, the leaflet dangling between my fingers.

"Maybe they can help you find somewhere to sleep?"

"Thanks. I'm good. I'm sleeping in the graveyard."

"What?"

He shrugged. "I'm sleeping in the graveyard tonight. I slept there last night, too. Safest place in town. Everyone in there's already dead."

There was a twisted logic to that – unless you believed in ghosts, the living nightcrawlers of a rundown town would be scarier than the dead.

"It's very quiet," he added, "And as I said, I like quiet places."

Afton was smiling, and I found myself smiling, too. It was weird. It felt like I had known him for a long time. Should I tell him? Tell him that I hung out in the graveyard often myself? I liked reading poetry there, even writing it sometimes, in the quiet calm of the place. It wasn't something I had ever shared with anyone, and it was an unfamiliar thrill to hear someone else talking along the same lines.

The library doors slid open, and I glanced over. It was Michael Pike. One of Gravestaff's tragic figures. I'd gone to school with him, but nowadays he looked about fifty years old.

Until a year ago, Mike Pike had been this clean-shaven, no-worries, rugby-playing fiancé to Ellis Elliot, the town's 2024 Spring Queen. But there wouldn't be a 2025 Gravestaff Spring Queen. There would never be a Spring Queen again. The title would die with her. No one felt like replacing Ellis.

Mike limped across the worn-out carpet. He was hollow-eyed, unshaven, and wearing the exact same clothes he had been wearing every time I had seen him lately – his old rugby top, now hanging a little loose on his slimmer frame, and tracksuit bottoms with that same beer stain down the front.

He grunted hi, or something like it, as he limped past my desk on his way to the Jobseeker's desk. The limp was one of the external wounds he'd gained the night Ellis died.

"I should go," Afton murmured to me suddenly. He put down his plastic cup, and stood up quickly. "Thanks for the tea, and, um, everything." He grabbed his rucksack and hitched it onto one shoulder.

A couple of metres beyond the desk, Michael stopped suddenly.

His back was still, his fists clenched. He turned slowly, and fixed Afton with his bloodshot stare. "You."

It was obvious, even from a few metres away, that Michael was shaking. His shoulders, and his hand, when he brought it up to his days-old stubble, was trembling, almost out of control.

Michael moved towards the desk, his eyes still locked on Afton.

"You were there. On the road that night. Why did you tell us to turn back?" He was at the desk now, closing the gap. Afton stood there, off kilter from the weight of his rucksack.

The low smell of beer crawled from Michael's pores like ghosts from a fetid sewer. It was on his breath, it was woven into his skin and nails and hair.

"*Why* did you tell us that? Eh?"

I felt this rising tension, like clouds full of thunder, full of lightning. "Hey, Michael?" I began.

Afton didn't look scared, even though Michael was a good head and shoulders taller than him. His weird eyes just looked sad. He held direct eye contact with Michael's furious gaze.

"Well?"

"I warned you because I had a bad feeling." Afton's voice was so quiet.

Michael stared at him, his mouth twitching. He went perfectly still for a moment, like a dog just before it strikes. Suddenly he barked with harsh laughter.

"You had a 'bad feeling?' Did you? A bad feeling. Guess what— all my feelings are bad, now. 'Cos, you— you were right, dude."

The most unnerving thing about him - not the filthy clothes, not the stink of his unwashed body or the sharpness of the fresh alcohol on his breath - was the unwavering stare as he yanked down the front of his T-shirt and pulled out a pale pink gemstone on a silver chain. It was the same colour as Ellis's hair.

"*This* was hers. She was wearing it when she died."

Afton glanced at it. "I'm really sorry, man."

"Sorry? What," Michael wrenched out, "are you sorry for?" He shoved his face closer to Afton's. The hitchhiker didn't flinch at the bared teeth and bloodshot eyes.

"You sorry for sp— spooking her? Yeah? For freaking her

out, m— making her drive too *fast?* Is *that* what you're sorry for?" On the last 'that', his hand shot out and he grabbed Afton's shoulder, his fingers going white as he squeezed. He crushed the fabric of Afton's striped shirt, the skin beneath. "You should be sorry, man. This is on *you.*"

"Michael!" I shouted, hopping out from behind the desk, "Stop."

Michael didn't seem to hear me, he just squeezed harder.

Afton's eyelids fluttered, and he swallowed, hard. But he was letting Michael hurt him. He wasn't making any attempt to defend himself.

"Is that what you are sorry for?" hissed Michael in a strangled whisper, his mouth almost touching Afton, his fetid saliva spattering the other man's cheek. He snarled and switched his grip to Afton's face, crushing his fingers into his jaw. With his other hand he grabbed Afton's neck and the rucksack banged to the floor.

*"Michael!* Stop it!"

"Maybe a freak like you should be dead instead of Ellis!"

His voice echoed around the library. The door of Alex's office was flung open and he came running out.

"Hey! Break it up! Michael!"

Alex and I each grabbed one of Michael's arms. As soon as we caught hold of him – I felt how damp and sticky and covered in sweat he was – the fight ran out of him and he turned into jelly. He sank down, sobbing onto the carpet.

Alex hovered his arms awkwardly over Michael's shoulders. "Come on. It's going to be all right, kid."

Michael allowed himself to be helped up, and Alex walked him to his office, shut the door with a soft 'click' behind them.

In the sudden silence, I looked at Afton. He was rubbing his jaw, but he looked okay.

"What was that about? You know Michael Pike?

Afton shook his head. "I don't know him. I was hitching on the road that night. He and his girlfriend spoke to me before the accident." Afton glanced at the closed office door. "He blames me. But it wasn't my fault. I was just there." His face had gone moonlit-pale, his dark eyes in shadow. "I should go."

"No, wait." I was surprised at my own words. "What... what about your poetry books?"

Afton shrugged. "I'm not a member of the library."

I gathered up the books he had been reading and laid them in his hands. "Borrow them off the record... if you promise me, you'll bring them back. But you know. *Shh.*"

Afton gazed down at the books, then he laughed quietly. "Okay. My lips are sealed."

And that's how it started. He *did* bring the illicit poetry books back, the very next day. The books were damp and smelled slightly of earth. On top of the stack, Afton had placed a small bunch of young white bluebells, their stems trailing veinlike roots and fragments of dark soil.

Afton himself had a bruise on his jaw in the distinct shape of Michael's fingers. His eyes still looked like the northern lights.

We started hanging out every day. He would come into to the library, drink that chemical-tasting machine tea with me, and we read poetry while I was on shift. We hung out together on my breaks, too. Afton showed me where he was sleeping – he wasn't joking about the graveyard.

He had hidden himself well, in a sheltered corner of the yard, near some fancy white mausoleum. His black sleeping bag was almost invisible tucked between the tombstones, spread on the gravel. It was nestled in a bed of shy white bluebells. A peaceful spot.

"I love quiet places," he smiles.

"Yeah, you mentioned that."

He settled back against a headstone, his skin paler than the faded concrete, his eyes deep and haunted like they had been chiselled into his skin.

"I never stick around a town this long. I usually move on after a day or two."

"So why *are* you still here?"

He opened his eyes, and smiled his tired smile. He didn't answer, but we both knew.

\* \* \*

Our relationship – if I could call it that – was strange. I didn't know how to define it, and I didn't want to. Was it friendship? Was it more? I'd never really had a friend before, so I didn't know the rules.

Sometimes we would talk for so long, I would asleep in the graveyard with him, lullabied by starlight, beneath the growing moon. We would wake in the morning among the white bluebells, morning dew glistening in our hair, listening to the birds in the graveyard trees. Gravestones made our shelter, and we were nestled there, somewhere between life and death.

One night, about a week after I met Afton, I woke up at 3 a.m. in the graveyard, alone.

It all looked different by night. I wasn't scared, not exactly, but the stretched shadows under the moon looked unnatural. Creepy. There was no birdsong. There was no Afton.

Just a strange, chilling, keening scream.

I drew my knees up to my chest, my teeth clicking together, my skin prickling. The screaming was coming from the far side of the graveyard, where a silver stream ribboned. I wrapped my blanket around my shoulders, got to my feet, shivering, and stole between the silent graves. My feet crunched on the gravel, and my own breathing sounded fast and loud. Before I reached the stream, the screaming stopped, and the running water trickled coyly in the sudden silence. An owl hooted in a nearby tree.

Afton was kneeling at the edge of the stream, his hands in the mud, head dipped down with his long black hair almost touching the flowing water.

Nightmare, sleepwalking, panic attack? I hurried over to him and put my arms around his freezing, trembling shoulders.

He twisted his head and looked at me. Water dripped from the tips of his hair, and his tears were silver in the moonlight. He didn't seem ashamed of them.

"It's not my fault," he shuddered, his strange and lovely northern lights eyes flashing in the water's moonlight reflection. "I want you to know that it's *not my fault.* I'm just here."

He wasn't making a lot of sense, but he must be talking about Ellis.

"I know," I assured him. "Nothing's your fault."

Kneeling together on the bank like this, we must have looked like lovers. Like he was my boyfriend. I held him a little longer, by the water, under the almost-full moon.

* * *

"Alex is dead? But... he was in work yesterday."

It was a stupid thing to say. It hung, deservedly unanswered, in the silence of the meeting room. We had been called in by the assistant manager, and I could hardly absorb the news. Alex. My boss. Dead?

I gripped the edge of the meeting table, watching all ten of my black-painted fingernails as the skin beneath them turned livid, then white. Someone was crying, one of the other librarians. Oh, man – Alex. Heart attack, they said. Pretty sudden, they said.

I looked away, out the window to the library garden. The sudden daffodils crowding round the bench were a jarring, neon highlighter-yellow. I had never noticed them until this moment; they were new. Everything was shifting, changing.

*It's not my fault.*

Afton's words sliced cleanly through the muddle in my mind. What had he meant by that? Did he mean Alex? He had said the same thing about Ellis. *"It wasn't my fault, I was just there."*

I was still in a numb, cold state when I arrived at the graveyard later that morning. Afton was packing up his campsite. I watched in silence as he rolled up his sleeping bag, as he stuffed everything into his rucksack. My throat felt horribly tight. I found myself staring and staring at the discoloured patch of gravel where the sleeping bag had been spread.

"I have to leave. Today," Afton told me, not looking at me. He was kneeling on the gravel, dismantling his camping stove. "I can't stay any longer."

I didn't cry, because I never do. But my heart went into a mini-freefall. Why did I feel like this? I had known him a week. Just a week.

He finished zipping up his rucksack, stood up, and gave me a hug. Although it wasn't cold, I shivered in his arms.

"I could come with you," I heard myself mumbling into his shoulder. "I don't have anyone here. I could come."

I felt him tense up. "If you knew more about me... you wouldn't want to."

A sudden warm breeze moved the trees over our heads, and I watched the leaves rustling from the warmth of Afton's arms. He was connected to Ellis's death; he was somehow connected to Alex's, too. But how?

"Afton—"

The words stopped in my throat. Because I had just locked eyes with Michael Pike. He was standing on the path, holding a bunch of candyfloss-pink flowers. He glared for a moment, then vanished between the graves.

I hugged Afton tightly and closed my eyes, shivering. I had forgotten. It was the anniversary of Ellis Elliot's death, a year to the day since the Spring Queen had died.

* * *

I drummed my fingers on the library desk, watching the clock on the wall. Afton had promised to meet me here after work – he wouldn't leave town without saying goodbye, I just knew he wouldn't do that. I was feeling something like panic. I had only known him for a week, but it felt like forever. I did not want to lose him. My chest and throat still felt tight, an anxiety I couldn't swallow or get rid of.

"Are you okay?" asked a customer, passing me a book.

I nodded quickly, stamped the book as quickly as I could, and turned to look out of the window. The daffodils out there were so bright, they should have been exuding warmth, but there was nothing.

*It wasn't my fault. I was just there.*

I checked the clock. Ten past three. Where was Afton?

My heart beating loudly under my tongue, I paused.

Ten past three.

Michael Pike had missed his Jobseeker's appointment.

* * *

The blue *POLICE DO NOT CROSS* tape looped across the graveyard entrance fluttered broken in the spring breeze. Afton's blood – I knew, immediately, without anyone telling me that it was Afton's – was all over the graveyard. His blood was spattered all over the white bluebells, his blood was bright red violence against the innocence of spring.

At the hospital I huddled in my chair, my fingers curled around a scalding cup of tea. I didn't even want it, but the chemical taste and the thin, plastic cup reminded me of Afton, and the shared daily rituals I'd become attached to over the past few days.

I sat there, staring at a vase of daffodils on the nursing station. Who *was* this man, anyway? All I knew about him was that he called himself Afton – I didn't even know his second name. And that he liked quiet places, and poetry, and that trouble seemed to find him. *Death* seemed to find him.

There was so much blood at the graveyard.

*It wasn't my fault. I was just there.*

I crushed the plastic cup slightly in my hand, and the heat intensified.

A doctor stepped out of the room. "You can pop in for a few minutes," he told me. Unsmiling.

Afton was lying in bed, his eyes closed, his heart monitor blipping steadily. It was just like the first time I saw him: same harsh lighting, same flat-on-his back position. But... he was different. That brutal scar, a monument to Michael's pain over Ellis, would be with Afton forever, long after the dark purple bruises around his eyes had healed. Michael had changed him forever.

And I was different, too.

Afton stirred, and his eyes opened. Just like the first time we met, he stared at me with that same slightly dazed expression. The long line of neat stitches looked so much worse alongside the beauty of his eyes, and I swallowed hard.

"Hey," I said softly. "How are you feeling, okay?"

Afton turned his head painfully, looked at the monitor, the blipping on the screen getting faster. "No," he murmured. He struggled to sit up on his elbows. "No... no...I can't be here." He pushed back the white bedclothes and put his hand down the front of his hospital gown, ripped the monitor leads away from his chest. He looked wildly around the room. "No! Not here. We have to go, we have to get out, *now."*

"Afton..."

He grabbed my hand and yanked me to my feet.

"Afton! Let me call the doctor, you're acting—"

"There's no time." He pulled me towards the door, peered through the glass. "There's too much death here."

Clearly, his head injuries were deeper than just that slash wound on his face. He opened the door and I let him lead me out into the corridor, because I didn't want to upset him any more, but I looked up and down for a doctor, a nurse, anybody.

Afton pulled me into the elevator and scanned the map, then he hit a button. He sat down in the corner of the elevator and put his bandaged head on his crossed arms.

"Please," I begged him, crouching down next to him, "Tell me what's going on."

"I can't be around death," he whispered. "I can't control myself, it's not my fault – I'm just *here.*"

I stared at him, and the lift doors opened behind me. Afton scrambled to his feet and grabbed my hand. In a daze, I let him lead me along.

The signs on the walls read *MRI.* Afton rushed me into one of the empty rooms with this huge cylindrical machine, and started tearing the room apart. He threw open drawers and came up with a set of ear defenders, then hurried over to me, fitting them down over my ears. He kept them covered with his hands.

"Afton?" Bewildered, I couldn't hear my own voice; it was like being underwater. I stared at his face in terror. "What's happening? Please!"

He moved to the window. My heart pounded as Afton collapsed onto his knees. I took one step towards him just as he threw back his head. His mouth opened wide, the cords on his neck standing out, his veins pounding as a howling scream ripped through his body.

I think I started screaming, too.

Then, total darkness.

* * *

Darkness.

I was on the linoleum floor, lying on my side. My throat was raw from my terrified screaming, and I groaned. Something sharp dug into my cheek. The air around me was suddenly cold, and my hair moved in the sudden breeze.

With shaking hands, I lifted off the ear defenders and tossed them aside. There was a gentle ringing in my ears, a high, faint whine. It was total darkness, and as I moved, the floor seemed to move too, with soft high sounds like a handful of coins.

It was so cold. The window was open, suddenly wide open. The only light in the room was a green, glowing emergency exit sign. I staggered to my feet. The floor was crunchy under my boots, and as I stepped, I realised it was covered with broken glass.

"Afton?" My whisper sounded loud in the sudden silence.

From somewhere else in the building, I heard a faint, but insistent screaming.

A sudden cold hand fitted into mine, in the darkness.

"It wasn't my fault," whispered Afton's voice, as he hugged me. He was shaking, and his face felt damp. "I shouldn't have been brought here. There's too much death here."

I gazed around in a numb horror. As my eyes adjusted to the darkness, I saw the jagged shapes in the window frames. Every window was shattered.

"Come on," whispered Afton.

Out in the corridors, people were roaming around everywhere, some wounded by shards of glass, some with spectacles smashed around their eyes. Every computer screen, every monitor, every syringe – Afton's scream had shattered them all. Our boots crunched over endless destruction as we ran along the corridors of the ruined hospital, past the crying and screaming patients and the frantic staff.

Outside the hospital, we slipped through the darkness of the hospital grounds, across the car park. The streetlights in the car park were broken and black. Car sirens wailed, and our feet pounded the glass of shattered car windscreens into the tarmac.

"This way," Afton said grimly, his hand still gripping mine. I was panting a little as he led me into the trees, scrambling uphill.

We reached the top of the slope. The town of Gravestaff lay spread out in front of us, and the wailing of sirens drifted up to us through the warm spring night air. Hanging in the sky above the town, brighter now due to the lack of light from the town itself, was the Flower Moon. In its light, I turned to look at Afton's face.

Moonlit pink and purple shadows moved in the darkness of his eyes. His brutal facial wound was illuminated in the Flower Moon's light, and the tears were still wet on his damaged skin.

"Tell me," I begged. "How did your scream do this? Tell me."

He sniffed deeply, took a deep breath.

"When death is near me, I... I scream." He threw a tortured glance back at the hospital. "And there was so much death in there." He finally met my eyes, and he spoke the word clearly. "Banshee," he said. "That's what they call it. So, I guess that's what I am."

* * *

The sirens went on all night.

We were under the trees, our backs resting against their comforting, solid trunks. The floor was a damp carpet of moss and dead, rotting winter leaves. I pushed them aside and skimmed my fingers over the new green shoots beneath. The innocence of the white bluebells, the warm spring air and the beauty of the Flower Moon made me feel peaceful, despite the fact that I was sitting with a literal monster, staring at the ruin of my hometown, wondering what the future held for me.

I thought of the library. The floor-to-ceiling windows, the computer screens: all would be blasted into pieces. I pictured the books, their pages fluttering in the breeze from the open windows. My *'Librarians Do It in Silence'* mug would be shattered of course, a thing of the past – but that seemed fitting. I knew I would never be back there.

My hand found Afton's, nestled among the white bluebells of spring. I didn't know what was next for the two of us, but I knew, there under the Flower Moon, that the goth librarian and the banshee were right at the beginning of something brand new.

Fiona Simpson, Scottish YA fantasy author, is excited to be featured for the first time alongside the many talented writers of this anthology. Her stories explore the myths and legends of her homeland. She currently resides in Scotland while studying creative writing at Oxford. Fiona's writing blends Scottish folklore with magical realism, featuring ghosts, banshees, merfolk, and other aspects of local lore that she is drawn to. She particularly enjoys combining the supernatural with mysterious, lonely characters living life on the fringes of Scottish society.

You can find her on Instagram at fionasimpson007.

# Spring Tide

**Kate Longstone**

Celinda placed the last of the neatly-tied packages into her wicker container, the contents kept safe from the salty sea breeze by their brown paper wrapping. She waited while Tomas grabbed a bulging hessian sack from his wooden cart, and together they started walking up the slope that led to the lighthouse.

"The basket feels heavier than usual," she said. "Did my father ask for extra meat?"

"No, he didn't. But I don't think I'll be able to make it next week, so I brought more today," he replied.

"Are you going away?" she asked. Aside from her parents, Tomas was the only person Celinda got to talk with regularly, and she looked forward to the weekly visits from the old merchant, who would regale her with tales from his time as a fisherman.

"You're full of questions today, aren't you, lass?" Tomas stopped and shook his head, placing the bag full of vegetables onto the gravel path. "I'm not going anywhere. Sofia says there's a mighty storm brewing out to sea – hasn't felt anything so strong in her bones since the spring tempests twenty years ago. She reckons the tides will rise so high the causeway will be completely under water."

Celinda's stomach lurched. She trusted the old man, but wasn't sure the water could rise so far. She'd lived in the lighthouse all her life, and although the waves would occasionally breach the top of the stone road, she'd never seen them cover it.

"Are you certain the sea will be that high?" she asked. "We've never been cut off like that before."

"Oh, it happened back then. It was this time of year as well, right at the start of spring. The squalls and storms lasted for days; I risked my life every time I had to take the boat out, though I doubt you would remember how bad it was." Pausing, he tapped the ends of his fingers. "You would've been just a baby at the time."

"I should warn Father," Celinda said.

Tomas snorted a laugh. "You can tell him, but I doubt he'll listen." He stooped to pick up the sack. "Now let's get these inside, and I'll be on my way."

After they had deposited the food in the lighthouse pantry, Celinda accompanied Tomas back to his horse and cart. As he climbed into the seat, and started to move off, she called out to him and waved.

"See you next week!"

He stopped the cart and turned to face her.

"I hope so, lass. Just remember what I said, and make sure you stay safe when the storm hits. And keep a watchful eye for whatever the gods of the sea and sky send your way."

\* \* \*

Celinda cleared the remaining plates and cutlery from the oak table and took them into the kitchen, placing them next to the sink, ready to be washed. She'd spent the remainder of the morning carrying out her daily chores – winding the old grandfather clock that stood at the base of the stairs, filling up the iron bucket from the coal cellar, and cleaning the oil lamps.

Her parents had had their own tasks to perform; her mother prepared the food for lunch, while her father worked at the top of the lighthouse, as he did most days – cleaning the glass and mirrors, ensuring the panels were kept spotless, so the beams emanating from the beacon could be seen from as far out at sea as possible.

Celinda stole a few minutes to step outside and stare longingly across the waves, wistfully wondering what it would be like to traverse the ocean – far better she imagined, than being trapped in the monotony of the lighthouse routine.

Returning to the dining room, Celinda returned to her chair and waited for her father to perform his post-lunch ritual – she had learned as a small child never to disturb him at this time. She watched quietly as he meticulously emptied the contents of a tortoiseshell pipe into a glass ashtray, and then wiped the inside with an old handkerchief. Taking a small pinch of tobacco from the tin, he placed it into the pipe and tamped it down with his fingers, repeating the process until the bowl was full. Selecting a taper from the container on the fireplace, he held it above the flames, removing it from the heat when the end began to glow. Then he settled back into his chair and held the embers above the pipe, coaxing the tobacco alight.

Only when the smoke had started to drift upwards did Celinda tell him about the extra food delivered that morning; he laughed as she told him why.

"Tomas is getting cautious in his old age," he said.

Rising from his chair, he walked over to the sideboard, upon which an ornately carved barometer held pride of place. He gently rapped its glass front with his knuckles and waited for the hand to settle.

"There is a storm coming, I'll grant him that," he

acknowledged, retrieving a leather-bound book from the shelf above and thumbing quickly through its pages before continuing. "And with the tides higher than usual, because of the close proximity of the new moon to the spring equinox, they could well be the highest we see this year. But enough to completely cover the causeway... no, I don't think so."

"Tomas said it had happened before, though," she insisted.

Celinda saw her father glance at her mother, who had stopped knitting mid-row.

"That was a freak occurrence," he said firmly. "A once in a century event – there's not a chance of that happening again."

\* \* \*

Celinda jolted awake. The sound of the rain being driven against the window, and the wind whistling through the small hole below the sill, suggested the forecast storm was on its way. The rhythmic pulsing of the weather felt strangely comforting as she lay in bed, letting her eyes adjust to the darkened room.

The thump of a shutter against the wall shattered her reverie and she clambered out of bed. Slipping on her dressing gown, she wrapped it tightly around herself as she moved to the room's only window. She jerked the curtains aside and stretched up to release the catch, lifting the heavy lower frame just enough to get her arms through. Pulling the left shutter towards her, she struggled to keep hold of it as a gust of wind sent a blast of rain inside. After securing the bottom catch in place, Celinda reached out for the other shutter. She stopped midway when, during a brief lull in the gale, she heard a voice crying out in the distance.

Raising the sash higher, she stuck her head through the opening, into the rain. The storm clouds obscured what little moonlight there was, but the illumination from the lighthouse allowed her to scan the tempestuous waves. She swept her gaze from side to side, ignoring the cold water running down her face as she followed the path of the beam of light. Twice more she heard the calls, but could not identify their source.

She dragged the frame down enough to stop the rain and hurried out of her room. Shuddering as her bare feet touched the cold stone steps, she descended to the floor below. She knocked loudly on the wooden door of her parent's room, until the door was yanked open by her father.

"What is it, girl?" he asked gruffly.

"I heard a voice calling—"

"Where?" he interrupted.

"It was coming from the ocean," she replied.

Grabbing the lantern from the nightstand by the door, her father pushed past her and started climbing the stairs. Celinda followed a few paces behind and as they reached the small alcove at the top of the lighthouse, her father pulled on the thick wax coat that hung on a hook by the door.

"Go back to your room, Celinda," he ordered. "No point in both of us getting soaked."

She returned to her bedroom and lifted the window back open. She could see the distorted shadow of her father stretching across the sea as he moved around the platform above her. She thought she heard the cry again, and her father's form paused.

Maybe he could hear it too.

Celinda focused on the expanse of water stretching out before her, ignoring the chill and dampness spreading through her hands and arms, only withdrawing when she heard the slam of the platform door. She quickly closed and fastened the shutters and window, and was seated on the bed when her father entered her room.

"There's nothing there," he stated. "You must have imagined it."

"I was sure I heard something."

Her father's toned softened, and as he was leaving the room, he turned to her. "Ocean storms play tricks on the mind sometimes. It happens to us all now and then. Try to get some rest; there'll be plenty to do in the morning."

Lying in bed, her eyes closed, she struggled to get back to sleep. She knew her father was probably right, but there was a small voice nagging at her – what if he wasn't?

\* \* \*

Celinda brushed strands of hair away from her eyes for the umpteenth time that morning. Although the rain was lighter now, the winds were still strong and gusty, and she knew that the worst of the storm was still to come.

Her father had not mentioned the events of the night before during breakfast, and she knew better than to bring the subject up. Now, in the cold light of day, as she stood on the apron at the base of the lighthouse, staring out to sea, she was certain she must have imagined the sounds.

She picked up the broom and resumed brushing away the small pools of water that had been left on the stone. When she reached the narrowest point, underneath her bedroom window, she caught a glimpse of something glistening between two rocks below.

Passing through the gap in the railings, she carefully climbed down the small iron ladder and cautiously made her way across the slippery surface. Reaching down, she retrieved what she could now see was a large scallop-shaped seashell, unlike any she had seen before. Its ridged surface was a mixture of pink and white, covered in tiny pearlescent flecks. She tried to gently open it, but its two halves remained stubbornly clamped together. Intrigued, she placed it into her pocket to study later, and returned to the apron and her duties.

\* \* \*

That night, Celinda's slumber was interrupted again by the hammering of rain on wood.

But was there something else?

Driven by instinct, she jumped out of bed and hastened to the window. She yanked the frame up high and flung open the shutters. The waves were rising higher than the night before and as she stared out into the fierce storm, she heard the voice calling once more. No, not calling; singing – and much clearer and louder than before.

Celinda scanned the choppy sea, stretching out as far as she could. Suddenly, as the enchanting melody started again, she spotted a head protruding above the water's surface. Leaving the window open, she rushed across the room and yanked the handle of the door, nearly falling over when it didn't open. She tried again, slower this time, but it wouldn't budge. The door was locked.

Banging on it with clenched fists, she shouted for her parents. After what seemed an eternity, she heard the key turn, and the door slowly opened.

"There's someone outside in the waves. I can see them, hear them crying out. We have to help—"

"I'll deal with it," her father said, and pulled the door closed.

Celinda stood with her mouth open, listening in disbelief to the click of the lock. Not understanding what was happening, or why she'd been locked in, she moved back to her window.

Helplessly, she watched the figure draw slowly nearer, occasionally catching a glimpse of an arm and hand raised above the waves. The rhythmic sounds tugged at her heart, pleading with her to join the mysterious presence in the sea.

But her reverie was shattered by the voice of her father yelling from the platform above.

"Be gone, foul temptress. We shall not let you take her!"

Celinda heard a despairing shriek echo across the waves, and watched the head disappear below the ocean surface. She stood motionless at the window, hoping for the figure or the beautiful song to return, but the only sounds were the wind and the rain dashing against the glass.

When she heard her father returning, she went back to the door and called out to him, but there was no response. She clamoured for her mother and father until her throat ached, to no avail. Finally – exhausted – she collapsed into her bed and slept.

\* \* \*

Her parents were already seated when Celinda arrived for breakfast the next morning. She wasted no time, starting to ask questions as she took her place at the table.

"Who was in the water? Why didn't you help them?"

Her father speared a piece of bacon with his fork and placed it into his mouth.

Celinda tried again. "Why did you lock me in my room last night?"

When there was still no response, she shrieked, "Why won't you answer my questions?"

Silence.

Then her mother spoke quietly. "We should tell her, Soran. She has a right to know."

Celinda looked at her father who, with a small tilt of his head, gave his wife permission.

"There are... creatures," she began. "They live in the ocean depths but in stormy weather, when the tides are high, they come closer to land."

"Do they need our help?" Celinda asked.

"No. They do not," her father interjected.

"No," her mother confirmed. "They come to lure unsuspecting folk into the sea."

"What happens to them... the people, I mean?"

"No one knows for sure. Very few of them return, and those that do are... changed." Her mother took hold of Celinda's hand. "So you see, we're only doing what's best for you."

"I understand." Still tired after the disturbed night's sleep, she felt in need of some fresh air. "Can I be excused? I'm not that hungry this morning."

Her mother nodded, and Celinda left the room and went outside.

Standing with her hands on the railings, she stared out to sea, her long hair billowing as the wind gusted around her. Although the rain had temporarily abated, the storm was still in progress, and not likely to peak until that night.

Celinda found herself humming a melancholy tune, and realised it was the same melody the creature in the sea had been singing. On impulse, she looked at the rocks where she had found the shell yesterday, and wasn't surprised when she spotted another similarly coloured object in the same place. It was another shell, and although this one was long and thin, it was sealed just as tight.

She took it back to her room and placed it on the bedside table next to the first one, then went downstairs to carry out her chores.

\* \* \*

Celinda couldn't sleep. A tempest was raging outside, far worse than any she had experienced before. Thunder boomed, and lightning flashes briefly illuminated her room despite the closed shutters and curtains. Tomas had been right – a storm surge had caused the sea levels to rise and cover the causeway. Waves were crashing against the lighthouse walls, and she had spent the evening helping her father pile sandbags against the doors to prevent the lower floor flooding.

As she lay on her bed, she heard a female voice singing a familiar, enticing tune. Pulling the drapes aside, she went to release the catch, only to find an old padlock preventing her. She knew her father had locked her door again, but this was unexpected.

She pressed her ear to the glass; whoever the woman was, she was close enough for Celinda to hear the words she sang. The refrain was simple, with the same lines repeated, and although they were in a language she didn't recognise, she started to sing along.

Short snapping sounds from her bedside table interrupted her. The two shells she had found had cracked open. Inside the scallop was a ball of fine silvery thread and in the other, a strange looking key made from coral.

Taking the key, she tried it in the padlock and with a little wiggling about, it sprang open. She lifted the sash as high as possible, but the shutters had also been fastened together. This lock also yielded to the key, and she flung the wooden coverings apart.

The sea had completely covered the apron, and a short distance away, amidst the undulating waves was a dark-haired woman. Raising her arms upwards, she called out, "Come. Join me. Use the cord."

Filled with a desire to join the stranger, Celinda unwound the string and tied one end securely to the bedpost. She didn't recognise the fibres that had been used to create it, but it was obviously very strong. Wrapping the other end around her wrist, she edged out of the window and started lowering herself down.

"Celinda!" her father shouted from beneath her, water swirling around his thighs as he pointed upwards. "Go back to your room. Ignore this foul creature!"

"Do as your father says," cried her mother, who was now leaning out of Celinda's bedroom window.

"Father!" shrieked the woman in the sea. "He's not your father. You're my daughter. They stole you from me when you were a baby."

"Don't listen to her!" Soran yelled. "She's trying to entice you with her lies."

When Celinda stared down at him, his face was contorted with anger. She turned to look up at the woman who had raised her, whose eyes were full of fear. Then she fixed her gaze on the woman in the sea, with hair as long and dark as her own, and she saw only warmth and love, and knew deep inside the right choice to make. Lowering herself to the ledge of the window below her, she loosened the thread from around her arm, then turned and leapt into the sea.

As she plunged beneath the waves, the storm-driven currents dragged her downwards. Her nightclothes hindered her attempts to swim upwards, and as she struggled to hold her breath, she started to panic – had she made the wrong choice? Had she been lured to her death?

But then she felt a strong pair of hands grasp her shoulders, dragging her to the surface. Gasping for air, she came face to face with her rescuer; with her mother.

"My child," she said, her eyes welling with tears. "I have waited so long to hold you in my arms again."

They embraced, Celinda trusting her mother to keep her safe in the water.

"Ever since that fateful night, I have beseeched the gods to grant me this chance to return to you."

"What happened?"

"You were still a baby strapped to my back, and the tempests caught me by surprise. I was exhausted and looking for a place to rest out the storm, when I saw the light upon the waves. As I approached the rocks, I saw them. I thought they would help me, but instead they took you from me and pushed me back into the sea."

Celinda gasped.

"I was too tired to fight back and let the currents take me. A fisherman found me, gave me food and shelter, and listened to my tale. He promised to look out for you, and with that glimmer of hope, I returned to my home."

There was a splash as a small buoy with a rope attached hit the waves nearby.

"It's not too late," shouted Soran. "Grab the rope and I'll pull you to safety."

Twisting around, her mother yelled to the couple who had raised Celinda. "You stole my daughter. Now feel my wrath."

She started to sing, but it wasn't the gentle song from before. These notes were filled with anger, and as her mother's voice rang out, Celinda could feel the ocean swelling around her in response. Her ire at being deprived of her mother for all those years built inside her, and she joined her in a powerful harmony. As they reached a crescendo, a huge wave was sent crashing against the lighthouse walls. There was an ear-splitting crack as the upper portion of the building toppled into the sea below.

There was no returning to her old life now, although Celinda was sad she wouldn't get the chance to say goodbye to Tomas and thank him. He had been a good friend to her over the years.

She took hold of her mother's outstretched hand, and without a backwards glance, they swam out into the ocean.

Kate Longstone is a writer of fantasy and other fiction.

She has a passion for telling the stories of strong female protagonists overcoming adversity, drawing inspiration from her interests in myth, folklore, history and nature.

Kate lives in Essex in the United Kingdom with two adorable cats, and when not writing can be found enjoying the local countryside, or exploring fantasy realms in books and games.

# To Name a Rose

Elanna Bellows

*What carries the hurt is never the wound*
*but the red garden sewn by the horn*
*as it left—and she left. I am rosing,*
*blossoming absence—a brilliant alarum."*
*-Natalie Diaz, "The Cure for Melancholy Is To Take The*
*Horn."*
Postcolonial Love Poem, 2020

The wind was cold as it wrapped around Rhiannon's ankles and wrists, a cool arm around her waist that bore her into the sky. The forest had smelled like wintergreen when she'd walked through its boughs to the Lake of Seeing, but the breeze she rode now carried with it the unmistakable earthy scent of roses in full bloom.

It was too early for roses.

Nevertheless, there they stood, red and gold in the fading

light, filling the courtyard of her town. They had bloomed when Zephyr breathed on them, after the unicorns had come and gone. They would not bloom again until she returned.

As her world shrank beneath her and the wind carried her up, and up, and further still into the endless sky, Rhiannon remembered the stories her grandmother had told her on starry nights when they sat around the campfire sipping sweet cocoa milk, though she could no longer trust in their truth.

*The Unicorns walk with silent steps, through the shadows and through the light. When the first of our men set foot on this land, he did not see their prints on the forest floor, or hear their singing on the wind, and he foolishly set his flags in the dirt.*

*They found him at night, and he covered his eyes, for they were too great and too terrible to be seen.*

*They told him that land could not be claimed, that he could not take for himself without giving back. He did not understand how land could belong to nobody, but promised to keep to his own.*

*And so our people have been good caretakers of our land. We built our fences and tilled our soil, felled trees and built our towns. The coast is studded with our settlements, and our roads spiderweb across the land.*

*The Unicorns no longer sing in our dreams, nor do they step out of the shadows and frighten us with their great and terrible beauty. But we cannot go to the Lake of Seeing, for that is their sacred ground. Some say the lake holds power beyond any we could imagine, but none has ever been able to tell what secrets lie beyond the glade. Do not fear the Unicorns, child, for they will keep to the shadows so long as we keep to our own.*

The years since had stretched as long as the height of Rhiannon's flight. As she watched the Earth spread below her, the horizon further than she had ever seen even from the tallest mountain, she could no longer point to her town.

When Zephyr had descended into the glade on his wide, silent wings, her people had not recognized him, thinking instead that a piece of the sky had torn itself free and fallen to the Earth, for his feathers were blue and gray, and reflected the dawn light.

But when he spoke, they knew him for what he was.

"Traitors," came the whisper from the great maw of Zephyr's beak, his voice breathy like skittering gravel over rock. "You have forsaken the promise made on your behalf by your predecessors, in the time of first stepping on this land."

Rhiannon's father had not blinked, though he held in his hands a waterLily still dripping lakewater like diamonds onto his shoes. It was the first Lily he had taken, but he did not intend that it be the last.

Zephyr opened his long, slender beak and rasped, "They are coming."

Suddenly the air grew silent and heavy, saturated with light and empty of sound, and everyone, including Rhiannon's father, had closed their eyes and shivered. They could no more look at the creatures than they could stare into the heart of the sun.

*He has taken from the Lake of Seeing, and yet he cannot see,* said the leader, Nini-anne, to Zephyr, but all the people heard was the stamping of a hoof.

*Neither can he hear,* said Bri-hinne, who stood beside her. *We cannot negotiate with one who cannot understand the harm in his own hands.* He swished his golden tail, but all the people heard was the rustling of leaves.

Their offspring stepped forward. *I will go,* he said in a voice soft as spring rain. He turned from his mother's steady gaze, past his father's glare, to Zephyr's still wings. *Send me a youth with a mind as open as this man's heart is closed, and I will teach them to listen as well as they speak.* But all Rhiannon's father heard was the whispering of the wind in the tall grass on the other side of the hill.

And then the glade buzzed once again with the chatter of cicadas and the quiet lapping of the lake against the shore, and the stillness in the air had gone.

When the townspeople opened their eyes, Rhiannon's father stared into Zephyr's golden gaze and waited for his sentence.

The great bird craned his long neck and ruffled his feathers. "The ones you have wronged have offered a deference, for the ceremony of renewal cannot be witnessed 'til one of your people understands the true value of what you have taken. Therefore you must return the Lily to the lake and promise to take no more. And your town must send a daughter to live in a castle in the clouds for a year, with the prince of their people, and learn to love. When next the roses bloom, she will return to you, and your debt will be repaid, if she can keep her promises as you have failed to uphold yours. She must go willingly, for love cannot dwell with suspicion, and she must know the terms, for daughters must not be lied to."

Surrounded now by clouds, Rhiannon could see no more than her father had in the presence of the Unicorns. Though she'd feared the sharp point of anger this prince must surely feel, the sting of punishment and the blunt kick of revenge, she could not let the burden fall to her people. She had volunteered, and gone to the Lake of Seeing at dusk to meet the prince.

Zephyr had met her there, shimmering like a tower of mist at the edge of the water. "Your intercessor awaits. Do you see him?"

As she scanned the edge of the lake, Rhiannon had walked her eyes from moonbeam to moonbeam, seen nothing but trees waving in the soft breeze, smelled nothing but the crisp of Zephyr's breath, heard nothing but the quiet lapping of the water on the shoreline.

"No," she'd said, "I see only the beauty of the Earth and the things that grow on her skin."

"Look again," said Zephyr in his gravelly voice.

This time Rhiannon searched the shadows, the shapes hidden in the interstices between shafts of moonlight. When her eyes caught on his silhouette, her breath caught as well, sharp and halting as it trickled into her lungs.

"Do you see him?" Zephyr whispered, though he knew the answer already.

Word-blank, Rhiannon nodded.

"What do you see?"

Studying him as he walked toward her on the mists over the lake, Rhiannon struggled to translate his features into feeling, the feeling into song, her voice soft as moss and quiet as dew sliding down a leafstem. "He is sleek and dark as a moonless night, and looking at him is like stepping blind down a path that you cannot see, but must feel foot-first with each step. The stars of the Milky Way dot his haunches, and his hooves shimmer like flakes of mica, as if his toes have been painted with rainbows. And he wears a band of moonlight as a bracelet."

By this time the prince had stopped in front of her, blowing warm air from his nostrils. Rhiannon reached out a hand, and he pressed his soft velvet nose to her fingers. "Here," she whispered, "is white like the last spark of every fire as the coals exhale their smoke and begin to cool. And from his forehead sprouts a horn that shines like abalone shells."

"And will you go to the castle in the clouds and live with him for one year, that you may repair the ruin your father has wrought?" Zephyr asked.

"I will."

At her words the prince vanished, his nose suddenly gone from her fingers.

Zephyr spread his wings. "Then let us depart," he said, and bore Rhiannon into the sky on the gusts of a flowery gale, trailing rose petals behind.

⋘ ✳ ⋙

When Rhiannon opened her eyes with the dawn, the castle walls around her sparkled. She had never thought of clouds being made of ice, but she saw now that the water had woven itself into crystal floors and halls for her to live in. As she walked through the arched halls, Rhiannon felt neither cold nor heat. The prince stood beside the pool of a fountain, the drip of water flowing through its channels of ice the only sound until Rhiannon raised her voice.

"I do not know your name," she said, holding out her hand. "I am called Rhiannon."

The prince reached with his muzzle and blew warm air over the skin of her palm.

"I do not understand."

He twitched his ears and stepped closer. His whiskers tickled her chin, and again he gave her his breath, flaring his nostrils so the warm air flowed over Rhiannon's nose.

She rested her hand on his cheek and watched his eyebrows sink over his eyes. "I do not understand," she whispered.

He blinked and sighed, ears folded away from her voice.

Rhiannon thought he looked disappointed.

He blinked again and touched the soft white patch of his nose to the tip of hers, then turned and walked down the corridor. When he paused and looked back out of the corner of one eye, swishing his white and black tail, Rhiannon followed.

So he led her through the crystalline halls as the sun walked shadows from one side of the fountain to the other. He showed her the places where she could find any sustenance her body and mind desired, the studs on his shoes leaving prickly indentations on the ramps where he stepped. As the castle glowed orange and the sun prepared to sleep, he showed her the gardens, where roses grew around the pavilion, and Rhiannon knew that these roses spoke to the roses in her town square, and would bloom at the same time.

Careful to avoid the thorns, Rhiannon cupped one flowering bud in her hand and breathed in the scent. She did not hear when it told her its name.

When she turned, her beautiful companion was looking at her with one ear turned back and one ear pricked in her direction. He dipped his head, and she followed him to the room where she had woken. Despite their icy hardness, the castle rooms were comfortable, and the food she had eaten had been both filling and delicious.

He left her to bathe, and when she had done, she found in the wardrobe fresh garments that smelled like lilac and April rain. She put on a simple silk shift and curled up in the blankets to sleep.

But as she sighed out all of the feelings she had collected during the day, a warm breath fluttered over her lashes, and she opened them to the startling blue eyes of the prince. He dropped a black band of silk on the blankets before her and stepped back, dipping his head.

Pulling herself to sit, Rhiannon picked up the opaque cloth and saw that it was wider in the middle and thinner at the ends, with a notch at the center. She looked at him. "A blindfold?"

He breathed and blinked.

So as the last light faded and the sun lay down to sleep, Rhiannon tied the silk over her eyes, understanding that it was necessary, but not knowing why.

"I am not a prince," came a voice, quiet and low, from the place where the unicorn had stood. The voice was careful and slow like molasses, but bitter. Rhiannon could not tell whether he was disappointed or angry, but she was not afraid of him.

"I am sorry; I did not know what else to call you."

"Twice I told you my name," he said. "You did not understand." Wherever the line fell between patience and impatience, his words walked it.

Rhiannon swallowed. "No, but I understand you now. Will you tell me your name?"

"Your tongue cannot say it, nor can I in this form, with my tongue clumsy as yours." He licked at his own words. "Your language is rough, like pebbles and sand. My language is sleek, like the ripple of water over the surface of a lake." He paused, and when he spoke again his voice had less tang and more sweetness in it. "You may call me *Eh-lue.*"

"Eh-lue." The name tasted like roses on her tongue.

"It means *beautiful* in one of the languages of my people, the Nyhála-inn. It will suffice until you can learn to understand. Then I will tell you my name."

"Nyhála-inn?" Rhiannon said, and the prince had her repeat it until she said it correctly. "I did not know your people had language. You do not speak during the day."

"Do I not?"

Rhiannon was silent.

"Just because you do not hear does not mean I do not speak."

Rhiannon could not help but frown. She ran her fingers along the edges of her blindfold. "In day I do not hear. Is that why now I must not see?"

"In time you will learn to listen, but you may not see me in this form. That is the condition under which I have been allowed to take it."

"Why? Are you ugly now that you are like me?" Rhiannon

could not imagine the florid, breathtaking beauty of Eh-lue reduced to the inelegance of humanity.

"I would be as lovely to your eyes in this form as I am in the other. But I am not myself."

There was something complicated in his voice that made Rhiannon's brow furrow.

"There is a consequence if this boundary is broken," she guessed.

"Yes."

"What is it?"

He did not reply.

"You cannot tell me?"

"No."

"Not being able to tell me is a silly condition."

"Were the circumstances different, I would agree. Nevertheless, it was a condition of this arrangement, and I have gambled on your integrity."

Rhiannon nodded. "Very well. I promise I will not look on you when you are not yourself."

"Thank you."

"Must I wear the blindfold all night?"

"Yes, for I must sleep beside you in your bed, or you beside me in mine. That is the other condition we must both uphold."

"Then I will trust that you will not touch me unless invited."

"Of course."

So they lay beside each other and slept, and Rhiannon did not know whether or not Eh-lue turned away his face.

And the year waned thus: in the daylight Rhiannon learned the language of the Nyhála-inn, and at night Eh-lue met her in hers.

"Do you think I am ugly?" Rhiannon asked on their second week together.

"Your people think of beauty in very simple terms," he said. "For the Nyhála-inn, it is not a way of looking, but an act of love. It is a way of being in balance; a way of seeing, and knowing, and hearing, and feeling, and doing. For your people, beauty lies in the curve of a nose, or the smoothness of the skin. For the Nyhála-inn, beauty sings in the swing of a step, in the flutter of a butterfly's wings as it takes to the sky, in the cycle of giving and taking that is all life, and the keeping of harmony between oneself and the world."

"You have not answered the question," she observed.

"It is not for me to determine your beauty. It is for you to reflect. Do you feel beautiful?"

"I am not sure I would recognize the feeling." For reasons she could not explain, Rhiannon had always felt out of sync with the world, the ways of her people, and the roles she was expected to fulfill.

Beside her, the bed shifted and she felt the slight edge of Eh-lue's breath tickle her shoulder when he said, "It feels like swimming with the current, every stroke in sync with the way the water wants to move."

The blindfold brushed her cheeks as they sank in dismay. "In your way, I do not think I can be beautiful if I do not know how the water wants to move."

"This," Eh-lue said, "you can learn, if you wish." And for the first time his words carried with them not only a drop of hope, but two of tenderness.

The feeling in Rhiannon's chest at the softness in her companion's voice was entirely new to her. She struggled to name it. It was bitter, like sorrow, and brittle, like disappointment, but also tart, like an unripe fruit not ready to be eaten. She let it creep into her mouth and soggy her speech when she replied, "I do."

"Then I have every confidence that, come spring, you will be more beautiful than the roses that will spell your return."

The next day she braided flowers into Eh-lue's mane and listened to the movements of his ears.

As the shadows crept across their pillows, and Rhiannon fixed the blindfold over her eyes, Eh-lue broke the silence first. "I wonder why you did not see me the first time you looked," he said. After a pause he asked, "Do you wish you could see me now?"

"No," she said, "but I cannot read your expression, so you must be clear with your words."

Eh-lue agreed, and they talked about the difference between words and truth.

As the days grew longer, they danced in the hippodrome and Rhiannon learned to read the movements of his mouth, how he stretched his jaw and sighed when she traced two fingers down the length of his spine. She was beginning to piece together the syntax of his language, how some movements mapped to a specific word or phrase, while others spoke in shades of an idea, or radiated an emotion too thick and layered to articulate. The ones she could not parse she would ask at night when Eh-lue could explain in familiar terms, and slowly Rhiannon began to understand.

"I wonder why you are here with me at all when you could be walking the stars and watering the flowers," Rhiannon said when the summer below simmered hot and dry.

"I wonder why you think those would be worthier endeavors than speaking with you," Eh-lue said.

"My people have broken the word they gave when they came to this land. My father has taken from your sacred lake. If beauty is a balance of giving and taking, then my kind are hideous, myself included. And yet you are here, for a year, with me. I do not know what I have done to deserve your generosity." Every breath hung thick in Rhiannon's lungs while she waited for Eh-lue's reply. By this time, she knew he would not rush, for he always chose his words carefully, but she could neither see nor hear him think. Rhiannon reached a slow hand into the blind darkness and held it there, missing the certainty of Eh-lue's body against her fingers that she so often had during the day.

With a gentle brush of skin, Eh-lue's hand closed around hers, and she waited patiently while he thought over his reply.

"It is not about deserving," he said finally. "Generosity is a gift, is it not?"

"I suppose."

"Then it should not, nor could not, be earned. It can only be given."

"Why give to such a one as hideous as me?"

"First, I contend that 'hideous' is much too strong a word. Second, I may as well ask why you agreed to this bargain."

"I could not bear to let my people suffer. Not when I could save them."

"Nor could I. The balance cannot be restored without first establishing a common ground. Your people do not see how their actions spread ripples through the world. We must work together. I give you my time, and my trust, and my tongue because I ask the same from you. We must give what we hope to receive. Otherwise, there is no balance: only breaking."

"Thank you for these gifts. I know their value, and will use them well."

"Of this, I have never had any doubt."

So they slept, and Eh-lue did not let go of Rhiannon's hand, nor she his, until the dawn came and took it away.

"I wonder why I could see you in the shadows but I could not hear your name," Rhiannon whispered in Eh-lue's ear when the leaves began to fall, and the bare trunks cast their silhouettes against the sky. "It carried so clear on your breath when you gave it to me today."

Eh-lue snorted and rubbed the side of his face against her shoulder.

Rhiannon combed her fingers through his ebony forelock, relishing the silky texture of the hair between her fingers. She was careful not to touch his horn, for the magic he held there was not hers to take.

"What did you mean, that night, when you said that you are not a prince?"

*My people do not think in such terms,* he said, slowly and carefully with the twitch of his ears and the swish of his tail. Rhiannon could understand him now, so long as he gave her time, and he always did. *Though my mother is our leader, we are not what you would call royalty. We do not set ourselves apart so, nor is our name associated with deeper respect or higher wealth. I am one of my people, as a prince would not be.*

Rhiannon frowned and placed a hand on the soft black of Eh-lue's shoulder. "I wonder that Zephyr would call you such, when it is inaccurate. Does the west wind truly know you so little?"

*It is the most similar word in your language to what I am.* He shifted, and turned his head. *Were you disappointed that I am not what you understood me to be?*

"Of course not!" Rhiannon reached for Eh-lue's nose and wrapped her arms around it, stroking the side of his face with her thumb. "You are extraordinary, and I am glad to know you. And anyway, a presumption of your royalty is not why I am here."

*I do not think you would have seen me in the shadows if stately wealth had been your goal.*

"No, I imagine not," she chuckled. "I wished only to learn how to make things right."

Eh-lue rested his chin on her shoulder. *And now?*

Rhiannon stroked his long, sleek neck. "I wish the same," she whispered, her voice thicker than the curve of each word. She saw in his eyes that Eh-lue could read what lay in the difference. "And you? What did you wish?"

He blinked at her. *To be understood.*

"And now?"

The young Nyhála-inn lifted his head and blew warm air across her cheek. *To be loved.*

Rhiannon nodded. "Me too." And she threw her arms around his neck. Eh-lue, in turn, pressed his chin against her back.

When night came to swallow the daylight and Rhiannon secured the blindfold over her eyes, she found Eh-lue's hand in the dark and squeezed.

"Do you wish you could see me now?" came the low voice of Eh-lue's human form beside her.

She rolled to face him. "You are not yourself," she said simply as she stroked his hand with her thumb. "But this listening feels one dimensional. In this form, your voice carries only a fragment of your speech. I do not miss the sight of your loveliness so much as the meaning that must be compressed to one sense."

Silence stretched between them for five breaths before Eh-lue said, "There are senses other than sight we could explore in this form," his voice as quiet as his words were careful.

"Yes," Rhiannon whispered, "we could. What do you think you might enjoy?"

He was so silent she could almost lose the sound of his breathing as it mingled with the night, but he was there, his hand in hers, and she knew he would find words to meet hers.

The wait was not brief, but Rhiannon was patient.

Eh-lue's words, when they came, were curious. "It is strange, in this form, to be so... flat."

Rhiannon heard his far arm flop down on the other side of the bed and imagined his wrist dangling off the edge. He'd spread the fingers of his hand and laid it over her palm like a starfish. "I am like an island, drifting on the sea." A rustle as he turned his face away from the ceiling toward her. "Would you anchor me?"

Rhiannon smiled. "What do you mean?"

"Would you come closer?"

"I will go wherever you would like."

"Would you give me your other hand?"

She offered it to him and his hand closed over it. Softly, like a wave slips from the shore into the depths of the sea, Eh-lue guided Rhiannon's head to rest upon his shoulder, her arm wrapped around him and her fingers interlaced with his.

"Are you comfortable?" he asked, and he sounded concerned.

"Yes," Rhiannon replied. "Is this your boundary?"

Eh-lue unlaced his fingers from hers. "It is strange, to have fingers with space between," he said. "In day, you comb your fingers through my mane. I have long been wondering what that is like."

Rhiannon smiled against his skin. "My hair is not as soft as yours, but I would enjoy that sensation if you would like to try it."

And so he did, his touch growing more sure with every stroke.

"Is this your boundary?" she asked him again.

"For now," he said, and there was no uncertainty in his voice. "We can renegotiate as our feelings change." He stilled, and Rhiannon opened her senses to hear in every detail whatever he was about to say. "Beautiful woman," he whispered, and his voice was tender. "I must tell you now, for it is only fair, that even if we discover love, no matter what kind, and no matter how deep the well of feeling digs, I will not ever desire to mate with you." He took a breath, so deep Rhiannon thought he must have swallowed all the air in the room. "It is nothing to do with you; it is simply not something I desire in either of my forms. I... desire only intimacy like this." With his fingers in her hair he cradled her head, following the movement as she tipped her face up as though she could meet his eyes even through the blindfold.

"This is enough for me," Rhiannon said, "I want most to be close to you. Everything else is merely frosting." She rested her fingers on his collarbone and nestled into his arms to sleep.

As the seasons changed, Eh-lue told Rhiannon about his childhood, about the trees that appeared to be many but were in fact only one, how the caterpillar did not simply grow wings, but gave up everything to reform as something entirely new. And he told her about the Lilies.

He brought her to the courtyard where she had found him on the first day, and she looked into the pool at the base of the fountain for visions of the land below. The Lake of Seeing sparkled in the morning sun, but the Lilies on its surface were sparse, and the water less clear.

"What have we done?" Rhiannon whispered, every syllable heavy with dismay.

*The Lilies are the lifeblood of the land. We tend the land, and the Lilies flourish with the Earth's gratitude. We receive the Lilies with honor, and take only as much life as we can return to the lake in exchange for the sight we have been given. And so we are one with the world.*

"My father does not know what he has done."

*No. He continues to take more than he gives, and the land suffers.*

"What does he need the Lilies for?"

*That is a question only he can answer.*

Rhiannon looked at the bare stalks of the roses in the garden on the other side of the archway. They were hardy, and they called to her, so she went. Eh-lue trailed behind. She could see from the color in their stems that, though dormant, they still held life.

"There is still time," she said, and Eh-lue blinked.

Turning back to the roses, Rhiannon ran her fingers over the stalks, careful not to prick herself on the sharp thorns, and she could almost hear them speak to her. But not quite.

When noon banished every shadow, Rhiannon wrapped her arms around Eh-lue's neck, now fuzzy with the thick hair of winter, and breathed in the musty smell of his skin. He rested his throat on her shoulder and pressed his chin into her back, and she knew that he loved her.

"Do you miss your home?" Eh-lue asked as the short days grew long again, and the snow on the Earth changed to rain. He had curled his body around Rhiannon and held her in his arms.

"Not nearly as much as I will miss you when I return home." She could feel the time passing as the Nyhála-inn felt the wind blowing their mane when they ran across the steppe, just as she could feel Eh-lue's arms try not to pull her tighter against him, and fail.

⟨⟨⟨ ✳ ⟩⟩⟩

On the day the roses bloomed, Rhiannon stood in the garden beside Eh-lue, brushing his coat with a rubber comb. With every stroke, the hair of his winter coat fell from his sides like waterfalls. It was a soothing sensation, one he had never before experienced: a relief from the itch that happened every year as he let go the safety and protection of winter and stepped, vulnerable, into the sun. Eh-lue relaxed into Rhiannon's touch as they waited for their summons.

Zephyr arrived on a warm westerly wind, alighting on the rim of the fountain in the ice castle's central courtyard. His head swiveled on his long neck until his eyes found Rhiannon, and he blinked.

Putting down her combs and brushes, Rhiannon laid a hand on Eh-lue's shoulder and he turned to face her.

"It is time," she said. "I must speak to my father so we can make it right."

The soft skin of Eh-lue's nose twitched. *Yes.*

Rhiannon cupped his chin in her palm and planted a kiss on the white spot between his nostrils. Eh-lue pushed his forehead against hers, his horn resting on top of her head and his nose pressed gently to her chest. He lipped at her collar.

With her hands on his poll, Rhiannon stayed in the embrace until Eh-lue pulled away.

He blinked and swished his tail.

"I will take all that you have taught me and help bring our peoples to parley," Rhiannon told him, adjusting his forelock to curl in a single wave around his horn.

He stepped back. Nose to the sky, Eh-lue called out and snorted.

At the sound of Eh-lue's call, Zephyr raised the winds and bore Rhiannon back to her people the same way they had come. Even though the whirlwind was as rosy as it had been before, it did not smell as sweet on the descent, watching Eh-lue's dark form disappear behind the icy walls.

≪⊪ ✳ ⊪≫

When Rhiannon walked through her father's door, he put down his tools – with more clatter than he would otherwise have made – and rushed to embrace her.

"I thought to come rescue you," he said, "but I could not find your castle."

"I did not need rescuing," Rhiannon assured him. "I was never a captive."

At this, he stepped back and frowned at her, in the way he always had when she'd misbehaved as a child. "I do not trust anyone who would take one of our daughters and lock her away to pay for her father's crimes."

Rhiannon found it encouraging that Owen seemed to acknowledge, at least, his wrongdoing, but she would not be able to bring their peoples to an agreement if he hated the Nyhála-inn so dearly that he refused to meet them. So she said, "They did not take me; I volunteered. You were there when I left that night for the Lake of Seeing."

"Yes, but they gave us no choice. They ordered that someone should go, so of course you would; you are too good to let anyone else sacrifice themselves."

The hope Rhiannon harbored dimmed. "Father, is that what you think that I have done?"

He stood silent, his face hard as stone. "You have always thought too little of yourself."

"Perhaps that is true, but I can tell you that I did not feel that I was sacrificing myself, nor have I been lost. I am still here, only now knowing more of the world than when I left."

"And did you do as you were instructed? Did you learn to love that cruel beast who stole you away for a year?"

"Father, you are not being fair," Rhiannon chided gently. "He did not steal me. He gave me the greatest gift anybody could give: the opportunity to learn and grow. He is like the Lake; in seeing the world through his perspective, I learned to see myself and find my place in it. It is like the world is always dancing, and I was always out of step. But now I can hear the beat; I must only practice stepping to it."

She spoke with such passion that Owen could not but believe her sincerity. Worse, he could hear the devotion that glittered in her voice. "And you love him for it?"

The radiance of her smile drove away any doubt that otherwise may have lingered from her previous statement. "I have grown quite fond of him, yes, and in your terms the affection I feel would be called *love*. But in his language love is much more than that; it is an action, a stepping in time with others, with the birds and the river and the mountains and the Lilies. It is a commitment to listen to the lifesong of the Earth, and do your best to sing in tune. This I have learned, but it is not enough."

Owen could not understand. "But you fulfilled the request. You lived with him for a year, and learned to love. Did you fail to uphold your promises?" Although he knew she could not.

"I have kept every oath I have made."

Owen's brow grew deep and broody as the furrows in the springtime farmer's fields. "Then our debt should be repaid."

"Yes," Rhiannon said, "it must be repaid, but it hasn't yet." She waited as her father stared at her, but when it was clear he had no response, she continued. "We must repair the damage that was caused when you took the Lilies."

"The lilies are gone. I have fed them to my machines, and they cannot be returned."

"Nevertheless, we must repair the harm." Rhiannon answered in the same calm voice she'd used all afternoon.

"Then what do they want from me? I have nothing else to give but you, and you have already been given."

"Absolution is never so simple. We must meet with the Nyhála-inn tomorrow to negotiate how the damage can be repaired."

It took only a few minutes more of persuading before Owen agreed to meet with the Nyhála-inn. Although he was still far more hesitant than pleased, he would come.

«««  ✳  »»»

The following morning, in an open meadow, Rhiannon stood beside her father and waited for the Nyhála-inn to arrive.

"You need not fear them," Rhiannon had said as they walked through the meadows.

"Is it not wise to fear someone who perceives you have wronged them, and passes judgment?" he'd asked.

Rhiannon had smiled at him. "It is wise to keep your mind and ears open, and listen to what they have to say before passing judgment of your own."

Now, in the meadow, she could only hope that she had done enough – that her father would be able to let go of his fear and hear the voices he could not now understand.

As the sun peaked noon, the meadow stilled as though even the bees that bounced from flower to flower had paused in their work, and the wind held its breath. This time, at Rhiannon's prompting, her father did not close his eyes, but instead watched the two magnificent creatures that seemed to glide across the meadow. One shone a brilliant marigold, his pale mane and tail flowing around him like the rays of the sun. The other moved like a shadow, her blue roan coat like steel gray granite misted in white, with mahogany undertones and red-brown highlights in her mane. They walked side by side, the lighter one a half stride behind the darker, ears pricked forward in greeting. When they reached the spot where Rhiannon and her father stood, the mare stepped forward and offered her breath.

Rhiannon returned the greeting, then spoke the introductions for her father's benefit. "Nini-anne, this is my father, Owen." It was difficult, Rhiannon found, to juggle the dual tasks of translating and greeting, and she worried that the palomino stallion might be feeling neglected, but his ears were pricked and patient, and he watched her with curious eyes. After she had repeated the introductions with him the same as she had with Nini-anne, he added, *you carry yourself differently than your sire. It gives me hope that we may reach an agreement.*

Rhiannon smiled at him, then translated for her father the part that was meant for him, "He says that he is hopeful that we will reach an agreement." Turning back to the Nyhála-inn, she said, "Thank you, Bri-hinne. I am likewise optimistic."

Nini-anne then pushed Bri-hinne aside and began asking Rhiannon questions about her year with Eh-lue, and Owen questions about the town and its people.

When Eh-lue arrived with Zephyr, he greeted Rhiannon with an affectionate nicker and offered his breath to Owen. Rhiannon translated for her father as best she could.

Once the introductions were finished, they arranged themselves in a circle, which Nini-anne explained gave them all equal voice and equal respect, so each could hear all the others clearly. And the circle began.

*We gather here to discuss the relationship between our peoples, so that we may come to an agreement of mutual respect and repair the harm that has been done,* Nini-anne said. *We will do this by answering four questions. First, we begin by coming to an understanding of the specific breaches in trust. Please describe, in your own words, what happened.*

And so they went around the circle.

Bri-hinne spoke first. *The border to the sacred ground of our people was crossed, and our sacred Lilies were taken. This is in breach of the treaty that was made between the Nyhála-inn and the humans when first they came into this land. Over the course of the past year, despite being asked to cease, this man has continued to steal the sacred Lilies from the Lake of Seeing.*

Zephyr spoke next, his gravelly voice cutting into the silence that followed Bri-hinne's offering. "The Nyhála-inn have lived on this land for many years, tuning themselves to the cycle of the seasons and the ways of the earth. Generations ago, the humans landed on these shores, and a treaty was set to establish boundaries of land. However, the treaty was insufficient to teach the humans a respect for the natural order, or the agency of the land. And so their society has grown to think of the land merely as a material good. This misunderstanding led to Owen crossing the boundary and disrespecting the sacred spaces of the Nyhála-inn, just as his people disrespect the Earth in their everyday lives."

Owen had raised his chin, and now that it was his turn, he opened his scowl in his defense, though he kept his tone even. "I have lived on this land all my life, and it has given my people a home, food to eat, and flowers to admire. But it is unpredictable, sometimes, and inefficient, so my people have sought to improve our lives by developing technologies, and harnessing the power of the earth to do better than nature alone can provide. So I have taken some lilies from the lake because they hold great power. I understand that this is in breach of the treaty, but I had honestly thought this treaty to be a folk legend, since I had never seen nor heard a Nyhála-inn during my lifetime until the day we first met at the lake."

And so, in turn, Rhiannon, Eh-lue, and Nini-anne shared

their perspectives, each in part distinct and yet sharing elements of the others.

After, they went around the circle again and each spoke, and the Nyhála-inn explained that the loss of the Lilies had choked the Earth, and Owen explained that he needed the nectar from the Lilies to power his machines.

"I do not see how the earth chokes, nor does it stop my innovation. The land on its own is not reliable; we crave consistency and so have invented machines to maintain it for us."

*Your species is creative,* Eh-lue said. *Can you not power your innovations in other ways that cause no harm?*

Hesitation squatted on Owen's brow. "They are only flowers," he said. "Surely the Lilies will grow back."

Nini-anne shifted her feet and swished her red-black tail. *They will not renew at the rate at which you will need them, especially if your technology grows. Are you not already running low on Lilies?*

Owen raised his chin. "Surely I could find more elsewhere once this supply runs out."

Rhiannon blanched. "Would you leave a trail of dead lakes in your wake?"

"I would do what I must for the sake of progress."

*It is important for both our peoples,* Nini-anne said, *that as you build advancements, you keep balance with the world around you. The Lilies hold potent power, but they are limited in number, and the Lake of Seeing cannot breathe without them.*

Rhiannon nodded. "Would it not be easier to engineer a machine that would not be limited by the Lilies you may or may not find? Surely to live in desperation, always seeking more of what you do not have, is a stressful existence. Would you wish that on future generations? Would you wish that on me?"

Silence trailed her words like the light trails the sun as it crosses the horizon.

"I think," said Rhiannon, her voice slow and calm and sweet as springtime sap, "it would benefit us all to build systems we can sustain for many more years. Why risk running into problems later when we could solve them now, before we are caught in the scarcity we ourselves created?"

Owen frowned. "I see that you have heard me, and that we all have similar goals. However, I do not know how to harvest any energy other than what the Lilies provide, and I fear for the stability of my people through the hard seasons. Although I now better understand the impact that my machines have on your sacred land and the Lake, I don't see any alternatives. And since I am not willing to put my people in danger, I see no other way forward than the path I am on."

Rhiannon's heart sank, and despair began to creep into her body until Eh-lue raised his magnificent head.

*This is not your problem to solve alone,* he said, and Rhiannon did her best to capture the gentle patience in his tone when she translated for her father.

*No, indeed,* Nini-anne said, *it is ours to solve together.*

Bri-hinne eyed Owen before adding, *We have heard your critique of our absence. We would like to be more present in the lives of your people, that we might all be neighbors.*

In the slowly shifting evening light, Rhiannon's face was even brighter than the golden shafts that pierced the canopy of the forest. "This," she said, and her voice barely contained her joy, "would surely benefit both of our peoples." And in the corner of her vision, Eh-lue's eyes glimmered with such glee that she could almost feel the strength of it, radiant on her skin.

Such was Eh-lue's excitement at his own revelation that he could not contain it, and he stamped all of his feet in turn. Everyone turned to look at him, and he managed to speak clearly after he'd shaken out his mane. *Owen, I am very grateful for all that you have given up to this point, and now I must ask you for more, but I hope what we offer could be an equal exchange. In my time with your daughter, I have learned that our peoples have different strengths, and different challenges we seek to overcome. I suggest that we continue to collaborate.*

Owen nodded in agreement, but his body was tense with hesitation.

Rhiannon, however, thought she knew where Eh-lue was headed, and picked up the thread. "Indeed, I have seen the lovely architecture of the castle in the clouds, and how the elements bent to create such a safe and accommodating environment that suited both of our needs. Perhaps the Nyhála-inn, with their knowledge of the land and the cycles of seasons, could consult and help us build new innovations to keep our supplies of food and water more stable."

*We would be happy to share such knowledge*, Nini-anne replied.

A frown still squatted on Owen's brow, but his shoulders had relaxed. "This would help our farmers to better work the land and store the surplus, but it does not solve the problems of the Lilies. I am not willing to give up our new technologies so easily."

*No*, Eh-lue responded, *we are not asking you to give up your technology. But perhaps we could find a way to revise it to run on an alternative power source.*

Bri-hinne blew a stream of air in agreement. *Yes, we are not experts in machines, but the Earth holds great power, even more powerful and vast than the elixir of the Lilies. We could help you learn how to harvest it.*

*And*, Eh-lue added, *perhaps you could help us build technologies to help us solve some of our own problems as well.*

Both Bri-hinne and Nini-anne turned to look at Eh-lue, and

their nostrils spelled surprise.

*In the spring and the fall, we suffer from great itch as our coats shed to prepare for the changing weather of a new season.* He turned to Rhiannon, reaching his nose toward her hand. *Rhiannon's brushes brought me a great deal of relief.*

Rhiannon smiled. "If you would like, I am sure the people of our town, especially the children, would enjoy grooming any Nyhála-inn who asked."

Nini-anne added, *It would be a great joy to bond with your youth, and to feel clean and sleek even through the changing of the seasons.*

"Then we will help each other," Owen declared. "And perhaps, once we have fixed my machines, we can build something the Nyhála-inn could use to groom yourselves as well."

The Nyhála-inn nodded an emphatic and enthusiastic agreement.

"And," Rhiannon suggested, "perhaps we could braid baskets for you, that you might carry with you the things that you need."

And so it was decreed on the fifteenth day of the fourth month of that year that the Nyhála-inn and the humans would live in peace and mutual respect, and an ambassador would be appointed from each group to walk between them.

At this consensus, Nini-anne turned to Zephyr. *Wild wind of the West, we implore you to aid us in this collaboration by appointing representatives for our peoples.*

"Eh-lue," Zephyr croaked, "You have already taken on this mantle. Do you wish to continue?"

The dazzling black stallion inclined his head. *Although I find it unpleasant to take on the human form, it is convenient for the purpose of communication and cultural exchange, and I glean great joy and excitement from learning about other cultures and philosophies of life. Therefore I would like to continue in my role, so long as I retain agency over my transitions between forms, and can choose to be seen or not, in either form.*

Zephyr clacked his beak. "It shall be done," he proclaimed, and with his wings flapped a gust over Eh-lue so that his black mane flew back from his face. Then the great bird turned to Rhiannon. "Child of the wind," he said, his voice crunching like pebbles underfoot. "You have lived a year with this son of the Earth and learned to speak his language. Would you take up the mantle of ambassador and walk between the worlds, as he has done for you?"

Rhiannon blinked in surprise, catching her breath and organizing her mouth to speak. "Yes," she whispered, "I would like that very much."

"To walk with the Nyhála-inn, you must be as they are. Do you consent to the transformation of your body?"

Rhiannon met Eh-lue's eyes. "I do."

The young Nyhála-inn stepped forward. *Do not be afraid,* he said, even as Zephyr raised his voice in a great cacophony of sound.

Rhiannon closed her eyes and braced herself against the gale from Zephyr's wings and the prick of Eh-lue's horn against her heart.

Like the moon pulls the tide away from the shore, cool magic prickled over Rhiannon's skin. In the place where her lifefire burned, she felt a seed bloom, prismatic and shifting like the stars pulling together, like the spark that ignited in the Nyhála-inn's eyes, like the dart of a fish at the bottom of a stream. She could hear Eh-lue in every note it sang, every breath it invited her to breathe, so she opened herself and let it flood her.

Like the moon pushes the tide to crest and break against the sands, cool magic spread through Rhiannon's body, clean and damp like fog rolling in to smother a mountain, and breathless as the wind tossing dunes into the sky.

When next she breathed, Rhiannon's skin had sprouted a coat of sleek hair, and her feet were tough as a rock standing against the tide, dynamic as the light splitting into colors through the rain. When next she stood, Rhiannon flared her wide nostrils, swished her chestnut tail, and blinked. Before her stood Eh-lue.

She stepped to him, reached out her muzzle, and gave him her breath, warm and musty as a rose after a rainstorm.

⋘ ❋ ⋙

Every spring when the last rose opens its petals to the sky, the townspeople host a great feast to celebrate the beauty of thorns and petals, of giving as much as they take from the Earth, and they toast to a new year of prosperity. Rhiannon and Eh-lue can always be seen amongst the crowd, Rhiannon sometimes in one form, sometimes in the other, and Eh-lue with his Nyhála-inn elegance, gamboling with the youths and teaching their languages.

Now when the sun sets over the plains and the hills glow red, the Nyhála-inn send beautiful dreams to the people in the town, and Eh-lue and Rhiannon walk among the host that come to the Lake of Seeing, swishing their tails and drinking of the sacred water, that they may never lose sight of the Earth that breathes beneath their feet.

And when Rhiannon bends to kiss the roses that bloom in the town square every spring, they whisper their names, and she whispers them back, and the west wind swells with their joy.

As a child, Elanna Bellows pretended to be a horse, wrote stories on the back of napkins to fend off boredom, and had the audacity as a third grader to try to teach her much younger brother multiplication. Now she teaches for real at a public school in Massachusetts, writes in notebooks instead of on napkins, and pretends to be an adult. You can find her on Instagram at Elanna_Bellows_Writes.

# It Started with Bluebells

M. J. Weatherall

Content warning: suicide

*"I'll sweeten thy sad grave: thou shalt not lack
The flower that's like thy face, pale primrose, nor
The azured harebell, like thy veins"*
*Shakespeare*

Winter is a hard time for my kind. It's a hard time for anyone, but we're different. We're dying out. As shapeshifters, stewards of the spring, it used to be that without us there would be no spring, or a late spring, or a poor spring. But now, with pollution punching holes in the atmosphere and the climate warming, we aren't needed as much.

That winter I was a young woman out in the world on my own for the first time. I'd refused to marry, refused to take vows to a god I didn't believe in. I was exiled from my village. It was nearing the end of winter and my family were starving; they couldn't support us all. I was the one with the least prospects. My older siblings had left home, and my remaining sisters would all make good marriage matches. That's why they chose me.

"Go find your place in the world. Find your fortune and return to us." Father had said.

I knew he was lying, but I spared us all the pain and embarrassment and went along with it.

I took one last look at the shack we called a home, the grave faces of my family in the window watching me go. I wouldn't let them see me cry. I turned, feeling the frosted mud beneath my thin boots, and started walking. I didn't know where I was going, but I knew it would do none of us any good for me to hang around outside the family home.

The people of my village shunned me, said that I was getting what I deserved, that a peasant girl like me had no right to be so picky. I wandered for days, my meagre supplies wearing thinner and thinner each night. The surrounding villages were no kinder than my own, saying that they couldn't afford to help a stranger when their own were suffering. That was understandable. But it wasn't the truth.

It was an unwritten thing that exiles were left to die. A sacrifice of sorts. I knew it was a death sentence, but I was still young enough to think that they were just cautionary tales told to young children who dared to misbehave.

The supplies ran out, and I gave up on selfish people. I went to the woods. I knew enough about the wild to survive a little longer. What plants and roots were edible, how to catch and cook small rodents and birds, where to find water that was safe to drink. Every day I prayed for a bountiful forage and every night I prayed for spring. I wasn't even sure who I was praying to; I didn't believe in gods. It was more like I was asking the trees themselves to deliver.

Eventually they did.

* * *

I walked barefoot and delirious among the brittle undergrowth. My body was emaciated and frail, my mind was lost; I knew it wouldn't be long until I felt Mother Nature's final embrace, but then the trees gave way to a glade, vibrant and welcoming. I felt like my prayers had been answered, that this was the start of spring. I summoned enough energy to smile and thank the trees.

With the sun's rays warming me and the new grass bouncy and soft beneath me, I took a nap. I felt safe with my tall sentinels towering around me as I curled up on the mattress of green and felt darkness pulling at the edges of my vision.

In the darkness I felt calm.

Until the pain began. My whole body seized with cramps, and if I'd had anything substantial to eat, it would have come hurling out. I cried out in desperation and opened my eyes. Before me, the glade had transformed into a waking nightmare. The tall trees that had made me feel so calm and protected were now bending over me like I was prey – their clawed hands reaching out towards me, the springy grass writhing with the tiny bodies of insects and nocturnal creatures, all racing to be the first to devour me.

I screamed as I raked my fingers over my exposed skin. My only thought was of escape; I had no concerns regarding the direction. I was too heartbroken, too frightened, too naive. I fled through the glade and into the dense woodland, towards a road, or village, or river. Anywhere but there. It wasn't long till my body crumpled with the weight of fatigue, so close to death that I couldn't wait for the sweet release, the dreamless sleep that was just out of reach. I lay defeated on the ground, unfeeling and flat.

A glowing white apparition flickered before me. I had to squint to make it out. A white bluebell, luminescent and inviting, appeared before me. I tried to remember what they said about bluebells. That they pointed south, that they were a witches favourite, that they were used in poisons and love potions, that they... They said a lot about bluebells. Most of it probably wasn't true. But, I thought as I lay shivering and weeping on the ground, they were probably poisonous enough to finish the job.

"Thank you, trees, for providing me this kindness. In return you can have my body to feed your roots," I chanted as I clawed my way over root and stem to the bright white light in the darkness.

I reached out and plucked the soft white bells from their fragile stems. The ivory petals glimmered in the moonlight, looking ethereal against my rough, filthy hands. My tongue knew they weren't food the moment they landed in my dry, greedy mouth; what started as a soft sting quickly turned into a deep, searing burn. My body screamed in protest against the poison I had ingested, but I continued, fluttering from patch to patch of the shining flowers, coughing and spluttering blood as I forced myself to eat.

The path of bluebells, illuminated by magic or just the moonlight, led me south to the crags overlooking a valley. The white flowers were in abundance here, creating a blanket on the crag top. I sighed and watched the sun threatening to rise over the horizon.

"Thank you," I said to the bluebells as I lay my unkempt head against them, the soft and the rough. I thanked them for letting me see the sun one last time, for helping me with death, for being a beacon of light in the darkness.

I closed my eyes.

\* \* \*

It was a strange sensation, being reborn. At first it was like waking up with a hangover, trying to figure out what had happened the night before – why everything hurt, why was I waking up in the woods. And why was I an animal? I looked down my whiskered nose to the long, strong legs underneath me. A hare.

My vision was distorted; it felt like things were clearer, but at the same time, the colours were duller and not how I remembered them. I wanted to call out, but I couldn't summon my voice, only strange squeaks and chirps.

The sun had risen, and the view was glorious. Spring *had* come. Mist floated from the ground, leached from the earth up into the atmosphere. I don't know how long I watched from my craggy birthplace, but when I decided to move, I felt a pull of determination and purpose. She had chosen me. Mother Nature had chosen me to help her spread her gift of spring.

I looked around and saw a pile of rags. I hopped over and sniffed the bundle. My new nose was more sensitive than my last and I staggered back, overwhelmed by the rancid stench. It occurred to me then that the pile of rags were my human clothes, shed and replaced with short, wiry fur. From the smell, I could tell that I had been dying for a long while, slowly decaying inside myself. I wanted nothing more than to leave that pitiful life behind and start fresh.

I hopped around the top of the ledge, wondering what to do next, when I heard a squeak behind me.

Assembled in the treeline was an army of hares, glaring at me. One bounded forward and sniffed me warily. I flinched and looked at the ground.

*Welcome, Sister.* A voice inside my head echoed.

My head snapped up to find the speaker. The hare stared at me knowingly. In life, I had only seen hares from afar, but I could have sworn they didn't normally look like the one before me now. It had large eyes that looked... human. Like they had been plucked from a human skull and inserted into the hares. They seemed to look right through me, like they knew what was inside my head, inside my soul. Not the usual vacant stare of a large rodent.

*You are one of us now, my sister. We are the spring, the reborn chosen by our mother to bring fresh gifts to her children.*

The hare spoke without using its mouth, not the squeaks I was able to conjure, but directly into my head. The other hares in the treeline nodded and thumped their feet in approval. Reborn? Were all these hares once people like me? Did they all suffer hopeless deaths like mine?

*Come, Sister, march with us and spread the seed of new life.*

I felt a tug in my gut. I knew that this was what I was destined to do, that this was the reason I had never fit in in my human life. I nodded.

*Then let us run! Let us usher in the new season together!*

A chorus of thumps followed their leader's proclamation.

\* \* \*

That was hundreds of years ago. I was the last one to hear our mother's call. There have been none since. My brothers and sisters died with the changing of the weather and the times, and only few of us remain. It was slow at first, just the occasional straggler getting caught in wildfire, or under falling trees and bulldozers, or not making it through the other seasons. Every time one of us fell, our mother's voice became fainter in our heads and our purpose became a little dimmer. It was harder than watching my family wither and die of old age, it was harder than seeing other outcasts perish on the ground like I did, but not be reborn. It was harder each time one of us didn't return to the hunt at the end of winter.

We didn't have names anymore; we didn't need them. But there was one brother I liked more than the rest. He was the one I ran next to and talked to the most. One year he just vanished.

It was winter, the time when our mother's pull calls us, and we returned to the husk to run. I knew where he liked to roam during the winter months, so I went to find him, trusting my remaining brothers and sisters to take the same route we always did. He'd grown up in a village not far from mine, close to the husk's meeting place, so I didn't have far to go to pick up his scent.

I bounded the well-worn paths around the outskirts of his

village, finding a burrow large enough to be one of ours and not that of one of our smaller cousins. I sniffed the air deeply, closing my eyes and focusing. I could smell the woodsmoke from a nearby fire, a rotting corpse of an unfortunate animal, the sweet nip of tree sap, and... there, just as I was about to give up. My brother's scent, weak but familiar. He hadn't been home for a while. I opened my eyes and homed in on the scent, blocking out all other distractions. I could sense the path he had taken, away from the village and our husk's meeting place. But why would he abandon us, so close to the coming of spring? He had to have a good reason; he was not the sort to shun our mother.

I followed his trail, remembering all those years ago when I followed the trail of white bluebells to the crag where I was to be reborn. Despite it resulting in my human death, I was fond of the memory of the pearlescent petals. My brother's scent led me to the woods behind a sprawling city, hastily erected and poorly built by invaders from across the seas. More specifically, it brought me to a little cabin in the woods, adorned with drying herbs. I thought the worst: my brother had been killed and eaten by the owner of this cabin. That's why he hadn't answered the call. That's why he was so far from home.

I froze, wondering what I should do now. Should I go and check? Make sure that he wasn't trapped? Confirm whether or not he was dead?

I didn't have to make up my mind, because the door to the cabin opened and a human woman strode out. Her hair was grey and fell in wisps around her hips. I flattened myself to the ground, hiding in the long grass by the stump of an old oak tree. If she was responsible for my brother's death, then I didn't want her to catch me before I had the chance to relay the information to the husk.

The human closed the door behind her and ambled her way up the path leading towards the city. She didn't look back towards her cabin.

I waited until she was completely out of sight before loping over to the cabin. I knew that there was no way I would be able to get in through the front door, so I made my way around the back, hoping that there would be a window or something I could enter through. At the back of the cabin were several neatly dug vegetable plots, all with different delicious-looking leaves sprouting from them. My nose twitched and I became very aware of the hunger gnawing at my stomach. I ignored it, looking instead towards the back of the building. There was a back door and two windows, but all appeared to be shut tight. Whoever this human was, she took her security seriously. I knew that not only because of my life as a human, but because I had broken into several human homes in search of food on the harder days.

A noise roused me from my scheming. A distinct and spine-tingling hiss. I looked around, blessed by my extensive vision, and saw the maker of the noise: a very round, very mangled looking black cat grimaced at me with its milky eyes and gap-toothed snarl.

*Leave me be,* I commanded.

The cat looked bemused. It continued its hissing as it came closer.

*You will not win this fight,* I threatened, drawing myself up onto my hind legs. As I did so, I glimpsed a cage through the window of the cabin. Inside sat my brother, unmoving.

*Get me in the cabin and you will be greatly rewarded,* I offered.

The ancient feline ceased its hissing and pondered my proposal.

I held my breath in anticipation, sinking back onto all fours. The cat looked from me to the door and realised what I was here for. It waddled to the back door and leant against it with its vast weight. The cat looked back at me impatiently and I finally realised that it needed both our weights to open the door. It was waiting for me. I joined the foul creature, pressing my body against the solid wood, trying not to breathe in the scent of my accomplice. The door shuddered, trying to resist and then gave in, creaking open. The cat looked over its shoulder at me as if I was a mere inconvenience, then entered the cabin. I hopped up to the door and peered inside, my eyes adjusting quickly to the dimmed light.

*Brother?* I called out, still hovering in the doorway.

Silence for several beats. *Sister? What are you doing here? You have to leave now!*

I could hear his claws scrabbling frantically on the cage floor.

*Fear not, Brother, I have come to rescue you,* I assured him.

*I do not need rescue, Sister. You must leave,* he begged.

I hopped closer to his cage and looked up at him. *What do you mean, you do not need rescue? You are trapped in a cage and it's the first day of spring. I must free you.*

He groaned at me angrily. *I am here of my own free will. If she catches you here she will kill us both.*

*She's going to kill you?* I gasped, my ears suddenly bolt upright.

*No, not exactly, but if she catches you here, then she'll think I called you here. She will think...*

*What are you here for, Brother?* I interrupted.

*I have asked this witch to make me human again, Sister. I know you won't understand, but answering our mother's call is my greatest regret.*

I staggered back from the cage, unable to believe what he was saying. I stammered, S*he's brainwashing you, making you sick. You would never be saying these things otherwise.*

*It is not so, Sister. This is what I want. The Horned God's witch will make me human again.* He wouldn't look directly at me, the shame fixing his gaze to the cage.

*You would work with the Lord of Death against our mother?*

*You are corrupt.*

I turned, hoping to leave, to catch up with the husk and tell them what I had learned.

"Well, well, well." The witch was standing in the doorway, the ancient black cat purring around her heels. "Two for the price of one."

*It's not what you think,* my brother began, his eyes pleading.

"I told you what would happen if you betrayed me, rodent," the witch spat.

*I followed him here. He didn't tell me what he was planning, I promise,* I blurted, trying to take her attention away from my brother.

"I don't care. The way I see it is I have two of Mother Nature's servants and my lord will be twice as happy," she cackled.

*But I don't want to die!* I squealed.

"Save your appeal for The Horned God," the witch said, as she closed and bolted the door behind her.

I tried to repress the terror rising in me. Tried to avoid the instinct to run. I knew it wouldn't end well for me if I ran. I would probably feel like I was getting away for the first minute, but once I realised that there was no exit, then I would be exhausted and have no energy left to fight.

The witch and her cat flanked me, closing in slowly. I weighed up my options, which were slim – I could either strike first, the cat or the witch, or I could try and go for the cage to free my brother. At least with the latter, it would make it a fairer fight... Time was up. The witch closed her eyes and muttered under her breath.

I ran for the cage, hoping a sharp kick would be enough to unlatch the door. I never made it. A strong hand yanked me out of the air by the scruff of my neck and held me firmly in place despite my wriggling desperation to be free. I spun my head to see the form of my captor: a spectre. A ghostly apparition with the strength of ten men. My ears flattened to my head reflexively.

The witch chuckled, "Gets me every time."

*Let me go! I don't want this. I won't make a deal with your Horned God,* I complained, trying to wriggle free.

"You will. See, fate has landed you right where you need to be... again," the witch said with a sly grin. "Just like the day you met your precious *mother.*"

*How do you know about that?* I whimpered.

"I know a lot more than you think, Sister," she replied with a malicious glare.

*Sister?*

ENOUGH, the spectre announced.

"Oh, you're no fun these days, Gerard," the witch teased.

WE MUST PREPARE FOR THE WILD HUNT, Gerard replied sternly as if he had given the witch a sufficient answer.

Gerard thrust his hand towards the cage, not concerned that, unlike him, I was a solid creature. The witch flicked her wrist and the door to the cage flew open, just in time for my whiskers to brush against it as it passed. Gerard deposited me without a second thought, and the witch wasted no time in latching the cage door.

Without another word, the spectre and the witch began their preparations, putting items away, getting different items out. Honestly, there seemed to be no reason or rhyme to what they were doing and I could only look on and wonder. I wasn't ready to talk to my brother yet. He still filled me with rage and sadness.

Eventually the pair stopped and looked pleased with themselves. Candles were placed equidistantly along patterns made with chalk, several offerings were placed inside the shape, and the air smelled sweet.

"Gerard, take *them* outside and watch them," the witch ordered.

Gerard did as he was asked without complaint. He even faced us away from the window and door to give her some privacy.

*Please, Gerard, let us go,* I begged.

NO.

*Why not?* I whined.

BECAUSE THIS IS WHAT SHE NEEDS.

*What* who *needs?* my brother chirped in.

THE EARTH MOTHER.

Before we could interrogate the spectre any more, the door blew open and a storm thundered out. It spilled out of the cabin like it was starving, whipping the remaining leaves off the trees, cooking the ground with its bolts of lightning and swallowing the landscape in its thick blanket of cloud.

We had no choice but to watch as an army of spectres on ghostly white horses stampeded out of the electrified gloom. I didn't recognise the uniforms, but I imagined that they were dressed as soldiers from every era, every discovered country, every side to every war that ever was.

*The Horned God's Wild Hunt,* my brother whispered.

*This is all your fault,* I countered.

Gerard shushed us and gestured for us to look. He pointed to the eye of the storm, crackling high above the neatly planted vegetable plots. Lightning flickered, intensifying every few seconds.

A huge crash of lightning hit the ground in the centre of the spectres' stampede, a flash of light so bright a mortal's eyes would have melted from their heads in an instant. When I could stand to open my eyes I saw, standing where the lightning had struck, a man. I blinked again, clearing the residual lightning from my vision. It wasn't a man completely. It had the body of a man, stripped to the waist of clothes, showing his strong muscles through his dark skin, but the head of a beast. A beast with deadly sharp horns and thick mahogany hair.

I could feel my brother trembling beside me before the Horned God spoke. The spectre army saw their master materialise; they stilled their steeds and sank their heads in a respectful bow.

"Rise," he ordered, his voice thick and warm.

The spectres obeyed. Everyone was waiting. Everyone except the witch, who, now that the clouds had departed into a thin fog, was visible through the doorway exsanguinated in the centre of her chalk shape. Had she realised that calling her Horned God and his Wild Hunt would carry such a high price? Beside her the ancient black cat lay stiffly, following its mistress to death. Was it the connection between them, or the fright from the Wild Hunt that had killed the pesky feline? I was trying not to focus on the deity before me, trying to linger my attention elsewhere in the hope that he spare me.

"You did well, General," the Horned God said to Gerald the spectre.

THE WITCH HAD GREAT LOVE FOR YOU, SIRE.

"And she will be repaid in the next life," the Horned God replied, closing his eyes and giving a moment of silence for his loyal subject.

The spectres of The Wild Hunt looked around the garden, trying to find the source of energy that didn't belong. They looked right at us, trapped in the cage. I found myself searching for The Horned God's kind gaze, wanting him to come to my rescue despite everything I knew about him. He was nothing like I had expected, not that I had ever imagined that I would meet him. He wasn't the bloodthirsty, evil-looking lord of death that I had been led to believe; instead, he had the same energy as our mother, gentle and respectful.

The spectres fizzed and hissed when they saw us, their auras turning spiky and malicious.

"Calm," the Horned God commanded. "These two willing volunteers are only here to offer you their scent, so you can find the rest of their kind and bring them to my domain... alive."

I would have relaxed, if that hadn't meant that several hundred terrifying, giant, battle-torn ghouls pressed their faces against my cage, inhaling with enough force to pull at the fur on my skin.

*What will you do with us?* I'd plucked up the courage to ask, but not to make eye contact with The Horned God.

"I need all of Mother Earth's stewards to return. She is dying. This cursed land is killing her, and she isn't strong enough to call you back herself. She needs every particle of her being restored to her if she stands a chance."

It took a moment for me to process what he said. *She's dying?*

"Have you not noticed that year on year the woodlands shrink and the paths become more dangerous? Have you not noticed that many of your kind have blinked out of existence?" the Horned God replied, pain thick in his voice.

*I was the last of our mother's stewards to be called. I didn't realise how bad it had become.*

*Until it was too late,* my brother added angrily.

*If you knew, then why didn't you warn us? Why didn't you do everything you could to save our mother?* I yelled back.

*I did! For years, I ranted to anyone who would listen, even you. No one heard me, no one cared. The witch was my last chance. The Wild Hunt is her last chance.* The anger had gone from his words now, replaced with sadness and desperation that his kin had failed him.

*Don't go pretending to be the hero. You wanted to trade your brothers and sisters for your human life,* I accused.

"Your brother has been brave. He saw what no one else could, and for that I thank him." The Horned God bowed his head with gratitude, and if it was possible then, I believe my brother would have blushed. "The Hunt must begin. We must save my other half."

It had always been said that there were two sides to the world. I had always believed them to be 'good' and 'evil'; that Mother Nature was 'good' because she brought new life and we celebrated everything she gave to us, the harvest, the light, the love. It was only now occurring to me that the Horned God, her other half, wasn't the 'evil' to her 'good'. He was the 'death' to her 'life'; the 'moon' to her 'sun'; the balance in the universe. It shouldn't have surprised me that the lord of death was so kind and compassionate, when he was the one tasked with the perished souls his other half had cherished so much.

*Anything you wish, Father.* I bowed my head.

With a crack of lightning as sharp as a whip, The Horned God unleashed his Wild Hunt into the world. Once the dust had cleared and the spectres had begun to follow my scent back to the husk, The Horned God collapsed the earth beneath us and we fell, far, far down into oblivion. That was the last time I felt the sunlight on my skin, smelled the fresh scents of spring, and the life in my lungs. The Horned God was kind to us, and our mother lived another day. I can only hope that she returns to her full power one day.

<u>M. J. Weatherall</u> is one of those people who loves writing but always struggles to write about herself. She always feel like she's bragging (which in and of itself sounds like a brag according to her).

She is a young author from Sheffield who moved to the Lake District to get her BSc (Hons) degree in Outdoor Adventure and Environment. More recently she has qualified as a primary school teacher and is now fulfilling her calling as an educator.

**M. J.** loves climbing, kayaking and spending all her spare time in nature. A lifelong bookworm, she takes pride in growing her book knowledge (an asset to any pub quiz team to be sure!). She likes to think that she's a fun person to be around...at the very least, her cat seems to think so.

# RADHAKRISHNA

Bharat Krishnan

In Spring, when the sun hit Davana at just the right angle, the native bay-backed shrikes would come out to bathe in the warmth of this hidden village. The white underbellies and small, grey tails of these birds did nothing to distinguish them on their own, but a black bandit mask over their eyes made them universally recognizable as the *Mascots of Davana*. Ubiquitous and yet unique, the portrait of colors was what made them so beautiful...

\* \* \*

"Krishna!"

Yashoda called into the neighboring woods for the God of Love to return home after a day of school and then playing with his cousin, Balarama. She heard his bare feet crunching leaves and twigs below before seeing his cherubic face emerge from the trees nearby. It was impossible not to smile. It had been thirteen years since his birth, thirteen years since his birth father had entrusted her with his well-being. The eighth avatar of Vishnu had been born to Vasudeva and Devaki at that time, but Krishna was not safe with them. The boy-god's uncle was the evil king of Mathura, Kamsa, and he knew of a prophecy that his nephew would one day rise up to slay him. And so, Vasudeva had broken out of jail for one night with the help of the gods themselves to deliver this baby to Yashoda. Kamsa had tried coming for the boy, but after many years of trouble they were now secure enough to wait. To wait until the boy was ready to fulfill his destiny.

"Coming, Mother!"

He did not know the truth about himself, not yet. How could a mother place that burden on her son? No, Yashoda would not rob her son of his innocence until it was absolutely necessary...

\* \* \*

The boy would leap over the threshold of the house in previous days, his black feet landing with a thud to shake the foundation of the building. Landing on one foot with the other raised to his hips, he'd extend his arms out and strike a pose as Shiva, Lord of the Dance. Today, though, he tiptoed inside as if worried about waking a lion. His face was bowed in deep thought, and the cricket bat he'd brought in from outside dragged mud into the house when he entered.

"What's wrong, *beta*?"

The God of Love did not even acknowledge his mother, simply choosing to sit down at the table and wait for dinner. She'd heard from her friends about the hormones of teenage boys; perhaps not even the gods were freed from them. Setting a stack of thepla down as she sat next to him, the pair ate their multi-grain flatbread in peace. She had prepared his favorite curry of okra and spices, but he ate it all so fast she wondered if he could even taste it.

"Tomorrow you can spend more time outside if you want," she said.

A smile wandered across his face as if it was lost. "Thank you, Mother. I'll go to bed now." Cleaning his plate, he retreated to the safety of his bedroom and closed the door. As Yashoda listened at the door, she heard Krishna's sniffles...

\* \* \*

Krishna woke the next day before his mother had a chance to pester him. Explaining his pain to her would be like sharing a secret with one of the village's bay-backed shrikes – pointless and unnatural. The burden and beauty he held in his heart was between no one but himself...and Radha. He'd first seen her yesterday, while playing cricket with Balarama and the others. The boys organized their own season of cricket each Spring. He'd hit a ball so hard it went soaring into the forest from the schoolyard, and when he chased after to retrieve it he came across her group. The girls sat on stones and gossiped about boys by the river, and their skin was as fair as the payasam dessert his mother sometimes gave him and his friends as snacks. Krishna dreamed her skin smelled as sweet too, but he didn't dare approach her. Even through leaves and shrubbery, her body shone like Lakshmi herself.

"Whoa..." Krishna dropped his cricket bat in awe, and the sound was enough to alert the girls to his presence. Mouth agape, he bent down to grab the bat and lost ball before turning around and racing back. He never saw Radha's smile as she batted her eyelids at him. He missed seeing her blue and yellow saree up close as she moved towards his hiding place with the lithe grace of a dancer. Krishna might have pretended to be the Lord of the Dance, but in Radha he had accidentally found the real thing...

\* \* \*

All Krishna could think of during school that morning was whether or not he'd get the chance to glance at Radha's face once more. He'd figured out that she was a year above him, which filled his body with relief, as he could not bear the thought of sharing a classroom with her. It would've been impossible to mask his longing to brush his hands against the same wooden desk she sat at and smell her hair as she walked past him at the water fountain and smile when she laughed upon hearing a joke. Their separation was agony, but it was what kept him sane as well. What did school matter? He would be fine knowing nothing else as long as he knew her.

"Krishna?"

"Hm?"

His math teacher had asked him to come up and write an equation. "Sorry, ma'am." She chided him, but he did not hear that as well...

* * *

During lunch, Balarama gathered another group to play cricket.

"We have another half-hour, man. Let's make the most of it."

She would be in the forest again, he knew it. He would hit the ball as hard as only he could when Balarama bowled it at him, and it would fly into the forest and then Krishna would have an excuse to go talk to her. He dared believe she might even be impressed at his strength.

And so, his friends rose and he followed until they found themselves in the field by the school once more. Though just a day had passed, he saw flowers painted yellow and violet and orange had bloomed around him. Krishna agreed to bat first, swinging the bat so fast it kicked up dirt from the ground that stained his white pants but matched his skin. The sound was like thunder when bat and ball connected, and again Krishna ran to secure maximum points before going to retrieve the ball. This time he would leave the bat behind lest he disturb the girls like yesterday. The wind whipped against his muscles as he darted to the forest; he'd never been so alive. When he saw Radha once more, her eyes carried a kindness in them he had only read about with fairy godmothers.

"Who's there?"

This time it was Krishna's bare feet that had alerted the girls to his presence. For a moment, he locked eyes with Radha and he knew his mind was not clever enough to pull tricks on him like this. He could not have imagined her mouth breaking into a grin or the whiteness of her teeth or how her neck reflected the sun when she threw her head back in laughter.

"Come play," she said. "Come join us if you are so keen on our company."

As she stepped towards him, he hesitated before looking down at his bare hands and feet; he had never before been so aware of his dark complexion. Turning away from her, he ran.

"Who was that?" Radha asked one of her friends.

"I think that was Yashoda's boy, Krishna..."

* * *

Krishna returned home that night as glum as Yashoda had ever seen him, and it was then she'd decided she'd had enough.

"Enough of this moping, *beta*." She rolled her eyes as she doled out a potato and eggplant curry for them to eat with tonight's thepla. "What ails you?"

"You would not understand, *amma*."

"Oh," she nodded in mock thought. "What a puzzle you are. It's a girl, right?"

"*Amma!*" He almost knocked his plate over in shock. Had he not been as cool as he thought?

"Your mother is no fool," Yashoda said as she sat down. "I could even tell you stories about boys in my day."

"Please don't!"

She smiled before taking a bite from her food. "Then tell me about this girl."

"Oh...how could I begin?" His appetite evaporated when he thought of her, for their love provided all the sustenance he'd ever need. "Describing her with words would be like trying to explain math by dancing...besides, nothing will ever happen."

"And why not?"

Looking down at his dark complexion, he gave voice to his fears at last as only a boy who trusts his mother can. "She is as fair as the law of dharma, while I was born as black as a bull."

"My child," Yashoda crooned. She was as flexible as any other mother; strict in one moment, teasing in the next, and soothing thereafter. "Has anyone ever made fun of you for that?"

Krishna stared at the ground so hard Yashoda wondered if he aimed for it to swallow him whole. "No...but that does not mean she could not be the first."

Staring at his long legs and sharp jawline, his mother sighed. "You are good-looking by any conventional standards."

"Mother," Krishna sighed before standing up, his plate of food untouched. "Even the term good-looking is a subjective word imposed by the masses to enforce antiquated ideals about what is beautiful and what isn't. What does conventional matter? The only opinion to value is Radha's."

"You are good at sports and decent enough in school," Yashoda said. "Any girl would think you're a catch."

He paced like a caged lion across the kitchen, yearning to break free and yet nervous of strength he had never tested. "Radha is not just any girl."

"No other boys in town have your sensitivity to complement their muscles and brains," Yashoda pleaded. It was not good for her son to deny himself food. More than anything she wanted to end this matter by telling him of his celestial lineage, but it was not time yet. "With brains, brawn, and sensitivity, you are truly the complete package."

"A package she still might ship away," he lamented.

Pulling at her black hair, Yashoda gritted her teeth and steamed in frustration as if she was a dragon. Her nostrils flared to a point that Krishna actually sat back down and tore a piece of thepla to eat. "*Amma*...it's good."

Returning to her calm self, she asked him again. "Why do you think she'll reject you?"

"*Amma*, my skin is as dark as the moon. Radha deserves the best."

Yashoda sighed. Even gods feared racism. Leaving the kitchen for a moment, she retreated to her bedroom to grab a few packets of something.

"Here," she said, holding out baggies of powdered color. "Radha deserves the best, right?"

"Yes, *amma*." Taking the baggies in his hand, he marveled at the blue and yellow and pink and green. "But I do not understand the meaning of this."

"You know we celebrate the coming of Spring, do you not?"

"Yes," Krishna said.

"The onset of such bright colors, as colorful as a peacock, is so majestic that the occasion demands celebration," Yashoda explained.

Krishna stared at his mother in confusion until she explained further.

"Who are you to say what is best for her?" His mother was smiling again, with her eyes and mouth and soul. "Give her these packets and tell her to paint you whatever color she desires."

\* \* \*

Again Krishna's friends wanted to play cricket the next day, and again he agreed. Only this time, he held the colored packets from Yashoda in his pant pockets. When he chased his ball out today, he called to Radha and she excused herself from her own group to meet him at the edge of the forest, where a boy's formal education and thirst for the wilderness of love intersected.

"I'm glad you've talked to me today." She spoke first; she had much to teach him in the way of confidence and intelligence.

Her lithe body sparkled when she moved, each step reflecting the sun off the blue and yellow saree she wore. She was all the colors of the rainbow, so of course his mother had been correct. Of course she deserved whatever colors she wanted.

"I was afraid you would not like my dark skin, so my mother suggested I give this to you, to decide what color I should be." He handed her the baggies, and she received them as a gift. Ignoring the giggling of her friends behind her, she opened the pink packet and scooped some powder out on her fingers.

"I have accepted your gift, and so now will you accept mine?"

"I will accept anything you give me for the rest of time, so long as we can be together." She giggled now as well before smearing pink across his forehead. Then Balarama and the other boys came to see why their friend hadn't returned yet, appearing just as Radha switched to green to smear across Krishna's cheeks. And when Radha's companions joined them, they looked on and marveled as Radha turned Krishna's nose yellow and brushed his chest with hues of blue.

"It does not matter what color you are born," she said. "It does not matter because it is our differences that make up the beauty of this world."

Then the two danced in front of their friends, uninhibited and fulfilled, and Radha withdrew a flute from her saree so that Krishna could serenade them all. The pair were seen together so often that they became known as Radhakrishna from that day forth, and their love and respect for each other grew as intense and blinding as the sun. And so every Spring, the pair would lead the rest of the town in a celebration of their love that became known as Holi. They would throw powdered color at each other to mark themselves in all shades and hues, for it was that portrait of colors that made them so beautiful...

Krishna and Radha, *Meena Vempaty, 2019*

Bharat calls himself a professional storyteller and amateur cook. He's always looking to make a political statement with his writing because he knows politics seeps into every aspect of society and believes we can't understand each other without a firm, constant understanding of how politics affects us in all ways. He just published the final novel in an SFF trilogy about power and privilege in America today. The first book, Privilege, won "Best Adult Fiction" for the Ohio chapter of the Indie Author Project.

Check out his Patreon at http://www.patreon.com/skingrafters.

# The Girls of Spring

Jenna Smithwick

I wake to the sound of water rushing over flat stones and blink my eyes open to the frenzy of spring. The high sun filters through the thick clusters of dogwood flowers, their white petals landing in my hair as I stretch out from a long nap. I take my time relishing the warm ground beneath my bones and the soft blanket of grass sprouting up along the forest floor. A bee flits from wildflower to wildflower, skipping over a lonesome dandelion puff in favor of one of its yellow-blossomed friends.

White seeds blow on a gentle wind and float over my face. I turn my head and make the same wish I always do.

It's my favorite time of year – when the meadow comes to life. I could spend days lying here, watching the blooms unfurl from their tight buds. I might do that. It's not like there's much else to do around here.

A peal of laughter echoes from the cave and yanks me from my peaceful state. I turn onto one side and sit up slowly, staring into the dark cavern as if I might catch a glimpse of the girl I was when I would play in its shadows.

So many of the memories from my youth are lost to the years gone by, but I remember coming here with Jakob and the things we'd whisper in the solace of the cave.

*You can tell me all your secrets. You can kiss me if you want.*

No one else ever ventured this far into the forest. The mothers of the village used to warn us about dangerous creatures rumored to lurk near the mountain's riverbeds: fanged beasts and beautiful women waiting to lure their victims to their deaths. The tales were enough to scare the others off, but Jakob and I knew they were only stories. We were the king and queen of the forest.

We had the whole place to ourselves.

I grind my teeth when another giggle bounces from the cave.

As much as I hated the ringing silence after Jakob left, this is so much worse. Nothing has been quiet since the new girls found our secret spot. The laughter fades, and a single high note pierces the air, carrying on until a breathier voice joins in, followed by another.

*Great.* Now they're singing.

I kick a rock downhill, trying to escape the noise. The last bit of snowmelt has flooded the crick. I focus on the bubbling stream and tune out the song that follows me on my way down. The branches thin out as I get closer to the muddy banks. Jakob and I used to skip rocks on the river with the others and sneak off when their games were over. It wasn't always this lonely in the outskirts of the forest, but all of our friends found new stomping grounds after the accident. Denny is the only one who visits anymore. Well, Denny and the girls who come in hanging on his arm, but they never stick around for long. He gets bored easily.

I'm about to make my rounds back to the cave when a twig snaps. Someone is here.

*It must be Denny.* I send up a silent prayer that he's alone today. I shouldn't get excited, but I've never been one to avoid things just because they're bad for me. Peeking out from behind a trunk, I wait for him to appear on the path.

He doesn't. Another man stands in the place where I'm expecting to see Denny.

*Jakob.*

My heart remembers him, even though his hair is thin and he's grown soft in the middle. I want to run into his arms and let the years melt away in one of his hugs. He always had a way of pulling me so close I never felt afraid. I bet he feels even cozier now. If he wrapped me up tight enough I might be able to pretend that we were never pulled apart.

I open my mouth to say something, but I can't find the words. Surely after twenty years I should have come up with a way to tell him I'm sorry. Maybe it's better this way.

He steps closer, and I hide behind the tree. I try not to let him see me as I trail up the hill after him. I don't think he saw me, but he seems to sense that someone is near. He checks over his shoulder constantly until he reaches the spot where we last stood together years ago. I remember peering over his shoulder as a group of men from the village pulled Irina's body from the current. I whispered something to him, then. I don't remember what I said, but I can't forget how his shoulders sagged as I spoke.

He sits down and swings his legs over the ledge.

A protest rises in my throat, but I swallow it down when he picks up a stone and chucks it into the water below. He heaves out a sigh and glances over his shoulder. I tuck myself away before he can notice me.

Would he still be angry with me if he saw me now? I'm not sure I want to find out, so I decide not to disturb his moment of peace. Besides, I know people whisper about me. They wonder why I've hung around for so long. Jakob and I used to talk about getting away and seeing the world. I've heard all about his travels. What could I possibly say to him now?

I never left this place. The village is all I know.

I watch him skip rocks until the sun sets, feeling a pang of regret when I see how sad he looks as he leaves, but I don't dare to follow him any further.

* * *

The next day I find more tufty dandelions in the meadow. I lie on my belly and make several wishes. If one came true, then why can't a few more?

I roll onto my back and smile at the thought of fulfilling one of my dreams, when I've had to give up on so many.

When the giggling starts up in the cave, I skip away happily. If Jakob is visiting his family, then he might come back. It would be enough to see his face again, even if I promised myself I wouldn't approach him.

I hum my own tune and weave a crown of daisies to place over my flaxen waves. Today I'm queen of the forest. Not even the girls in the cave and their eerie songs can get to me.

I stop what I'm doing when I hear footsteps approaching and twirl back behind the trees again, awaiting my king's arrival. My heart sinks like a stone when I see dark hair and a broad set of shoulders cresting the hill.

*It's only Denny.*

My mood plummets. I don't even feel like talking to him, but I'm bored and he probably knows I'm here, so I step out onto the path and laugh when he flinches at the sight of me. It doesn't matter how many times he sees me here, covered in dirt with flowers in my tangled hair. He always looks slightly frightened.

That makes me feel powerful. I like him being afraid of me.

"You're all alone today."

"Of course I'm alone." The corner of his mouth tugs up. "I came to see my favorite girl."

I hate that this works on me. I tell myself I only like it when he talks like that because it means there won't be another girl, but it's a lie. Being his favorite might not be a good thing, but it's almost enough to chase away my disappointment.

He's alone. There won't be another.

That's all that matters.

I take him by the arm. There's a chill in the air, but he's warm. "Should we go back to our spot?"

It's not *our* spot, but I lead him there despite the guilt flickering through me. It's nice to have some company in the meadow, even if we never say much to each other. Denny mostly keeps his eyes fixed on the green things sprouting from the earth as he presses his hands into the soil. I study his sharp features – the cut of his jaw and the ridges of his shoulders – and a pinprick of resentment starts to bleed when I wonder if the years would have made me softer, like Jakob, if he'd never intruded on our secret spot.

Would I have gray hair at my temples or lines from smiling too much?

At some point, Denny clears his throat and shields his eyes from the setting sun.

"I should be going."

I won't ask him to stay. I know he'll leave anyway. And tonight, I don't feel like clinging to him out of loneliness.

"When will you be back?" I ask instead.

"Soon," he answers, moving to his feet. "Very soon. I might bring another girl with me, though." He cocks an eyebrow. "You won't fly into a temper this time, will you?"

I can be a nightmare when I'm mad, and my blood is already boiling. *No. No. No.* He can't bring another girl here. A gust of wind shakes the dogwood trees, sending a storm of white petals swirling around us.

"I won't come back for a very long time if you do," he adds. "My family needs me at the shop. It's not easy to manage these little visits, but I always make time for you."

I bite my lip and squash my anger. "I'll be good."

"Good. You know you're still my favorite," he says. I close my eyes and listen to his retreating footsteps.

*"He's lying."*

Twinkling laughter calls my attention back to the cave. I wouldn't have brought Denny back here if I'd known the cave clique had set up camp while I'd gone looking for Jakob. The sting of missing him comes back stronger than it has in years.

"If you're his favorite, then why does he keep bringing others around?" a woman asks, her voice drifting from the cave.

"If he was telling the truth he would've stopped with you," another adds, laughing haughtily.

The trees begin to sway as my temper rises.

This is my spot. I lift my fingers to my crown of flowers. Who are these girls who think they can talk to me like that in *my* forest? I stomp over to the cave, pressing a hand to its damp mouth.

Shadows conceal the group within. The light hits the cave in strange angles, allowing small glimpses of the young women – a flash of white teeth, a knobby knee, a tumble of hair covering a swath of porcelain skin. We all look about the same age – barely twenty – with sharp smiles and dark eyes.

I want to take a closer look, but something holds me back.

"You need to leave," I say, trying to sound more confident than I feel.

I'm met with a fresh batch of laughter. "You want *us* to leave? Why don't you get rid of him instead?"

"Yeah, we could stop him before he shows this place to another girl."

I back away into the sunlight, but their taunting continues. It's bad enough that they've been eavesdropping, but now they're holding what they heard against me.

"Why are you being so cruel?" I cry.

"We're not." Slender fingers wrap around the lip of the cave, the nailbeds crusted with dirt. "We want you to come play. You're just like the rest of us."

"I'm nothing like you," I shout and flee down the hill before they can say anything else. My surroundings are a blur of brown and green as I hop over moss-covered logs and dodge flowering branches. I run until the edge of the riverbank comes into view and skid to a stop.

I don't like being here. But I can't go back yet.

I lean back against the trees and close my eyes. When I open them, I'm not alone.

Jakob is coming up the path with his hands shoved into the pockets of his light brown coat. I slide back behind a tree, but it's too late. He's already seen me.

He stops in his tracks and pulls off his hat. "Is that really you?"

I step around the trunk so he can see me fully.

His pale green eyes go wide with surprise, and then he loosens a breath and leans against the tree across from me, his shock fading away as fast as it came.

"I've heard you never married," I say, brushing my fingertips along a rough patch of bark. "But I'm guessing you didn't come all this way to flirt with me?"

He pulls a tight, sad smile. There are webs of lines around his eyes, but I still know that look.

"No, I didn't, but I was hoping I'd get a chance to talk to you again." He scrubs a large hand over his stubble. "I didn't think you'd actually still be around."

"I know we used to talk about all the places we'd go, but I stuck around. At first it was for my parents, but then I guess I got comfortable." I shrug. "Maybe I'll still get out of here someday."

"I hope you do. I'm sorry we didn't get to go together." I swear I see a tear gathering in the corner of his eye, but he swipes it away so fast I think I must have imagined it. "There's so much I want to say to you, but I mostly want to tell you that I'm sorry."

"You're sorry? I'm the one who fought with you that last night." I close up some of the space between us. "It must have been such a silly squabble. I can't even remember what it was about."

"It was silly," he says. "It was the first day of spring, and you wanted to dance in the moonlight, but I'd been working all day and wanted to go home. You said I was ruining your fun and told me to leave, so I did."

"You know I have quite the temper. I can be vicious when my fun is spoiled," I laugh, but his frown lines only deepen.

"I loved your temper," he says. "I shouldn't have left, and I'm so sorry I did. If I'd stayed, then maybe things would've turned out differently."

Memories of burning lungs and rushing water swim to the surface of my mind. I shove them back down. "I don't know what you're talking about."

"I came back. You have to know I came back so many times to look for you. I was there the year after—" He shakes his head like he's trying to rid himself of some horrible thought. "I was there when they found—"

"Stop."

"I heard you," he whispers. "I heard your voice in the wind telling me you were afraid of the girls of spring and what they might do to me. You warned me to stay away, and I did, but I've never stopped wondering what happened. I had to come back. I had to make sure..."

"I'm fine," I snip. "I don't know any girls of spring."

"Yes, you do. Remember the stories our mothers used to tell us about the mavki, how they'd come around in spring?"

"I hardly remember anything from when we were that young," I tell him. "And they were only stories."

"The mavki are the souls of—"

*No.*

"I don't know why you're telling me this." I spin away from him. "I wouldn't have spent the past two decades wishing to see your face again if I'd known you'd come here to ramble on about such things."

"Irina, wait. I need to know what happened that night," he calls out, but I've already covered my ears to muffle his pleas.

Irina was the girl they found in the river, and I... I don't remember who I am.

"You need to stay away for good this time!" I scream.

It doesn't matter how much I want to see Jakob's face again. I don't look back.

* * *

Rain drenches the earth, mixing up the soil.

When I return to my spot hours later, I invite it in. I lie on my back, letting it soak my outdated dress and weigh me down.

The heaviness feels right.

I'd cry if I could, but I make do with the droplets running down my face like tears as I wail into the night.

"You sound so lonely out there," a woman croons from the cave.

I shut my eyes.

Spring will be over before I know it, and everything will go black and quiet again. Next year will be better. Seeing Jakob will be a foggy memory by then.

"We feel sad for you, alone in this downpour."

But I don't mind.

"It's better than being like you," I rasp, and a lower voice joins the chorus of laughter.

I sit up in the mud and squint at the cave. There's a man in there with them.

"I promise it's more fun in here," the leader of the group says. "We have someone special to keep us company."

Long-forgotten panic has me up and on my feet in a matter of seconds. I haven't been this frightened since I was—

"Let him go," I command, lurching for the cave, trying to see past the water flowing over the stone entrance.

"Why should we? We've been looking for a new friend for ages."

I move in, running straight into the shadows until I see a flame flickering on the ground and cover my eyes. I know if I look straight at these women, I'll be crossing a boundary I can't come back from. I won't be able to unlearn the truth once it's known.

"Irina," Jakob says softly, and I drop my hand.

He's propped up on a log next to a small fire with four women forming a circle around him, their waist-length hair covering them better than their thin gowns do. They hunch over him, and in the meager light, I can see the gaping spaces between their shoulder blades, as if someone has peeled the backs of their bodies away. Jakob's eyelids drop heavy as they comb their fingers through his hair.

"Jakob!" I stomp my feet, but he doesn't look my way. He's lost in a trance, enticed by a sweet song being sung by several beautiful women. No, not women - *mavki*. I pluck the word from a memory, a fragment of a story my mother used to tell about the tortured souls of women who'd had their lives cut brutally short.

*"They wake in the springtime to gather in caves and lie next to riverbeds, luring men and tickling them until they're starved for air. Sometimes you can hear their laughter rolling down the mountain when they've claimed a victim."*

"Let me join you instead," I offer, noting how his chest rises and falls. I used to love resting my head on his sternum, listening to his heartbeat. I don't want it to stop when he still has years ahead of him.

The mavka closest to me grins through a curtain of auburn hair. "I don't know. You've turned us down so many times before."

My hand is shaking as I lift it to my ribs and slide it back beneath my shoulder wing to feel the emptiness between my bones. Water churns in my ears. I ache for air, but my lungs don't need it. I'm no forest queen. Only a dead girl they pulled up from the river.

"I'm just like you," I murmur, the illusion of my life slipping through my fingers. It's all empty space now. "You said so yourself."

"Then prove it." Another mavka turns to me, the firelight making the white flower tucked behind her ear glow orange. "Bring us another."

"Another?"

She points her chin at Jakob. "You need to find us another and bring him to the cave. He can't leave unless you prove you're really like us."

I dip my chin. I know what I need to do.

It's easy to wind my way back down into the valley now that I've accepted I can move through the trees, their branches passing through me like I'm made of air. I rarely go to the village anymore, but not too much has changed since my last visit. My family's bakery is boarded up, but it's still standing. The woodshop is in the same place it's always been, and although I've never been inside, I know a man is lying on a stale cot in the room upstairs.

I'm tethered to the one who made me like this.

"Wake up, Denny," I say, crawling onto his bed. He snaps his eyes open and bumps back against his headboard.

"How did you get in here?" he asks, clutching his blanket.

"I thought it was time I paid you a visit." I stroke my hand over his hair, remembering how the mavki had Jakob under their spell. I can be like them. "I want you to come with me."

I bring him to my spot one last time, and this time I invite him to follow me into the dark.

"Where are we going?" His bare feet splash through the puddles.

"You'll see. It's a secret."

The flames come into view, and so do the mavki, their pretty, pale faces distorted by thin, stretched smiles, and their long hair adorned with pink and white blossoms.

"I've brought you another," I say, shoving Denny to them. He stretches his neck back toward me, startled as if he's only now realizing he's left the safety of his bed.

"Irina," he pleads. "What is this? Who are these—" His cries are cut short by a string of cackling, each peal of laughter rolling into another as the women pull him into their circle.

I rush over to Jakob while they're distracted with my offering. His chest puffs up with a held breath, and even amidst the chaos, the world seems to go still around us.

Finally, he lets go with a warm exhalation, "*Irina*, you came back."

"So did you." I cup his face in my hands. "But now you have

to let me go."

He sits up, clearly horrified by his surroundings. I note the salt and pepper threaded through his eyebrows as he draws them tight together. "I can't leave you here."

Denny screams, and a wool sock is flung across the cave.

"Kuba, is that you?" he pants, gritting his teeth against a laughing spell.

Jakob's eyes slide past me, moving to Denny's head popping up from the circle of mavki relentlessly tickling his feet as he yells, "Help me! I'm not supposed to be here!"

I touch Jakob's wrist, my fingers going right through him this time. "Leave him."

His pulse flits in his neck as he clenches his jaw. The pieces are all coming together. "Did he do this to you?"

"He snuck into our secret spot after you left that night, and I told him to go away." I roll a shoulder back. "He did, but he was waiting for me at the riverbank when I was nearly out of the woods. I was planning on throwing rocks at your window so I could kiss you good night."

"All these years I've spent wondering, and it was one of our friends?" he mutters, pinching the bridge of his nose at the thought of a sweet moment that never came to fruition. His gaze is cold when he answers Denny's pleas with a question of his own, "How could you do this to her?

"You remember how she was," he says, the veins on his neck popping when he sees Jakob's face go slack, the empathy draining away. "Always stomping about as if she was some queen. When I caught her out alone, I only meant to dunk her head under the water and put her in her place. I didn't realize I'd gone too far until it was too late. I was trying to dim her light, not snuff it out. I'm sorry, Jakob! *Help!*"

Jakob turns away, ignoring his desperate cries.

"He's lying," I tell him. "There've been others. He likes to lure young women out here. He's hurt a few, planned worse for others before they caught on to him. If he was sorry, I would have been enough." A fresh wave of sorrow washes over me. "I won't let him bring another girl here."

"I'm so sorry," Jakob says softly after my statement sinks in.

"Me too." I touch my fingers to my lips and ghost them over his cheek. "But you have to finish seeing the world like you said you would. It'll make me happy."

"I can't." He sets his mouth into a hard line. "Not when you're like this. I came back because I hoped you'd be at peace."

"Oh." I glance back at the giggling group of mavki. "I am. Know that I'll be here whenever spring rolls around, having fun in the meadow like we used to together. Goodbye, Jakob."

I watch the rain pelt against him as he takes off into the night, and then I turn to my girls and join them. I don't hold back with my new friends; I let my laughter roll down the hill.

I want everyone to know that I'm as happy as can be.

<u>Jenna Smithwick</u> is a writer living in Virginia Beach with her husband, two sons, two wild cats, and one sweet pup.

She has an M.A. in International Studies, but she's more interested in the stories that tie communities together than foreign policy these days. Jenna writes Gothic romance and horror for adults and is always interested in new spins on old tales.

When she's not writing you can find her teaching yoga or reading a romance novel on the beach.

# ACKNOWLEDGEMENTS

H. L. Macfarlane, editor

Oh, what a ride this book has been. The previous volume, Summer, came out in June 2023, so it's taken a lot of hard work and deadlines (and extensions of deadlines) to perfect the third volume in the Once Upon a Season anthology series. But my wonderful band of authors rose up to the challenge with style and grace. I wouldn't expect anything less from them!

Getting Spring into publishing shape on time would not have been possible without the help of the amazing Adie Hart, who not only wrote the longest story in the book (when is that anything new?) but also co-edited the entire volume with me. Seriously, I could not have done it without her, and the thousands of pet photos that were exchanged between the two of us over the last few months.

I mentioned the authors already but I cannot thank them enough for their wonderful, original, heartbreaking, hilarious stories. This book exists because of all of you, and for that I am truly grateful.

Lastly I would like to thank, of course, every person who chose to take a chance on this book. I sincerely hope you love the stories found within its pages, and stick around for Once Upon an Autumn. It's due out in September - our most ambitious deadline yet.

I shall see you when the leaves begin to fall!